Heleen van Royen is one of infamous Dutch writers. Trained as a journalist, she worked for several newspapers, magazines and for radio where she met her husband Ton, a popular TV presenter. They have two children and now live in Portugal.

ESCAPE

Heleen van Royen

Translated by Jantien Black

BLACK SWAN

TRANSWORLD PUBLISHERS
61–63 Uxbridge Road, London W5 5SA
A Random House Group Company
www.rbooks.co.uk

ESCAPE
A BLACK SWAN BOOK: 9780552773799

Originally published in Holland by Foreign Media Books bv,
a division of the Foreign Media Group
First publication in Great Britain
Black Swan edition published 2007

Typeset in 11/13pt Melior by
Kestrel Data, Exeter, Devon.
Printed in the UK by
CPI Cox & Wyman, Reading, RG1 8EX.

2 4 6 8 10 9 7 5 3 1

Mixed Sources
Product group from well-managed
forests and other controlled sources
www.fsc.org Cert no. TT-COC-2139
© 1996 Forest Stewardship Council

FSC

For Ton

Stars are again like a teary ballad, and at nights
dogs tune their cloven violins.
I do not let sorrow come,
I do not let it near.
A thousand feet of snow over my heart.

Sirkka Turkka – The Dog Sings in his Sleep

Acting is not very hard.
The most important things
are to be able to laugh and cry.
If I have to cry, I think of my sex life.
And if I have to laugh,
well, I think of my sex life.

Glenda Jackson, actress

Not that it makes much difference, but my brother is dead. The earth is still rotating on its axis. My mother still believes in God. My father doesn't know yet.

Jimmy is lying on his bed, with a cooling system underneath him. The coffin arrives tomorrow – he will be buried. It is going to be exactly as he wished. I have written it all out, down to the last detail, and passed the instructions to the undertaker. He seemed surprised to be dealing with me; I explained that my parents are divorced and that my mother wasn't up to any of this. I found it hard to believe that he hadn't come across this kind of thing before.

My mother has thanked God because He took Jimmy before the doctor arrived. Jimmy had told the doctor he wanted an injection. He was nineteen, twenty next week, and so he was an adult. My mother was devastated. She said it should be God's decision, not Jimmy's. My brother told her it really wouldn't make the slightest difference to God if he came a bit sooner, He would understand.

My mother wasn't so sure. She changed her prayers, for the umpteenth time. At first she had begged and begged that Jimmy would be cured. When she realized this wasn't going to happen – my brother weighed a mere seven stone, could barely get to his feet, there was no hope – she asked God if

He would free him from his misery once he reached twenty. I suspect my mother hoped it would be just that little bit more bearable to lose a twenty-year-old son. She may even have practised in front of the mirror.

'How old was your son?'

'Twenty.'

It's shorter than 'nineteen', which is an advantage, and it does make him sound older than he actually was.

When God failed to answer her prayer for the second time, and Jimmy made a phone call to the doctor, she prayed fervently that God would at least come and get Jimmy before the doctor could send him; his twentieth birthday no longer seemed so important.

This prayer was heard. He died last night. In his sleep. At least, that's the official report – that he died peacefully.

The weird thing was that my mother became all elated. 'You see?' she said to Kaitlin and me. 'You see now? That's the Lord. When the going really gets tough, He is there for us. Amen.'

I don't understand her. I don't feel He is there, and certainly not that He's there for us. If I were God, and could have answered any one of her three prayers, which in itself seems a reasonable number, I would have known which one to choose. I would have saved Jimmy's life. He wasn't a bad guy. He had done nothing to make me think: that boy deserves to die.

Part One

I leave

Chapter One

My husband is asleep and I am awake. Wide awake. I've got my eyes shut but I might as well open them, it makes no difference. I sit up and look to my side. My husband's mouth is slightly open: beads of sweat glisten on his forehead. I clench my right fist. My nails dig into the palm of my hand. He has no idea. No idea of how I lie next to him in this state, night after night. He doesn't know strange thoughts enter my mind from time to time. Secretly I hope he will open his eyes and take me tenderly in his arms; I have the courage to tell him everything, absolutely everything, and then he comforts me and says he understands. That it doesn't matter. That he feels the same sometimes. Then we could get some passion going and make love as if for the first time.

Nothing happens. Paul never notices anything. Paul is asleep. Paul is snoring. He is happy, I think. And he probably thinks I am happy too. I could burst his bubble with one carefully aimed swipe. It seems very tempting.

I whisper my thoughts: 'I feel like punching you in the face.'

Very hard, as hard as I possibly can. Wake him

brutally with a sudden punch of the fist. How would he react? Would he leap out of bed, think I was a burglar? Attack me, and lash back? Or just stare at me in astonishment?

'Yeah, I'm sorry. I suddenly felt an urge to hit you. I thought our marriage could do with some fresh input.'

There are times when actions speak louder than words.

I take a deep breath and relax my fist. Not tonight. Tomorrow night perhaps. I sink back into the pillow. I must close my eyes, I must fall asleep. Everything is fine, I have no real worries. I must pull myself together. Everything will be fine again in the morning. Things seem better when it is light outside.

Half a minute later I am sitting up again. I am not a wimp, dammit! I want action. Always brooding and worrying, but never actually doing anything. I am letting life pass me by without ever achieving anything, or becoming somebody.

I clench my right fist again. I screw up my eyes, pull my elbow back, as if I'm drawing a bow to fire an arrow, I wait for a couple of seconds and all of a sudden, as if someone else has taken control, my fist flies forward and collides with my husband's temple.

His head jolts, he gasps for breath. For a moment I think he is going to sit up, but no, he is not. He turns over, away from me, and lets his breath escape with a snore.

All that time his eyes remain closed. He just goes on sleeping. Even when he is smashed on the head by his own wife he can't be bothered to wake up.

What am I supposed to do? Hit him again, harder? With a heavy object perhaps? There is a vase with dried flowers on the window sill.

No, that wouldn't work. You might hit somebody by accident, in a dream, a nightmare perhaps; you may temporarily have been in a state of semi-consciousness. But a shattered vase in the marital bed at three forty-five in the morning, while your husband is growing a bump the size of a football on his forehead: that's harder to explain. You could argue that the vase had long ago lost its appeal to you. The chance that he would believe you is slim, although it wouldn't be a lie. I went off that vase ages ago. And the dried flowers.

My daughter bought it for me, a gift set for Mother's Day from the Argos catalogue. Of all the presents that a woman receives in the course of a lifetime, Mother's Day gifts are the most repulsive. As if the world wants to make the point to you that you don't need anything beautiful any more: after all, you are the mother. That hand-knitted scarf might come into fashion, you never know. That necklace made of plain clay beads suits your neckline. Try it on, Mum, do you like it? I went to so much trouble making it, I'll varnish the beads another time, so that they look nice and shiny.

Anyone who lies awake at night with an inner urge to smash an earthenware Mother's Day gift against their husband's head has some thinking to do.

There must be a reason.

I know it. Deep inside, and for months now, possibly even years, I have known exactly what is wrong: I am unhappy. Maybe that's too big a claim. Unhappiness is a strong emotion, which I don't really seem to have. There are graphs with sharp peaks and troughs and, in between, straight lines. I am the straight line. Always on the straight and narrow. Neither up one minute, nor down the next.

I have a husband, two children, and we have our

own house; each year we decorate the Christmas tree; I am in good health and so are they, our lives are good: we have everything. And yet I couldn't care less. Sometimes I look at my family from a distance and wait, in vain, to be moved, which is apparently what's supposed to happen when you watch your own family. Why don't I feel anything any more? It is as if I am behind a panel of frosted glass. When the children were tiny I was constantly overwhelmed by my loving feelings. They were so dependent, like little pets, I loved them to bits – ten, twenty times a day I was ready to cry.

My tears have dried up. I must love them, enjoy them. Before you know it, they will have grown up. I must try harder, think of a way. I can't go on like this, every day and every night. I am slowly going mad. Soon I'll hate them, like I am already beginning to hate Paul. Not passionately, but even so. If he knew he'd be shocked.

Chapter Two

I have just come up with a thought: I am a train. One of those model trains you used to see in the windows of toyshops, going round and round the same track, always stopping at the same station. That is what I do now. I rush from home to school, from school to the office, from the office to the supermarket, and from the supermarket, if I can, to Mum's, because otherwise she'll just be on her own. In between, the children need to be taken to, or collected from riding and swimming lessons, helped with unsaddling the horse, getting dried and dressed, and then home again. That's my life in all its glory.

And as if all this isn't exciting enough, there is still the housekeeping. A household is a complex and elusive situation, which got going at some stage, but has spiralled out of control into something never-ending. At a certain point, if you have the misfortune to reach a ripe old age, the household shrinks again, but that coincides with the deterioration of your faculties and your growing inability to cope with things.

It could take my grandmother up to two weeks to buy a stamp, and then she would spend the next three weeks wondering if she had got the right one. I used to think that was ridiculous but now I understand her better than ever. For some time now, the housekeeping has been making me anxious. It's because of my husband.

Paul has recently managed to reorganize his job so that he can work from home three days a week. He loves it – I am less enthusiastic. He watches me like a hawk and comments on everything. According to him I can't get anything right: I am too sloppy, too careless, and I just let everything get into a mess. So he drew up 'The Complete Maintenance Plan for the De Groot Household'.

He began with the electrical appliances: the coffee maker, vacuum cleaner, washing machine, tumble-dryer, dishwasher, fridge, freezer, the lawnmower, the computer, the deep fryer, and the iron. The fact that I use all these machines is not enough for my husband: I should also be looking after them. Paul got the manuals out – he had kept them all – and wrote down how to keep each appliance in perfect condition.

I tend to forget that maintenance needs to be done all the time, sometimes daily, for some things weekly, monthly or annually. The coffee maker and iron need to be descaled, the tumble-dryer and washing machine need to have the fluff removed – there are special drain points for this, which you have to unscrew so that you can remove the gunge. Nowadays the washing machine even comes with a digital program which you are supposed to adjust one way or another. The freezer has to be defrosted at regular intervals, the fridge should be washed out once a week, the lawnmower needs to be oiled and have its blade sharpened, you should never use the fat in your deep fryer more than ten times, the vacuum cleaner has a filter that you have to shake out, the bag absolutely must be changed when it is full, and you mustn't forget to update the computer, both hardware and software.

Computers require more maintenance than any other machine. They drive you mad: it is a miracle when they work and when they don't, you spend days trying to find the problem, and then sorting it out. Networks collapse without warning, Internet connections go down, and firewalls are so effective that they block everything, whether it is coming in or going out.

When my husband had done the bit about the electrical appliances, he moved on to the next heading, 'General Housekeeping'. This covers how often to change the bedding, when to turn the mattress, how to clean windows and polish the floorboards. Then there is 'Administration', which deals with bills, renewing the insurance policies, claiming on the health insurance, doing your tax, and checking preliminary tax bills. 'Transport' takes care of the car. Julia, he had written, try for once not to forget this year, you don't want to find yourself stuck on the side of the road again. You have to take your car to the garage every time it has done ten thousand miles, it needs an MOT, and don't forget to check the tyre pressures regularly, that saves petrol. The bicycles also need to be serviced, the front and rear lights of the kids' bikes are usually not working. This can be _lethal_. The last word was in italics and underlined. 'Garden': the lawn needs to be cut and aerated, we have a special rake for that, the grass also needs compost, and has to be weeded. PS: When are we going to get rid of that rubbish from the pond?

We used to have a pond but I had it filled in. We had eighteen goldfish, which we never saw because the water was always murky. Trying to keep pond water clear could take you a lifetime – you can even get a degree in it now, people who have attempted it have ended up in mental institutions. Whenever another mental-health-act detainee manages to escape, I think: I bet that man used to have a pond he couldn't keep clean. Ponds can destroy you, people who live in flats have no idea how hard it is, ponds should be banned. The pond industry is vast – pumps, filters, additives – and worth millions. You can have your pond water tested at the garden centre, try and explain that to a dehydrated wretch in some far-off refugee camp. In our country they encourage you to buy additives, one kind for summer and another one for winter, costing hundreds of euros, which you dilute and then sprinkle over the water, producing a pond that will stay cloudy, even when pure desperation has driven you to install hideous filters and pumps. And then, when your neighbour's two-year-old son drowns in your murky pool one day and you send up a pale blue teddy-shaped balloon at his funeral, you finally know you have had enough, believe me.

Paul has written it all out and drawn up a schedule and I have put a name after each entry. We had to distribute the chores fairly; the children got some too. I showed Paul my plan. He said Isabel was too small to replace the fat in the deep fryer, and that he had a full-time job and really couldn't manage more than servicing the bikes and the things he had listed under 'Garden'.

'So will the rest have to be done by me?' I asked, waving the wodge of A4 sheets.

'It's not like you're overworking yourself,' he said. 'We've got a cleaner.'

Then we argued. We have been arguing a lot lately. We even argue about money, something that wasn't an issue before. It's because of the euro. Paul was dead against the introduction of the euro and still can't accept it now it is here. He gets terribly wound up about rising prices and is worried they are going to ruin us in the end.

Sometimes he'll suddenly want to go and do the shopping on Saturdays. Then he is off to Lidl or Aldi and brings back bags full of obscure brands of Coke, cheese, sausages and chocolate spread, which the children won't eat. Last Christmas we bought a Senseo coffee maker. Paul thinks the pods are expensive so he only allows me to use it once a day. The rest of the time I am to make normal coffee. Not with Douwe Egberts but with Aldi coffee. Of course I secretly drink Senseo and flush the used pods down the loo.

The problem is, we are in each other's way too much. I am never on my own any more. Before Paul changed his work arrangements I would occasionally have the house all to myself for a morning, say, or an afternoon. I used to love those peaceful hours. I could do whatever I liked. Not that I got up to anything special, I would lie in the bath and fantasize about being married to Tom Cruise, or I would finally get round to reading the paper. I was free to do these things without anyone watching me, or hassling me with questions.

That is the other thing: it drives me bonkers that everybody always comes to me with their questions. Most questions begin with, 'Mummy, can I . . .' (go on the PlayStation, watch TV, have a biscuit?) Followed by, 'Mummy, where's my . . .' (gym kit, fountain pen, hairbrush?) Day after day I get asked, 'What are we eating tonight?' and Paul's speciality, 'Why is there no toilet paper?'

Nobody seems to realize that I am a person, a woman, not a national information centre.

Nobody thinks I can manage anything more than keeping the bathroom supplied with enough toilet paper. When you are newly in love, you don't have a clue. You want to get married, have a beautiful dress and a big do, you think you are going to live a long and happy life, you enter into it blindly. But there is one thing they have neglected to tell you: a marriage usually results in a family, and a family generally ensures the end of your marriage.

Paul thought I was exaggerating. His maintenance plan was clear; it was simply a matter of getting on with it. As if that happens by itself. Nothing happens by itself, absolutely nothing, that is why I am lying awake now. I have too much on my mind, too many things to get on with, the aerator is going rusty, my mother, my sister Kaitlin, my kids, they all need maintenance. If you want to keep up with everything, you have no time to descale your marriage, let alone your own blocked drains.

Chapter Three

Thursday morning, ten o'clock. I am at the office and I want to scream. I work at an estate agent's, the family business. My father took over the firm from my grandfather who set it up. It was always assumed that sooner or later my brother would step into my father's shoes. But that is not how it worked out. Jimmy's death provided a convenient excuse, but if he had been alive he would never have gone into Dad's business for anything in the world. He and my father were like chalk and cheese. It is different for me, I am more resilient and besides, I have never done anything else, so I don't know any better. From the day I left school my father has been my boss.

The moment has come for the old man to retire. He keeps on churning out the same old sales talk with the same old smile. His clients have noticed it, I have noticed it – the only person who seems oblivious to it all is Dad himself. Meanwhile his rivals are overtaking him left, right, and centre. I should know, or rather I can find out, because that is my job: I do the book-keeping. Last year he sold an average of twelve properties a month, this year it has dropped to eight. At the height of his career he would shift twenty a month, but then that was when Juliana, the Queen Mother, was still on the throne. Those days are long gone.

He was so big-headed then. The spitting image of the boys who are now in the fast lane, poaching his business. I ought to feel sorry for him and I have tried; honestly, I have tried to find something approximating to warmth inside myself but it simply isn't there. As I look at Dad sitting at his perspex desk, I see the decline that awaits me and Paul, and the only thing it makes me want to do is give a hollow laugh. At the tailor-made suits that no longer fit him, and his hair that has been dyed far too dark a colour. In my thoughts I march into his office, at least once a day, to give him an earful: 'Just admit it, Dad. Admit that you've lost the battle. Throw in the towel. You were once a respected businessman, you were successful – that's not bad, is it? Some people fail in every aspect of their lives. Do you ever think about that?'

Sometimes I am determined just to speak my mind. To say once and for all how I feel, no matter who I am talking to. I imagine visiting everyone I know, and telling them exactly what I think. It could be cathartic but I worry I wouldn't know when to stop, that I would end up lonely and hoarse, perhaps in an empty cell lined with polystyrene.

'Dad?'

He moves a pile of papers and looks up.

'Do you still have Jimmy's car?'

'Why?'

'Just asking. I was wondering if I could borrow it sometime. Do you still have it?'

'It's at home, in my garage. Engine still starts, amazing if you think about it. That's Toyota for you –

indestructible. I let my cleaning lady use it once or twice before she got a car of her own. What do you need it for?'

'Nothing. Just want to drive it for a day, you don't mind do you?'

'As far as I'm concerned you can,' he says, shrugging his shoulders. 'Just be careful your mother doesn't find out.'

25

Chapter Four

'I'm going,' I say to my husband. It's Thursday night, half past six, we've just finished eating. The children have already gone upstairs. Jim is playing on his PlayStation and Isabel is preparing a talk for school. The table hasn't been cleared yet.

'Are you going to the gym?' Paul asks. He collects the dirty plates and puts them by the sink.

'No, I'm going. Going away, for a while.'

'How do you mean?' Paul sits down again. He leaves the dishwasher open. Paul's idea of clearing up is to open the dishwasher and stack the dirty plates by the sink. Once everything is on the worktop he disappears, assuming the rest will take care of itself.

'What do you mean by going away?' asks Paul.

'I'll be going abroad soon.'

I study his face closely. It isn't true actually, I am making it up as I go along, but I am enjoying watching his reaction. When I lie awake at night it is the only thought that can soothe me back to sleep. I can always leave. I've got the money, I can take Jimmy's car and disappear if I want to.

He draws his head back, giving himself a double chin. 'Abroad? Why didn't you tell me before? Has your

26

father finally got his eye on something, does he want you to go with him?'

'It's got nothing to do with the business.'

Paul frowns.

I decide to finish the game I've started. 'You really don't get it, do you?' I stand up and slam the door of the dishwasher shut. 'Your wife, your spouse, your Julia, doesn't give a fuck any more.'

'Can you just calm down, please?' asks Paul.

I move my face right up to his. 'No, I can't. That's my problem. I can't any more, and I don't want to either. I'm fed up, I can't face it any more. Do you understand?'

I can hear how shrill my voice sounds. I am a better actress than I thought. It frightens me.

'Just calm down for a moment and sit down,' he says. 'And tell me exactly what it is that you don't give a fuck about any more.'

'I don't want to sit down.' I pace up and down, hands on hips. I've got to keep going, this is a good experiment. I wonder how it is going to end.

Paul sighs. 'Don't sit down then. I just want to talk to you. This is completely unexpected.'

'But that's exactly what I want, darling. You may think this is some kind of hormonal outburst, but let me tell you, it's not. I am going away.' Oh my God, that just came out without thinking. That sounded good.

'Abroad, you said?'

'Precisely.' If you're going to go away, you go abroad. Even if you go no further than Germany or, if you like, Belgium, but you've got to cross a border, otherwise you might as well not bother.

'May I ask why?'

'You may.' I sit down opposite him.

27

We sit in silence. He hasn't picked up on anything, he hasn't even cottoned onto the fact that I am pulling his leg. Let's see who can keep this up the longest.

'Why?' Paul asks finally. 'Is there someone else?'

I leap up immediately, knocking my chair to the kitchen floor. 'God, why do you always have to be so simple? Is there someone else? No Paul, I'm not fucking someone else. Maybe if I was, you'd have noticed, but I'm seriously beginning to doubt that now.'

The sitting-room door opens. Isabel emerges in her bunny slippers. Our eldest. Good timing, well cast, fitting in perfectly with the rest of the picture.

She looks at the chair, then at me and her father. 'What's going on? Why are you making so much noise?'

'Mummy and I are just talking a few things through. Mummy has a problem at work,' Paul says quickly.

My fantasy is interrupted. 'The child is eleven, for heaven's sake, do you really think she doesn't see what is going on?'

I put the chair back. 'Mummy and Daddy are having an argument, Isabel. It happens.'

Paul gives me a vicious look. 'Shall we leave the children out of this? You go on up, sweetie, get changed, then you can hop right into bed in a moment.'

Isabel looks at her watch. 'It's a quarter past seven, Dad, way too early for bed.'

'Of course it is,' I agree with her. 'You carry on with your schoolwork for a bit longer, Mummy and Daddy will carry on arguing and if the noise bothers you, put on some music.'

Isabel shrugs her shoulders and leaves.

'Shut the door!' I shout after her. She comes back and obeys my order, Paul's jaw dropping.

'See how easy that was? Communication. Just simple,

honest communication. It's dead easy. People should do it more often.'

At last he gets up, exasperated. 'What the hell's wrong with you? If you . . .' He's about to raise his voice but pulls himself together. 'If you want to rant like an idiot you can do it some other time. Not in the presence of my children.'

My children, he said. Biologically speaking, I have entrusted my egg cells to the right man. Paul is the perfect father. He will never abandon his offspring, he is very protective of them. OK, a bit too much so sometimes, but so what?

'Let me tell you something about your children, Paul de Groot, I pity them. I think you're a hysterical father. You're overanxious, you've lost all sense of reality. Those absurd Smart-lights Jim has to wear when he wants to play outside make him look ridiculous. He looks like a walking Christmas tree with all those flashing lights on his sleeves. And that fluorescent safety jacket – the only thing missing is a helmet. Oh no, I forgot, he's already got one. When he goes out cycling he's the only one who has to wear a helmet, poor kid. You know what the nice thing about cycling is? That feeling of the wind blowing through your hair.'

'I think we've had this conversation before.'

'Yeah, yeah, I know. I'm an irresponsible, crazy mother. If it wasn't for you, they would have had I don't know how many accidents by now, but their short lives would have been more fun.'

Paul's voice drops an octave. 'I could never forgive myself if anything happened to Isabel or Jim. That's all. You know that, and I don't think it's fair that you're bringing it up now.'

'They've got to be allowed to live, Paul. When you're

around you're constantly interfering. You still wipe Jim's bum, you tie his laces, you cycle to school with them, you take them to all their clubs at weekends, and then you stay to watch. They're eleven and six. Jim's almost seven, you've got to let go a bit, you can't protect them for ever.' I get up. 'Do you want coffee?' Paul nods absent-mindedly.

Once we are sitting opposite one another again, he rubs his eyes. Good, he is getting tired and confused. I can go on with my experiment. I change my tone.

'Paul,' I say softly. I stretch my arm out towards him and gently stroke his hand. 'I don't want to argue with you. It's just that I need to go away. I love you, and I love the children, you know that. But there are times, at work too, when I feel crowded by it all. That's when I feel an urge to get out.'

His expression softens. 'Do you think it might be to do with . . . you know who? You visited his grave this week.'

Jimmy. Always Jimmy, every day, week, month, and year. He never goes away. Every year Jimmy dies on 13 July. Every summer, on 21 July, he fails to grow any older. Of course the thought has crossed my mind, I just don't want to abuse it; we can all think of some childhood experience or other to explain our problems. It's not right, it's too cheap, too easy.

Paul says my life has been tainted by grief, though I rarely speak about it and he only vaguely knows the story. In the early years of our marriage he thought that with his great love for me he would be able to alleviate the pain. Later he hoped the arrival of the children would bring me out of the shadows. He has never said it in so many words, but he must have noticed nothing has changed.

'It might be,' I say. 'Anything is possible. But what difference does it make? It's not about the past, it's about now.'

'Where do you want to go?' Paul asks. 'Perhaps you could rent a house on Crete. Where we went two years ago, remember, with that beautiful little beach?' He smiles. 'I'd go like a shot if I were you. Then you could get away from it all.'

Paul loved Crete. I wish I could say the same. All I remember is dragging two whining kids around in the sweltering heat. The mosquitoes. The begging for ice creams. Paul's never-ending inspections. 'Are the children wearing their life jackets? Have you put enough sun cream on them? Did you check if the coffee maker was switched off? Did you put the passports in the safe?'

Paul is prepared to let me go. Let's see how far I can go. In theory of course; this is still purely hypothetical.

'You still haven't quite understood what I'm saying. I'm not talking about a week. I want to go away. I'm going away. I don't know how long for yet, or where to, even. I just know I'm going on a long journey.'

That's how it goes in my dreams. I pack a suitcase and walk out. Just like that. Get a packet of cigarettes on the way. Mama was a rolling stone.

'Why?' He sounds slightly bewildered. 'There must be a reason? You can't really mean it. You can't just leave – abandon the children and me? That's what this means, isn't it?'

I nod slowly. Now that he puts it like this, if I really think about it, I begin to feel something. A glimpse into the future. A flicker of pain, nostalgia, perhaps even homesickness. I can't place it, I don't even know if it is good or bad.

Paul stays in control. It is an aspect of his character I both admire and loathe. 'When do you leave?' he asks abruptly.

So it is that simple. You drop a bombshell and you are coldly asked: when do you leave?

This is the moment I should tell him it was only a game. That I just wanted to test the ground. Of course I didn't mean it, I really have no plans to leave. 'As soon as possible,' I hear myself say.

'Have you packed yet?'

'No.'

'Have you thought how you're going to break it to the children?'

That is the part I always skip in my fantasy. I leave a note on the kitchen table and creep out in the night, without anyone noticing. By the time they wake up I am long gone. 'Can't we do that together? Maybe we could think of a reason why I'm leaving.'

'You want to lie to our children and you expect me to play along?' asks Paul.

'I can't think of anything better,' I say feebly.

He sees his chance. 'And you think I'm too protective, you talk about honest communication? No. If we're going to do it, we're doing it your way. We tell them the truth. You are leaving for no other reason than your own selfishness.'

'If you would prefer to tell them the truth then that's fine by me,' I say. I don't dare look him in the eye.

Paul lashes out. With words – he is not one for physical violence. 'I have been so wrong about you! I knew it. There's something heartless within you, something cold, just like your mother. Why did you even have children in the first place?'

32

So this is what happens when you experiment. You get to hear the unvarnished truth.

'I'm heartless and cold and you are warm and good, is that it?'

'I'm a normal husband, yes. And a good father. You may find me overanxious and ridiculous, but I don't care.'

He is so sure of himself. He has an answer for everything.

'Oh Paul, you're a marvellous father, I appreciate you enormously. As a husband I think you're less impressive. Can you remember when we last had sex? I think it was last year. Do you know why I never feel like it? Because of that physical handicap of yours which you'll never discuss. I can't get used to it, Paul, to that inch and a half. Nothing can make up for it.'

'Bitch!' In two steps he is next to me. He grabs me by the shoulders and shakes me roughly.

'You have an abnormal condition, Paul, has that ever crossed your mind? You have what they call a micro-penis. It's a disorder. You can count yourself lucky that you have a wife, a loyal wife. I don't suppose they ever told you, any of those ex-girlfriends you're always bragging about, but I'm sure that's why they pulled out—'

The flat of his hand lands on my cheek. Full on and forcefully.

I scream and instinctively cross my arms over my head. Should I run or fight? I have always been determined to give as good as I got, should any man physically assault me. I stand up and clench my fists. I am ready for him.

The door opens. Isabel runs towards us, Jim stays at the door. I bang my fists against Paul's chest, Isabel worms herself between me and Paul and tries to separate us. 'No, don't, stop it!'

Paul turns round and walks off without a word.

'Coward!' I shout after him.

Jim also rushes forward and flings his little arms around my legs. Unconsciously I rub my throbbing right cheek.

'Did Daddy hit you?' Isabel asks.

'He didn't mean to. It was . . . it was because we were having an argument.'

I lift Jim up.

'Does it hurt?' he asks.

'A bit.'

He gently kisses the painful cheek.

'I'm calling the police,' Isabel says. She walks over to the phone.

'There's no need, Isabel.'

She stops and looks at me searchingly.

'You and your little brother argue with each other all the time. And you hit him too, don't you?'

'That's different,' she says. 'Men are not allowed to hit their wives. It was on *Newsround* the other day. There are special houses for women who have been beaten up, houses where you can hide. Maybe you should go there.' She thinks for a moment. 'Has he done it before?' she enquires, sounding both matter-of-fact and curious.

'No, he hasn't. And I don't think he'll do it again in a hurry. It was just as much my fault as his. I was provoking him.'

Isabel sighs in a kind of suit-yourself manner.

I stroke Jim's hair. It feels all sticky from the gel. 'Come on sweetheart, you're having a shower and then it's off to bed. And you too, young lady, it's been a long day. We're all tired. Mummy too.'

Chapter Five

Before Paul came into my life I had had three serious relationships. My boyfriends were all completely different but they all had one thing in common: they all had a small penis. And when I say small I mean *petit*.

Jack, my first boyfriend, measured three inches when hard. I can't be 100 per cent certain, it's a guess I made looking back, and that was me being generous. Herbert was no more than two and a half, that's indisputably correct: I once put a tape measure alongside his early-morning erection while he was still asleep. Chris scored two and three quarters. And then there was Clark, a one-night stand, my only black man, who I had hoped would surprise me with a pole, a cucumber, a forearm measuring into double figures.

I met him at a funfair in Amsterdam, in the middle of summer. Clark was on his own, I was with Patrick, my brother's best friend. I never dated him. He had an attractive face and an OK body, but I didn't fancy him. He knew that, but he still lived in hope. He was convinced that one day I would change my mind, which kind of suited me. Whenever I called him, he was at the ready. From time to time I still think of Patrick and then I regret that I never did it with him anyway. I bet he was averagely endowed. I very nearly rang him once to ask. But I was afraid he would bring up my brother so I didn't bother.

Clark and I crashed into each other at the dodgems. We exchanged a few looks and very quickly the matter was settled. I just had to ditch Patrick. Luckily he was used to that. He wished me good luck and then left us to it. The next moment Clark and I were strolling across the fairground. I could barely keep my eyes off his crotch. I really just wanted to unzip his trousers on the spot.

'Shall we go and pull a lucky string?' Clark asked.

We walked over to the stall. A red-haired woman thrust a bunch of at least thirty strings at me. I picked one and gave it a tug. An enormous pink baby's dummy popped out from behind the wooden partition. That was when I should have realized I had backed the wrong horse. My intuition had failed me. With a stupid, unwitting grin I accepted the dummy.

'Suck, bitch,' Clark whispered in my ear.

One hour, five beers and half a slice of cannabis cake later, I was crouching down in the toilet of a café. Impatiently I undid his belt. Clark's hand was resting on my head and he said he thought I was unbelievably hot. I wasn't interested in his compliments, I could only think of one thing. Let's get the goods out. Was this the moment I had been waiting for? Unfastening the belt, unbuttoning his trousers, and sliding down the zip.

Behind the navy blue pants I could make out a knob the size of a champagne cork. I frowned. Not really the Hiroshima effect I'd had in mind. Maybe it wasn't fully hard yet. I pulled Clark's knob out of his pants. It felt hard but it could be harder still. Let's help him along a bit. Clark moaned. After ten seconds it was as stiff as a plank but still unremarkable: brown and undersized. I held his member between my thumb and index finger. My expert eye gave him no more than two inches. I stuck it back in his pants.

'What's the matter?' Clark asked.

I got up. 'Sorry, I'm feeling sick.' I wasn't lying, either. The combination of the cannabis cake and beer was affecting me badly. 'I think I'm going to throw up.' I opened the toilet door, pushed Clark out, shut the door again and quickly locked it. 'You go. It's not going to happen,' I shouted through the door.

'Are you sure?'

'Yes.'

'Can I have your number?'

'No!' Why would I hand out my number to a black man with a small cock?

'Did I do something wrong?'

'No, really.' I kept my disappointment to myself. Why do I always do that? Why couldn't I say how it really was, just for once? Dear Clark, I'd hoped your cock would be enormous, but it turns out it isn't. What you've got hanging there is a tiny, rotten thing. That's what always happens to me, it's as if I've been cursed by the devil. Do you see my problem?

After Clark there was no one for ages, and then it was Paul. The funny thing was that with Paul it didn't seem to matter. I wasn't particularly curious, I had no expectations – I think I hardly gave it a thought. The first time I got to see his manhood, I remember thinking: oh, another one. It registered, but nothing more.

Paul fascinated me. Right from the start he was more serious than my previous boyfriends and – very importantly – he was the antithesis of my father. I could depend on him. Paul was the first man in my life who always did as he promised. That offered me some peace and I felt safe when I was with him. I wasn't madly in love, but little by little I grew fond of him, in the same way you might become fond of an old chesterfield, one of those classic, indestructible sofas with lots of padding. It may not be the height of fashion but it is so comfortable you wouldn't part with it for the world. My husband was like a chesterfield. The fondness became love of its own accord.

Later, much later, it began to trouble me. Not that I wanted to trade Paul in – it was hardly his fault that the meter had got stuck at an inch and three quarters (when soft) – but because I was never going to enjoy the pleasure of a truly big one.

By the way, I think it was closer to one and a half inches than to one and three quarters. That's important, because penises below the inch-and-a-half mark are known as micro-penises. If you've got one of those you have a problem, an abnormality. Until recently my husband didn't even know he was suffering from an abnormality. He thought his equipment was a bit smaller than average. When erect, Paul's penis grows another inch. A two-and-a-half, none too thick penis is all he's got when it comes to his equipment.

The trouble didn't really start until after Isabel's birth. It doesn't matter how you look at it, the delivery of a baby doesn't exactly tighten up the space designed to be filled by the fully engorged member of the opposite sex.

Isabel was about six weeks old when we began to do it again. 'Is it in yet?' I asked Paul after a few minutes. He said it was.

I tried to bring it up, of course. Not immediately, only years later, when I'd finally given up any hope of our sex life ever improving. It was an awkward conversation. Perhaps I'd chosen the wrong moment. On the other hand, there never really is a good moment for these things.

Anyway, my mother had just been to visit us and Paul wanted to go to bed. My mother's visits always make him very sombre. He calls her 'the black hole'.

'I want to talk to you about something,' I said.

'Can't it wait till tomorrow?'

I had just plucked up courage. No, it couldn't wait.

'What is it about?'

'Sex.'

He snorted. Paul likes sex but he thinks talking about it is distasteful. 'Oh, come on,' I said. 'It's important. Since having the children, I barely feel a thing when we do it. That's because . . . well, you know why. Because of size.'

'Julia, please.'

'Well, I don't know how else to put it. You're not exactly well endowed and I've become roomier, so there are implications for our sex life. We have to do something about it.'

'Why?'

'Because I'm suffering.'

'You don't look like someone who's suffering, Julia.'

'Why do you refuse to take me seriously?'

'I am taking you seriously, but this just seems ridiculous. We're doing OK, aren't we? You've never complained before. OK, maybe you don't feel as much as you used to. Is that such a disaster?'

'It bothers me, yes.'

'What do you want me to do about it?' He brushed

39

his hand through his hair. I saw a window of opportunity.

'God knows. There must be a solution, there's a solution for everything. There was something on the telly last night . . . But then you wouldn't be interested.'

'Will you please let me decide for myself?' he said, irritated. 'How many more times do I have to tell you? Don't put words in my mouth.'

I held my breath and counted to five. 'Well, all right then, there are various options. Firstly, there's always things like having a penis enlargement, but that would be an operation . . .'

'Forget it.'

The idea had hardly surfaced and it had already been discarded. No point in saying anything more.

'. . . And secondly, there are all sorts of aids.'

'Go ahead and buy them if you like. You don't need me to come along.'

'But would you be willing to give them a go with me?'

'Do I have to decide now?'

'Jesus, Paul, this involves us both, doesn't it? Last night I saw a woman on television. In order to be able to feel her husband better, she'd bought an aubergine, hollowed it out and shoved it on his dick. Made a huge difference.'

'Was it the Menno Büch show?' Paul asked.

'Yes,' I said, surprised. He hadn't watched it, he had already gone to bed.

'They were all talking about it in the office. What a sick couple they were. They were total freaks, a danger to themselves. Do you want me to dress up as an Indian and parade around a wigwam? Is that how you want to invigorate our sex life?'

'That's not what I'm saying, is it? It just gave me an idea. I'm trying to approach our problem creatively.'

'Your problem, Julia. I'm going to bed. You go and enjoy your sex programmes tonight and see if you get some inspiration. Goodnight.' He got up and walked off.

'Paul! Wait a minute . . .'

He went upstairs. I didn't even get a kiss. To punish him, I refused to speak to him for several days and slept in the spare room. Once I'd grown tired of that, we simply went back to our old routine and put the size issue on ice. I imagine that is how many marriages stay together. The things that can't be sorted are put right to the back of the salad drawer of your fridge, until it gets too full. Until it all rots and the fridge begins to swell up. Until you are lying awake every night because of the stench.

Chapter Six

When Paul McCartney's wife died of cancer, the couple's sleeping arrangements were laid bare in the press report announcing the tragic news. Paul and Linda hadn't spent a single night apart since the beginning of their relationship. It was presented as a romantic fact, the ultimate proof of their love, which went deeper than most of us could even imagine.

Paul casually gave out a description of his wife's deathbed. Artists do this all the time: they experience something and, before you know it, it is a song, a poem, a press release or a combination of all three. It is hard to know when these guys are telling the truth or just making it up.

So, Paul had written her a letter, or a poem, whatever. In the week before her death Linda had been out riding for the last time. Her long blonde hair no longer billowed in the wind because she had lost it all during the chemo. Eventually, when she was about to draw her final breath, Paul held her hand and whispered in her ear that she should imagine it was spring and that she was in a beautiful meadow full of flowers. Linda McCartney, the biggest love of his life, had died peacefully, said the ex-Beatle. We'll just have to take his word for it.

No sooner had the love of his life been cremated than the widower fell in love with, and married Heather, a one-and-a-half-legged former model, twenty-six years his junior. The couple had a daughter and, according to the press release issued at this happy time, were in seventh heaven. Paul McCartney is one of those men who makes you wonder how many heavens there are for him.

If I die during the night, there won't be any press release. If I file for divorce tomorrow, it won't make the headlines. I am leaving no cultural heritage behind, I am leaving nothing but my money and my genes. If my children use up my money and don't reproduce, I will have vanished completely from the face of the earth.

I am almost thirty-seven and I have missed out on so much. It feels like I missed out on my youth: being carefree, doing loads of completely irresponsible things, a substantial penis. And if I carry on like this, none of it will ever happen. My youth is over. My life consists of responsibilities weighing me down, and they are getting heavier by the day: be a good wife to Paul, a good mother to Isabel and Jim, a good sister to Kaitlin, a good bookkeeper to Dad and, above all, a good daughter to Mum. Mum has had such a rough deal already: Jimmy's death, Kaitlin never showing up. I am the only one she has left.

I feel stifled, I am hyperventilating, I need a paper bag. I am afraid I am suffocating. Maybe I should explain it all to Paul. Maybe then he would understand me, but I don't know how to do it. I can hardly understand myself, and besides: I can't tell him about that one thing, the worst, which nobody can know.

I have kept my word, Jimmy, I have kept our secret, it isn't even in my diary. You made me swear to take it with me to the grave and so I shall, even though it sometimes makes me long for my own grave. Peace at last. You would probably think it was funny, your last sick joke. You are weighing me down too, Jimmy, I am not going to lie to you. You are a dead weight: a lead weight.

I have just taken some Valium. I haven't got any sleeping pills, unfortunately. I'd like to take them but I am afraid that if I start, I won't be able to manage without. I am rather prone to addiction. It runs in the family. Dad and I never have a glass; we have a bottle. Or two. Or three.

I always have some Valium handy – it all goes back to Jim. Isabel was an easy, placid little girl. Independent from an early age. Obedient. She was my first child, my only point of reference, and a girl, just like me. Then Jim came along: a tornado, a little hothead, a completely unpredictable lunatic. In other words: a boy. Jim was always noisy, he still is. Since he was a baby, he has been making sounds that none of us recognize. He howls, screams, sings and he never sits still. Paul was afraid he might have ADHD, but after a few birthday parties with other boys his age I concluded that Jim was perfectly normal. We would have to learn to live with it and we would have to bring him up. There was nothing else for it.

Jim listened better to Paul than to me. Maybe it had to do with natural influence, authority, a deep voice, I don't know. The fact of the matter is that, back then, Paul was working full-time outside the house, and I was part-time, so that while Jim was too little to go to school, he was always within a few metres of me. He got on my nerves. Nerves, which I didn't even know I

44

possessed. There were moments when I wasn't able to maintain my self-control. Those moments are stamped on my memory. Jim has long forgotten about them; he was two or three at the time. It used to trouble me more than him, afterwards. I would apologize to him, though I am not sure he understood. Whenever I had an outburst, he would be angelic for several days in a row, that I do remember. He would keep bringing me kisses, like a puppy constantly coming to lick your hand.

The worst incident happened two days before his fourth birthday. Why I lost my temper doesn't matter, it had been building up all morning and in the end I became so angry that I was on the point of smashing Jim's head against the nearest wall. I managed to hold myself back just in time. I shouldn't physically harm him. I dragged him out of the living room, through the hall, pushed him into a cupboard and locked the door: he got off lightly. I returned to the living room, put on some headphones and listened to Mozart's *Requiem*, with the volume full blast.

Jim is afraid of the dark. Isabel was at school and Paul at work. For several minutes he screamed, scared to death, in the cupboard under the stairs. From time to time I turned down the sound to see if he was still at it. Then all of a sudden it went quiet. Blissfully but alarmingly quiet. I opened the door. There was my son, curled up like a foetus, asleep on the bare floor, snot running from his nose, traces of half-dried tears smeared over his cheeks. That afternoon I went to the GP to ask for Valium, 'Mother's little helper'. I have a repeat prescription. After that I never abused Jim again, at least not physically, and I think he has come out all right mentally. For the moment.

*   *   *

45

Paul still believes that I am actually going away. Since our fight, we have kept conversation to an absolute minimum. Jim is blissfully unaware of the situation, he happily frolics about in his own little world, ruled by the creator of Gameboy; Isabel observes us, but doesn't ask questions. As I wait for the pill, OK, the pills, to take effect, it occurs to me that I could turn my fantasy into reality. I made an announcement; I could take it a step further.

Nobody knows, but I have a nice little nest egg stashed away. My father always left the bookkeeping to me. I was cheaper than a proper accountant. I would do all the admin for the day and then get down to managing the company's reserve funds. Over the years I accumulated a substantial sum of money, even though my father would often spend more than I thought wise. He would need a new car, or his office had to be refurbished. I don't know how many desks the man bought, each more expensive than the last. Rarely did he sit at one.

He also went through a phase of obsessively buying art. He was copying Ramses, a colleague and rival, who insisted on having only Real Art on his walls, because it looked classier for when clients came. My father wanted to outdo him, so he went for paintings *and* sculptures. Particularly the latter. There is a small garden surrounding the office, an area of only about 200 square metres, which he crammed full, hardly an inch of gravel left uncovered.

'Your clients come to buy a house, Dad,' I would reason. 'If it's sculptures they want, they can go to the Kröller-Müller Sculpture Park.' I sold off the collection in dribs and drabs, and ended up making quite a tidy profit on it.

The capital was intended to be my father's pension. A few years ago I began to invest the money. Initially it was just for fun. Or perhaps I needed to prove myself to him, so that when he reached sixty-five, I would be able to show how it all added up: look Dad, this is what your pension would have been originally, but thanks to my intervention, your capital has now tripled. That means you can finally pay your cleaner a decent wage. And you could make that trip round the world, after all.

I knew it could have gone wrong. That goes with the territory, but I didn't let that worry me. It wasn't my money and my father didn't expect much of me, anyway. If his pension did turn out to be the bare minimum, it would merely confirm his suspicions. Women and money, women and cars, women and business, women and power: ultimately they just don't mix. When he decided to let me have a job at the office, there may have been an element of fatherly love involved, not just stinginess. Of course, it is always possible he just didn't trust anyone else. In any case, he thought that keeping the books was such a doddle, even I wouldn't be able to make a mess of it.

I was a better investor than I had anticipated. I put my father's money mostly into Internet shares and it all went swimmingly. There came a moment when on paper I had a million guilders. Dad himself would no doubt have become greedy and wanted to continue, but I felt the moment had come to stop, and sold the whole lot, in the nick of time as it turned out. A week later the stock exchange collapsed. I felt sorry for all the other small investors, but I had made my pile. I was a millionaire, well, formally Dad was – thanks to me. A commission of 50 per cent didn't strike me as unreasonable. Paul and the kids would be flabbergasted.

Isabel and Jim would be able to go to university, we would be able to afford a second house. It was fantastic: I had won the lottery.

Once I had had some time to think, I redistributed the money. Thirty per cent was more than enough for the old sod; the rest was mine. The only question was how to transfer the money into my account without having to pay tax on it. The answer was simple. I set up a trust. It would have to be a charitable affair of course, in aid of some worthy goal that could never be achieved.

When I was trying to think of a possible cause for my trust, I came across one of those uplifting articles in the paper about a couple who had made an unsuccessful attempt at exterminating their family. First they had slaughtered the two dogs, then their three children and finally they had tried to kill each other, but that hadn't gone as planned. I think that in the end they lay down on a railway track somewhere, but of course there were leaves on the line so the train never came. When it became too cold, they got up from the ground and set to work on each other's wrists with knives, but that also failed. Anyway, after all that trouble they were left with a bloody but ultimately disappointing result.

The news gave rise to a small craze: in the ensuing weeks, several fathers and mothers followed suit. Some were successful in their efforts and, to their credit, managed to wipe out the whole family, themselves included. Half-hearted, sloppy attempts don't do anyone any good.

Driven by this news, I set up the Society for

the Preservation and Protection of Families. I became the Chair, drew up a constitution and appointed my mother treasurer, without informing her. I can forge her signature with my eyes closed. My father's property business regularly donated chunks of money, which the trust gratefully received. The trust's aims were clear: to preserve and protect the family as the cornerstone of society. The fact that it was aimed exclusively at my family didn't really matter. Each saved family is still a success, right?

My trust keeps a low profile. Financially it is thriving. Since I started, I have managed to accumulate a comfortable sum. There are seventy-five thousand euros in the bank. The Chair could easily travel abroad to see if any families need to be protected and/or saved. She could do some useful fieldwork. She could stay away for several months, she wouldn't have to go hungry.

I see swaying palms and white beaches, I can feel the Valium kicking in. Soon I'll be asleep. My worries are over, I've got an emergency exit. That's good, very good.

All that remains now are Isabel and Jim.

Chapter Seven

On Sunday mornings we always have a leisurely breakfast, the four of us together. Saturday is sports club day: Jim goes to football, Isabel to riding, I do the shopping, and in the evening we slump in front of the telly. On Sundays Isabel boils four eggs and makes the coffee, Jim lays the table, while Paul reads the paper and I try and have a lie-in, usually unsuccessfully. Occasionally I make a loaf with the bread-maker. You programme it the night before so that the following morning the whole family wakes up to the smell of freshly baked wholegrain bread. This always gets me lots of credit, which is why I am careful not to do it too often. If you want to be given compliments, you have to be sparing with your generosity.

'Are you coming to have breakfast?' Isabel shouts.

There's no fresh bread this Sunday.

Paul emerges from the bathroom, and I from the spare bedroom. We give each other a brief nod and proceed downstairs.

We eat in silence. Normally the children chatter constantly. Isabel slowly munches on her bread. Jim is making a mess with the Nutella. No one tells him to stop.

Paul breaks the silence. 'Mummy has something to tell you,' he says. 'Right?'

We haven't discussed it any further yet. He is setting the cat among the pigeons. I can still turn back. It is never too late to go back. It will only become real when I stop talking about it and take action. I put my knife down.

'Daddy and I had an argument last week. You heard us. It wasn't Daddy who started it, it was me.'

Isabel wants to say something but changes her mind.

'I'm not quite sure how to put this, so I'm just going to tell it like it is. I'm going away for a while.'

'Are you getting divorced?' Isabel's voice is shrill.

'No,' I quickly say. 'At least, I hope not.' I look at Paul. He takes a sip of his orange juice.

'I'll try and explain it to you. I'm not feeling too well at the moment.'

'Are you ill?' asks Jim. I shake my head. The children look at me in anticipation.

'It's been like this for a while now. I don't feel anything any more, not like I used to.'

It's not entirely true. I do feel some things. Just never anything pleasant. A pair of large hands strangling me. Walls and ceilings closing in on me, getting nearer and nearer, locking me in until I am completely trapped. Not really wanting to be here any more, fantasizing about getting some terrible news from the doctor, and then secretly feeling pleased; longing to be removed by the Big Claw, so that there can be an end to the incessant demands and constant requests, so that finally I can stop feeling responsible for it all.

This probably isn't suitable for kids. Let's try a different approach.

'You both like ice cream, don't you?'

'Yes!' Jim shouts enthusiastically. Brilliant, now he'll expect me to magically produce one in a moment.

'Imagine . . .' I slowly say, '. . . imagine you're eating an ice cream and you can't taste it at all. You can't taste how delicious it is, it tastes of nothing. Or, you're playing with your friends, but you're not enjoying yourself. It's really very boring, it's as if you're sleeping while you're awake.'

Jim glances at the slice of bread on his plate. He picks up his knife and sticks it in the Nutella jar.

'I can't taste my life. I can't enjoy it any more. I can't think of another way to explain it. It probably all sounds very strange, but I hope you understand a little bit of what I'm trying to say. I do know, for instance, that I love both of you to bits and that I love Daddy, but it's as if someone has built a wall around my heart, a very thick wall, which won't let anything through.'

Isabel frowns.

'The only thing I can come up with is going away. If I go away, I'll be completely alone. I never am, and I have to say the idea appeals to me. A sort of extended holiday. And do you know what I think will happen when I'm gone?'

'Don't!' Paul warns Jim, who's about to lick his knife.

'Tell us, Mum,' says Isabel, impatiently. 'What will happen when you're gone?'

'I'll miss you. That I'm absolutely sure of. It may be after a week or so, or perhaps a month, but I'm definitely going to miss you terribly – all three of you. And as soon as the wall around my heart is gone, I'll come back. If that's all right with you?'

'Of course it is. Isn't it, Daddy?' Isabel is putting Paul on the spot straight away.

He ignores her question. 'Mummy's taken a big decision, kids. You just heard her. I'm going to take care of you, Monique will have to come in more often, and maybe we'll need to get a second childminder. Everything's going to be different.' Paul has been thinking about the new situation, and has already been planning ahead.

'Shouldn't you see a doctor about your heart?' asks Jim.

'She doesn't really have a wall around her heart, silly,' says Isabel. 'That's just how it feels to her. And that's why she's going away. Right, Mum?'

'I don't want you to go.' Tears well up in Jim's eyes as the penny starts dropping. This is what I have been dreading – this is what I have been dreading all along. I should never have listened to Paul, I should have crept out like a thief in the night. So what if that makes me a coward? Anything is better than a family session around the kitchen table.

Jim climbs onto my lap. I lick my finger and remove some chocolate spread from next to his ear.

'Where will you be going?' Isabel wants to know. My daughter puts on a brave face. She is so sweet, so sensible, she is everything I am not. Not any more.

'Abroad.'

'Which country?'

'I'm not sure yet.'

'Shall I go and fetch the atlas?' Isabel is such a practical girl.

'No, sweetheart, that can wait till later.'

Unbelievable, she is taking it so well. Maybe she is pretending, maybe she thinks it is better if we get divorced, maybe tonight, when she is in bed, she'll be sobbing into her teddy bear, while Jim— No, stop thinking about it, they're here now: let them feel you love them, make sure they trust you.

Jim nuzzles up to me.

'It'll all be all right, sweetie,' I say hoarsely. 'Just think of that boy in your class, what's his name again? His father works on an oil rig . . .'

'Denzel.'

'That's the one. Doesn't his father regularly go away for long periods?'

He nods fiercely. 'Ages and ages. And when he comes home, the first thing he always does is measure Denzel to see how much he's grown, and then he gives him presents. Usually new K'NEX.'

'What a lucky boy that Denzel is. I should think there'll be a present in it for you too when I return,' I say with a smile.

Jim's face lights up.

'Angela's father's in prison,' says Isabel. 'In Belgium. He's been away for six months now. Every two weeks they go and visit him. Sometimes he's allowed out. Angela says he is innocent though.'

Paul and I nod. We are familiar with the story about Angela's father.

'You see? There are loads of parents who aren't always at home,' I say breezily. 'But I won't be going to prison, or an oil rig. I'm not going to do anything dangerous.'

'How are you planning to pay for it all, if you don't mind my asking?' my husband enquires. 'There's no way your father is going to carry on paying you if you push off.'

'I've saved a bit of money. And if the worst comes to the worst, I can always find a job somewhere else.'

'Yeah, yeah,' he agrees. 'But not with an estate agent. You'll have to work irregular hours behind the bar of some mouldy café. Is that what you really want? Do you think that all of a sudden you'll *feel* something again, when you're washing out filthy beer glasses at four in the morning?'

'Do we really have to discuss this in front of the children?'

'You're the one who's always going on about open communication.'

'You could try being a bit less hostile,' I hiss. 'Perhaps you could show some appreciation for the fact that I am trying to do something here. It's not just going to be a walk in the park for me, you know. It's an adventure.'

He scoffs. 'You see it as an adventure, do you? Julia on *Expedition Robinson*, excellent idea, why not? Take a camera, keep a video diary, sell it to a TV channel: you'll become famous, that's what you want, isn't it?'

He says it like it's something bad. As if no one else ever secretly has such dreams. I think life is a hell of a lot easier if your name is Oprah Winfrey. Famous people always look beautiful, even if they are not. They have got the money, the entourage and the fans. They only have to turn up and a wave of excitement rushes through the crowd. That's never going to happen to me. I can't even audition for *Idols*, I am just too old.

Paul gets up and throws his napkin on the table. 'Very moving that story about the wall around your heart, but I am not buying it. I know what's going on. You're having an early midlife crisis, you want to prove you still count. Apparently you've got some catching up to do . . .' He lifts Jim up. 'Nothing to worry about, kids. Mummy's going to have a lovely holiday abroad. She's going to have a whale of a time and we'll manage just fine without her.'

Chapter Eight

Monday night. The children have gone to bed. I have just been upstairs to kiss them goodnight. Paul is sitting at the kitchen table. He hasn't cleared away the plates, the dishwasher is open. I have taken some Valium. I can't afford to let this conversation get out of hand. I close the dishwasher.

'I'm going tomorrow.'

'Thanks for giving me plenty of advance warning.'

'Paul. Please.'

He opens his mouth, but shuts it again. I get the bottle of wine from the worktop and empty it into his glass. It is red wine. He's had more than usual. I open a new bottle and pour myself a glass too.

'How nice,' says Paul. I ignore his sarcasm. 'Who else have you told so far?' he asks.

'No one.'

He falls silent. I take my glass and sit down at the table. 'No one,' I repeat. 'Not Dad, or my mother.'

'Does Kaitlin know?'

'She's out of the country. I'll tell her later.'

I haven't contacted my sister because I want to explain it to her calmly. Kaitlin travels a great deal. I am her regular point of contact, her security.

'Are you even going to tell me where you're going?'

'I haven't a clue myself, I'll grab a last-minute flight. You're working at home tomorrow, aren't you?'

He nods absent-mindedly.

'I was thinking you could perhaps take the children in to school a bit later, so that they have time to say goodbye properly. Or they could stay at home the whole day, if you're here anyway. Would you mind?'

Paul rubs his hands over his temples. He goes to rest his elbows on the table but knocks over my wine. I get up and fetch a cloth from the sink. The glass is still in one piece; the wine drips off the tabletop onto the tiled floor below. I bend down and mop it up. Then I give the table a wipe. We are only a few inches away from each other. Since my announcement we haven't even touched.

'Don't rinse that cloth, just chuck it in the bin,' my husband commands.

My hackles are up. Paul has this thing with hygiene. When I see shares in cleaning products start to go up, I know he has been shopping. He buys multipacks of Brillo pads and dishcloths like there is no tomorrow. And floor mops. We have a cupboard full of those yellow cloths, scourers, and at least eight mops. He says I should replace them more often.

I pour myself a new glass of wine.

He picks up his own and takes a mouthful. His hand is shaking. 'I've been thinking,' he says. 'And you can be absolutely honest with me . . . is there something I should know about, is there a special reason for your going, something you're afraid to tell me? Is there someone pressurizing you, have you done something you shouldn't have?'

Paul is giving me the opportunity to confess. How sweet. I wouldn't say my conscience is completely clear, but that's a long story. Furthermore, it is a story that can never be told. With some things you just have to keep quiet, even where your spouse is concerned. I lay my hand reassuringly on his.

'If there was anything troubling me, I'd tell you. Honestly.'

'Why do you want to go away? Is it my fault? I know I no longer satisfy you sexually. If that's what it's about, let's find a solution.'

So now suddenly he does care.

'It's more than that. And what I was saying to the children is true, by the way: I don't enjoy my life any more. And I do want to. I want to know what it's like to have fun again.'

'Don't we – your family – give you any pleasure at all?' Paul can barely manage to be without Isabel and Jim. Every time he goes away on business he leaves with a heavy heart and phones practically every hour. He is a real family man.

'Perhaps I've taken too much on,' I answer. 'Too many people want something from me, including you. You're always on my back.'

He tugs his hand away abruptly. 'I *knew* it. I knew I'd get the blame in the end. You're the one who's walking out, but it's my fault.'

'That's not what I'm saying.'

'It is what you're saying.'

It's not going as I'd hoped. 'I don't want to fight on our last night, Paul.'

'*You* don't want an argument, *you* want to go away, *you* can't feel anything any more. Everything always has to come back to you.'

I had wanted to spend the last night in our marital bed. I wave that idea goodbye. 'I'm sorry,' I say flatly.

'I hope you realize what you're doing to your children.' Paul fires his last shot.

'Jesus Christ, Paul, I'm going away. I might be back in three weeks' time. I don't get it, what's the big deal? Am I a criminal now?' I stand up. 'I'm going to bed.'

'Yes, just you walk away again,' Paul shouts. 'You arrogant, fucking bitch!'

He grabs his half-empty wine glass and smashes it against the wall: sharp bits fly everywhere and the red liquid drips down. Never in my life have I seen him so angry.

'Stop it! You'll wake the children.'

'As if you care. You're running away from them, aren't you? Off you go! Pack your bags and get out.'

I run upstairs, into the spare room and turn the key in the lock. My heart is in my throat. I can hear swearing, more crashing of glass, and the sound of chairs being moved about. Heavy footsteps on the stairs. Paul bangs on the door.

'Open up!'

I climb into bed, fully dressed.

'Julia, open the door!'

'Go away.'

'I'm not leaving, I need to speak to you.'

I don't answer him any more, take the duvet and pull it over my head. He bangs on the door again and fiddles impatiently with the handle. It's a miracle the children are still sleeping. If they are . . .

'Do you want me to kick it in?'

'Go to bed, Paul.'

'Go to bed, Paul,' he mimics. 'Just listen to that fucking, arrogant voice of hers.'

He keeps ramming the door. I stick my fingers in my ears.

'Did you take Valium, Julia, have you knocked yourself out again? Don't think I don't know what is going on. I know exactly how often you take the stuff. You're disturbed. I'm quite glad you're buggering off, actually.'

Tonight will not go down in the history of our marriage as our finest hour.

'Answer me, damn you!' He rattles the door again. 'How much Valium have you taken?' There is a hint of panic in his voice.

I remove my fingers from my ears. 'Not enough!' I shout back. 'I'm wide awake. Go and clear up the mess you've made. You'll end up with stains on the wall, Christ, what a nightmare! And don't forget to throw away the cloth afterwards.'

For a moment it is quiet.

'I could cry, you know that?' His voice sounds muffled. 'You're destroying me. You're completely destroying me.' I hear his steps fade away down the stairs.

I am desperate for a Valium. They're in my bag downstairs in the hall. I daren't go and get them. I shut my eyes and pull the duvet over my head again. The next thing I hear is the sound of the vacuum cleaner.

Chapter Nine

My wide-open holdall lies on the bed. Paul is down-stairs. The children are hovering round me. They are still in their pyjamas. Jim is 'beatboxing', his latest obsession: he makes strange noises while beating his chest, and patting his hollow cheeks with his flat hands.

Normally I would have told him to do it somewhere else. Children really know how to invade your privacy. People get worked up about surveillance cameras in the street, improper use of government files, and the fact that their boss has access to their inbox. None of these compare to what your own children can achieve. They violate your privacy the whole time; they waltz through your personal space. You can't hide anything from them: they see, smell and hear everything. *Little brothers are watching you*.

Imagine it is half past four in the afternoon; you're tired and you feel like having a quick lie-down with a trashy magazine and a packet of crisps. From past experience you know to take the packet as quietly as you can from the cupboard. You hide it underneath your jumper (watch out for rustling!) and you tiptoe upstairs. No sooner have you settled down than they descend on you, like wasps to a honeypot, and demand their own bowl of crisps, and a glass of Coke. Caught in the act. You haven't got a leg to stand on. Eating crisps before the evening meal: a mortal sin. Your only option is to make them your partners in crime. So there you are, with two kids sitting on the edge of your bed, each holding their own bowl of crisps in one hand and a toy in the other. Jim's squeaks and flashes, Isabel's is a pack of cards and she wants you to join in with beggar-my-neighbour. Your moment for yourself goes up in smoke.

But this morning I am pleased to have them around. They provide a welcome distraction. They're acting like I am just going away for a couple of days and that makes it easier for me.

'Are you sure we don't have to go to school?' Isabel asks with a note of concern.

'I rang to say you'd be in a bit later.'

'Can I watch Nickelodeon?' Jim is already holding the remote in his hand. I nod. He switches on the TV and throws himself on our bed, next to my bag. Isabel joins him.

I am not taking much. Wherever I end up, I want to be reminded of myself as little as possible. I don't want to feel like I am mother to Isabel and Jim, or wife to Paul, or an estate agent's administrator. I want to find out who Julia is when the surrounding egos are taken out of the equation. I am curious to meet her. Who will she be most like? Kaitlin? Jimmy? Hopefully not my father or mother. Will she be unique? She doesn't feel she is. Far from it: right now she feels as if she could be anyone.

'Oh, there you are.' Paul puts his head round the door and immediately wants to retreat.

'Can I talk to you for a moment?' I ask. I take Paul to the desk in our study and open the deepest of the drawers. Tucked away at the back is a fat envelope. Paul frowns.

I open the envelope and show him the contents. 'Here are ten thousand euros for you and the children. I know you always worry about money, at least this way you won't have to for a while. You can get extra help with the children, eat out regularly, you don't have to count each penny you spend.'

Paul is so surprised that for a second he forgets that he is not speaking to me. 'Where does the money come from?'

'Does it matter? It's yours, ours. You can have it. I can get you more if you need it.'

'Are you out of your mind? What am I supposed to do with ten thousand euros? Is it dirty money?

'No, not strictly speaking. I think.'

'Phew, I feel completely reassured. Is it stolen?'

'Not really. Or perhaps it is. I really can't tell you too much about it, but I promise you that no one besides you and me knows this money even exists. Nobody is going to try and claim it. You can safely spend it.'

Paul smells a rat. 'Have you raided your father's account, is this his money?'

'If anyone can be accused of raiding my father's account, it is him, as you well know. Do you honestly think I could embezzle my own father's funds?' I put the envelope back into the drawer and close it. 'Maybe you should drop in at the post office later, and pay it into our account. It's unwise to keep so much cash in the house.'

'How long have you actually been plotting all this?'

I don't answer him. But it is a good question. Possibly for longer than I allow myself to believe.

'Am I such a bad husband, do you really think your life is that awful?'

'Can we please not start this again . . .'

He raises his voice. 'And why not, dammit? It might all be blindingly obvious to you. But it isn't to me. Can you not see that? Does it interest you?'

If I am not careful, he'll have another outburst, like last night's. We can't have that. Not now. The children are nearby, they'll hear everything.

'Paul,' I say softly. 'If I stay, it'll go wrong. We'll end up getting divorced. I need time. Time and space for myself. I need to do some thinking. Away from everyone. Not just from you and the children. From my mother and father too. Let me. Please.'

Hesitantly I put my arms round his waist. It feels slightly uncomfortable. He doesn't return my embrace but stares at the closed drawer. As he says nothing, I carry on with my speech. 'No matter what happens, you and the children won't suffer financially. You don't need to worry about that. I promise you.'

'Do you think that's all I care about? You can keep your money. The children need you. *I* need you. We want you to stay here. We love you. You belong with us, even though right now you might not feel it. I know you better than anyone, Julia.'

He's given me my cue.

'Trust me, then. Let me go.'

My bag is packed and waiting in the hall; the taxi is on its way. I check my handbag one last time. Passport, purse, sunglasses, Valium, tissues.

The children are dressed. Isabel has got nothing but

pink on, and is wearing lipgloss. Jim is in his Real Madrid shirt and a pair of jeans. They both rush to the front door when the bell goes.

'It's the taxi!' Isabel shouts. She opens the door. 'My mother's just coming.'

I walk to the door, forcing a smile, and show the driver my bag. 'Would you mind taking this? I won't be a moment.'

He picks it up and walks away without a word.

I hug my children. 'Will you look after each other? And Daddy?'

Isabel looks startled. 'Where is Daddy?'

'In the study. We've just said goodbye,' I lie. I don't know how to behave any more. Everything seems to have changed in the last few days, we can't even have a normal conversation now. Perhaps this is what it is really like, perhaps the rest was all an act. An attempt at marriage.

She lets go of me. 'Daddy, are you coming? Mummy's going!' she calls up.

My little Miss Busybody. She takes after me. We belong together. I am insane, completely insane, what am I doing? Jim clasps both his arms tightly around me. I lift him up, kiss him where possible, and pinch his tough little neck.

'Goodbye my lovely little man, why don't you go and think what you'd like me to bring you as a present. Mummy will be home again soon.' That is how it will be: two, three weeks, at the most – I can't see myself lasting longer than that.

'Come on, Daddy!' Paul can't ignore Isabel any longer. He appears at the top of the stairs.

'I told them we'd already said goodbye,' I say apologetically.

Slowly he comes down the stairs. I put Jim down. It is Isabel's turn next. She is too big to be picked up. I give her a huge hug – we haven't cuddled like this in ages. 'Promise me to take good care of Jim and Daddy?'

She averts her eyes; she doesn't want me to see how hard this is for her. I put my hand under her chin and turn her head gently towards me. Her little face crumples in pain; tears glisten in her eyes. I hate myself. 'Everything is going to be OK, Isabel. I love you. Don't forget that, hey?'

The taxi driver appears in the doorway.

Paul calls the children to him. We exchange glances over their heads. Neither of us makes a move towards the other. Thousands of words run through my mind, but find no voice. The only meaningful thing now is that I am leaving. I raise my hand.

'Wave Mummy goodbye, kids,' says Paul.

'Bye, Mummy!' they shout in chorus. I reach into my bag for my sunglasses and put them on. Then I walk out of the door, following the taxi driver along the garden path.

Jim comes running after me. 'Just one more kiss, Mummy.'

I turn around. In his haste he trips and falls on the path, landing flat on his face. I run back, lift him to his feet and brush the dirt from his trousers.

'I don't want you to go,' he sobs. 'If you go, I won't have a mother any more.'

I take his face in my hands. 'You will have a mother, Jim. I am your mother. Your mother is going on a trip. Some mummies do that. But wherever you are, and wherever I am: you are always going to have a mummy, and I am always going to have a son. And that's you.'

Gently I press my lips onto his, then I let go of his

face, turn him round and nudge him on his way back to the house. He staggers to the front door. Paul catches him in his arms. Isabel finally gives way to her tears, but bravely keeps waving to me the whole time. The image is etched on my mind's eye. Let it be worth it, I pray, please, let some good come of this.

A few more steps to the taxi. I just make it. 'In the back, please.'

The door swings open. I get in. The driver walks round the taxi and worms himself into his seat. We drive off.

'To Schiphol?' he asks. Isabel was standing next to me when I called the taxi, and it was the only thing I could say. I open my handbag to get another dose of Valium. I gulp the pill down. I don't care whether the driver sees me or not.

'I briefly need to go into work first.' I give him the address of my father's office. He enters it into his sat-nav. 'That's a short journey.'

'I usually cycle.'

Three minutes later we're at the office.

'What do I owe you?' I ask.

'I thought you wanted to go to Schiphol?'

'Yes, but I've just realized that I—' I want to give a detailed explanation but decide against it – just in time. Today is the dawn of a new era. This is the new Julia. I don't have to justify myself to anyone.

The driver glares at me.

'It's not important,' I say curtly. 'How much do I owe you?'

'Eight euros.'

I offer him ten and get out of the car. 'Can I have my bag, please?'

'Stupid cow,' I hear him mutter under his breath.

He shouldn't have said that. 'You still owe me two euros,' I say. 'And I would like a receipt.'

He hands me the change, fills out the receipt with a sigh, and waits for me to get my bag myself.

Chapter Ten

It is quiet at the office. My father is sitting in his chair, his feet resting on the table. He looks grumpy. 'You're so late. I was about to call.'

'I thought you had a viewing.'

'Cancelled.'

Aha. Hence the bad mood. 'Is there any coffee?' I ask.

'If you make it yourself, then yes.' It's his running joke. I stopped finding it funny a long time ago and today of all days it really bugs me. I have just left my family, been through hell – you'd think my father might pick up something. But no, not a thing. I should have known: empathy was never his greatest strength. It is one of the many reasons why Jimmy found him such a pain.

Dad lifts his feet from the desk and mindlessly goes through a pile of papers.

'Actually, I was just dropping by to let you know that I'm going away on holiday.'

He looks up in surprise.

'And I'd like to borrow Jimmy's car.'

'The Toyota? Why?'

'I told you: I want to get away for a bit. Have a break.' I don't really know why I want to travel in Jimmy's car.

It's just something I've felt like I wanted to do for a long time.

'Alone?'

I nod.

'And what about the office?'

Unbelievable, he only ever thinks of himself. I was hoping for a different response, like: what's the matter, dearest daughter? Why do you want to leave? Is there something upsetting you? Is there anything I can do? All my life I have been too nice, that is the problem. Servitude is not a virtue, it is the curse of women all over.

'The administration is completely up to date, most of the payments are standing orders. You don't have to do anything, just answer the phone.'

He stares out of the window. We both know the phone hardly ever rings. I am beginning to feel sorry for him.

'Why don't you take a week off too, Dad? Shut up shop. It's ages since you last did.'

'Do you think that would be all right?' he asks, sounding less confident than usual. He is beginning to see that business isn't so rosy; he knows nothing about the financial cushion I have created.

'Absolutely. I'll transfer some extra holiday money to your private account. Where would you like to go?'

'Ramses is always going on about Thailand. Apparently it's still a fabulous place to go to,' he says dreamily.

Ramses is a pillock. He was the first out sunbathing on the beach after the Tsunami, and got onto the television news. He never shuts up about it. However, I've got to hand it to him: he can wind my father up like no one else.

'Thailand is beautiful, it's true. Kaitlin was blown away when she went. Remember?'

'Oh yeah, of course,' Dad says vaguely.

He was on her mailing list, he received travel reports and photos, but he has already forgotten.

'Why don't I book something for you now? Then I'll quickly sort out the last few things here, we can lock up together, you pack your suitcase and we go and see if we can get the Toyota to start.'

Dad is so overwhelmed he doesn't protest.

'When do you want to go?' I ask. 'Tomorrow, the day after?'

'Hang on a minute,' he says, panicking. 'I might need some jabs before I go. Can you book something for next week? I've still got a few viewings; I don't want to cancel them. And I want to drop in on Ramses. The other day he was complaining about arrhythmia because of all the stress – his wife was threatening him with divorce. When he hears I'm going to Thailand, he'll go mad.'

'Just tell him business is booming and you can easily afford to go away for a while.'

'Brilliant, Julia, that's what I'll do.' Dad looks at me admiringly. There's a first time for everything. 'Are you sure it's OK? Financially, I mean?' he asks again.

'Absolutely.'

'Shall we open a bottle?' he suggests. 'To celebrate?'

My father slides the door open. The smell suggests to me that the garage has not been properly ventilated for a long time. The car stands majestically in the middle, underneath a cream cover, surrounded by boxes of tools and other junk. Neither of us says anything; we just stand there until Dad stirs himself again. Stiffly he walks over to the car, pushes a couple of the boxes to one side, and carefully rolls back the cover. The Toyota is unveiled. I don't remember it being such a bright shade of red.

'For the first few years I kept it in mint condition, Julia. But then I just couldn't keep it up.'

'I understand.'

'I couldn't sell it either. It was *his* car.'

Jimmy's Toyota. Most sons would be thrilled if their father gave them a car like that, but not Jimmy. My brother pretended he wasn't interested. He was angry. Jimmy was always angry with Dad. I was caught in the middle and tried to mediate.

'He went in it three times. He thought it was a fantastic car, that's what you told me, right?' I nod. I had told him that.

'I'm really glad I could do that for him,' my father says. 'Even though I wasn't there in person. That doesn't matter. He got what he wanted.'

I could have screamed at him. You could have been there, Dad. But you were afraid. You were a coward. You allowed yourself to be sent away. You allowed yourself to be sent away by your dying son. You could have done more, so much more, but you hardly even tried. You gave him a car, with a note that I had to dictate. I will never understand you, and if I did, I wouldn't have any respect for you because of everything you neglected to do. It's not like I have a choice in the matter. I have to be on Jimmy's side.

Thou shalt not judge, Mum would say, but we do judge. Myself included. The whole time. We are programmed to judge. Ourselves, but others as well. It is our only compass.

The moment has passed. Today is not Judgement

Day for my father. He is going on holiday to Thailand and I am going away too.

'Where are the keys?'

Dad rummages around in a drawer and hands me a set of keys. The road tax is paid, I know, because the car is registered under the business. I have brought the official registration document with me.

I pick up my bag and put it in the boot. I get behind the steering wheel, fling my handbag onto the floor by the passenger seat, and wind down the window. I turn the key in the ignition: the engine comes to life.

Dad hits the roof of the car with the flat of his hand. 'What did I say? Toyota. Indestructible. Always starts.'

'I'm off. You've got an e-ticket, so all you need to do next week is check in with your passport. The hotel will fax you a voucher.'

He nods. I am glad he is going on holiday too. He won't immediately be wondering where I have got to.

I drive out of the garage. Dad waves me off. My next stop is Mum. She'll kill me if I leave without having said goodbye to her.

The journey takes less than thirty minutes. Dad, Mum, Kaitlin and I all live in Amsterdam. Once we were a family: we all belonged together, Jimmy as well. Mum and Dad split up, Jimmy fell ill. The last time we were all together was at Jimmy's funeral. Officially we are still a family, but we have broken up. I am the only one who keeps in touch with everybody. I see Mum at her place, Dad at the office and Kaitlin in her flat – if she's in the country that is. Mum and Dad never see each other; Kaitlin is either too busy to see them or off on her travels. She hears from me how our parents are. She hasn't seen Mum in years, she can't cope she says. She only visits Dad when she wants something from him, like the other day when a friend of hers needed a house.

The Toyota is attracting a great deal of attention. The last time I was in it was with Jimmy. I was seventeen at the time. Patrick was behind the steering wheel; he went on visiting my brother until the very end. Patrick was a nice guy. I'd like to meet him again, but I don't feel brave enough. He is married and has children of his own now. I don't want to impose.

I call my mother to tell her that I am on my way. She says she'll put the kettle on for a cup of tea. I prefer coffee, but there's never any in the house, not even when her daughter comes. She lives in the same house we all grew up in, in the rural north of Amsterdam. After the divorce, Dad moved into the spacious storage area above the office. He has done it up nicely, it was a miserable hole.

I park the car half on the pavement, outside the front garden. The curtains are closed. They always are. My mother appears in the doorway. As soon as she sees the Toyota she crosses herself.

I walk across the concrete paving to the front door.

'You might have warned me.' Her face is ashen. Her hair is short and grey. She is wearing a white blouse, buttoned right up to the top, a navy blue skirt, and she is holding a rosary in her hand. I can't think of anyone who has changed course more drastically than my mother. Maybe I get it from her. Maybe I'll come out of this adventure wearing a peach-coloured garment and clutching a little string of bells.

When Jimmy fell ill my mother dug up her faith, dusted it down, and devoted herself completely to God. If the Lord had kept Jimmy alive I might have understood – who knows, I might even have bought a

Bible myself – but He never did a thing for Jimmy, and yet my mother persevered. In fact she got worse. Apparently that goes with the territory.

If an astrologer predicts that a meteorite is going to hit Europe the day after tomorrow, and you jump on the first plane to Australia only to realize you've travelled all the way round the globe for nothing (a week passes and no unusual changes to the planet have been reported), many people – you could call them diehards – will actually be encouraged rather than disappointed in their faith in the charlatan. Isn't that strange?

My mother is one of your typical diehards. After my brother's death, she hired a builder to construct an altar in the living room. She went to church every day, lost herself in prayer more often than the average Muslim extremist, and tried to convince us that this was the one and only way to keep Jimmy's memory alive.

'Hello Mum.' I give her a peck on the cheek.

We go inside.

'Shoes off, Julia.'

There's tea in the living room. We sit down.

'How are you?' I ask.

'Shall we light a candle first?'

'There's one burning already.'

She ignores my observation and stands up. I follow her. Jimmy grins from ear to ear from the altar. I can see that photo with my eyes shut; yet, each time I see it, I get a shock. He was so full of life. Or is that a misconception? Every person is full of life. He seems all the more alive because I know he is dead. Because I saw him at his most emaciated. I bite my lip. I really want to give the altar a good kicking. The phoniness, the puppet show, the nonsense. Jimmy doesn't exist any more. My mother is clinging onto a phantom. It is her phantom, her consolation: he is, and was her son. I have no right to take him away from her – that would be wrong, that's not what daughters do.

Go out for a change, Mum. There are flowers, there's sunlight. There are beautiful countries, hot places, luscious meadows. No, you won't find Jimmy there, but then you are not going to find him here in this stuffy room, or at that cold church with its hard benches, even though you are adamant you will. You have lost him. And you are not the only one. You think you are, but other people miss him too. We have all lost him. Dad, Kaitlin, me. And Patrick.

We live on – we laugh, we cry, have children – but we all bear the scar, though for some it is bigger than others. I wish someone could remove your blinkers, Mum. In fact, that would be the perfect job for that Lord of yours. We are suffering. We want to be comforted. You don't comfort us. You look for your own comfort, every day, which He gives you. But you have abandoned us. Completely dropped us, from the moment the lid of his coffin snapped shut.

To please my mother I light a candle for Jimmy.

She crosses herself again, and then we go and sit down. 'Why have you come here in my boy's car?'

'I was in a nostalgic mood,' I say breezily. 'I wanted to go for a drive in it again. That way, at least someone benefits from it.'

'I'm surprised your father hasn't sold it.'

There's something we agree about.

'Do you have anything nice to eat?' I have a sudden craving for something sweet.

'Are you here to see me, or to eat?' She goes and

fetches the biscuit tin from the kitchen. It contains one digestive. She takes it and breaks it in two pieces.

I soak my half in the tea and let it dissolve in my mouth. It reminds me of when I was small. 'I'm going away for a while, Mum.'

My mother sips her tea.

Shall I say that I have a brain tumour? That nothing can be done any more? That I want to see the sun go down over Cape Town's Table Mountain, and then die? I wonder what she would do:

a) tug at her rosary
b) burst into tears
c) a combination of the two, or
d) tell me my tea was going cold?

'Work is quiet at the moment and Paul can manage with the children.'

'Are you taking his car?' For a moment I think she means Paul's, but then I understand. 'No, I'll hop on a plane.'

'Your father would never have let me do that. Just push off like that.'

Undoubtedly true.

'Not that I ever felt the need. The best years of my life were when you were all small.'

And I know those years are long gone now, Mum. You've deleted the P for Pleasure, the L for Lust and the E for Enjoyment from your dictionary, and you insist on reminding me every time I come and see you – which is why I can't get enough of these little visits.

I stand up.

'Are you leaving already? You haven't even finished your tea.'

In one big gulp I empty the cup, burning my tongue.

At the bottom of the cup lie the soggy crumbs of my biscuit.

'When will you be back?'

'Not sure really. I'll send you a postcard.'

'You're beginning to take after your sister. I never see her any more, either.'

I want to protest, defend myself, defend Kaitlin, but I don't know how.

'Don't worry about me, Julia. I don't let anything get to me any more, I've let that go. You'll find out for yourself, as you get older. To live is to let go. To let go of everything: ultimately we're all on our own anyway.'

She walks with me and opens the door. The Toyota is waiting for me with two of its wheels provocatively on the pavement.

'Will you please not do that again? You're not supposed to drive that car, Julia. It's Jimmy's.'

For the first time she refers to him by his name. Dad never does that; my mother only rarely. When she speaks his name it is as if he is still around. As if he could walk through the door at any minute.

I blink a couple of times. 'Sorry, Mum,' I say hoarsely.

Fascinated, she watches my reaction. She has managed to make me feel it: the emotion she can no longer draw out of herself, despite all her attempts, despite the altar and the church. She is satisfied. Her ability to feel things for herself has gone, unlike her talent to get at others, which is as strong as ever. That weapon is still perfectly intact. She nurtures it and polishes it daily until it sparkles; she uses it to its full capacity. She reserves it for her own brood, or what's left of it. The brood keeps dropping in to take the stab wounds with open arms. Come on Mum, have another go, stick it in one more time, and don't forget to give it a good twist.

'Your brother is well,' she suddenly says. 'I saw him just recently.'

She is losing her marbles, she spends too much time on her own, it's my fault, I should visit her more often. More often and for longer.

'I went to see a medium. She made contact with him. It took a while, because he's very busy.'

Of course. Jimmy always was the enterprising type.

'What is it that's keeping him so busy?' I ask cautiously.

'The dead. He receives all the young people who have died and gives them a wash. A ritual wash.'

Jimmy standing at the gates of heaven, with a bucket of soapy water and a sponge. I try to picture it.

'Another time, you could come with me, if you like; then you can talk to him yourself.'

'I'm not sure, Mum.'

'Your brother is still with us. You'd notice it yourself if you'd allow yourself to be open to him. He sends you his regards by the way.'

It makes the skin on my arms crawl. Jimmy sends his regards.

'Well, next time you speak to him, say hello from me. I really have to go now.' I give her a kiss.

'Have a safe journey,' she says.

Once she has closed the door behind me, I realize she didn't even ask me where I am going.

As I get into the car, I think of Jimmy. It's probably because of Mum's story, but it really feels like he is sitting in the back of the car. As if he has been waiting for me on the back seat all this time.

– Hey, Jules, have you finally come out of your

coma? Congratulations, I wasn't counting on it any more.

I smile inwardly. Just the kind of thing he would have said in real life. I know it is nonsense, but I answer him all the same.

– Hello Jimmy. How are you?

– Couldn't be better, thanks.

– What are you doing here?

– I've come to help you. It's quite something, what you're planning.

– How do you know what I am planning?

– That's the advantage of being dead. You're omniscient.

– When you were alive, you always acted like you knew pretty much everything anyway, I tease him. It's fun talking to him again.

– Are you sure this is what you want, sis? You're stirring up quite a bit of trouble.

– Do you think I shouldn't go?

– That's not what I'm saying! I think it's a brilliant plan. You're finally remembering to fulfil your promise. Or had you forgotten about that?

I shut my eyes. I haven't forgotten anything, I remember it all. Every day, hour, minute and second. The weeks before his death were the most intense of my life.

– You were dying and I was still very young then, Jimmy. I would have promised you anything. I'm thirty-six now, I'm the mother of two children. It's a bit childish to pretend I'm still seventeen, don't you think?

All of a sudden he falls silent.

– Sorry, I didn't mean to sound unkind. You would have loved to live to thirty-six, and become a father perhaps . . .

He chuckles.

– Still the same serious girl, our Jules. You look fabulous by the way. Well, let's start the car and get out of here.

I do as he says and drive to the end of the road from where I head off in the direction of the motorway. It is quite nice, actually, that he's coming with me.

– Is it true, what Mum said? Have you been talking to her? I ask curiously.

– It's true for her, Jules, that's the important thing. Would you do me a favour?

I sigh. Here we go again.

– Could you step on the gas every time you spot a speed camera? I want to see Dad's face when the fines land on his doormat.

His years in heaven haven't made him more merciful. The idea appeals to me, I must admit. As soon as I reach the ring road, I put my foot down. Effortlessly the Toyota accelerates to 130, 140 kilometres an hour. Around me I see my fellow road users shake their heads, some pointing to the side of the road where the speed cameras are.

I switch on the radio, turning it up full blast, and push the accelerator down still further. Normally I spend more time watching the speedometer than the road, but now I can let rip: race without a single distraction. Something bursts open inside me, something warm and exciting flows through me, I feel alive and ready for action, it has been a long time, too long. I haven't forgotten our agreement about the Big Dream, Jimmy, I have done my best, but things haven't quite worked out as I expected. I am going to try and make it up to you. You are right, it is time to deliver what I promised. Presumably you are the only person who still knows the old Julia – I mean, the young Julia. I've lost sight of her a bit on the way. Occasionally I look in the mirror and see a grim expression, just like Mum's. With her it has become a permanent fixture, her facial muscles can't adopt any other position. I don't want to end up sour, Jimmy, no way. Is it any wonder I sometimes frighten myself?

I am driving towards the A9, I know a few more speed cameras along the way, and then there are some hanging above the A1. Today I am a road hog. When the films are developed someone is going to notice the woman who rampaged through Holland in a red Toyota. I am here one moment, there the next. My driving style will be unprecedented.

And I am laughing. The photos won't really show this, but I am. Every time the camera flashes, I clench my fist in the air, and give a yell. I sing along with the radio and laugh until my jaws begin to ache. Then I start talking to myself, the talking becomes shouting, louder and louder. I keep one hand on the wheel and with the other reach down to the floor for my handbag; I search for, and find a little jar, unscrew the lid, grab two pills and chuck them down my throat, while the car swerves across the road.

Before the start of the rush hour I turn off for Schiphol. The closer I get to the airport, the slower I drive. I leave the Toyota in the short stay car park, stroke its leather interior and say goodbye to it. I also part with Jimmy; it isn't the first time, and there will never be a last time. My head is empty, my hands cold. I take my handbag, lift the suitcase out of the boot, slam it shut and walk to the terminal.

Dad dropped in yesterday. Mum went out before he arrived –
I let him in. He went and sat by Jimmy's body for ten minutes.
I told Mum that Jimmy wouldn't like it at all, but she felt that my
father had the right to see his son one last time.

Jimmy and I have spoken to each other a great deal in
recent weeks. He discussed all the serious matters with me.
Not with my mother and not with Kaitlin. He appointed me his
posthumous spokeswoman. He loved the word 'posthumous',
and used it at every opportunity. Sometimes he shocked
people with it.

Most of my life is posthumous, he would joke. It was his
favourite sick joke. The fact that it was a sick joke made it
even funnier, of course. He would practically choke with
laughter, wondering who was sicker, him or the joke. We
laughed a lot during those final weeks, it's hard to explain.

He also invented a new word, 'prethumous', to refer to
anything predating the posthumous era, in other words: the
present. 'These are my golden moments, Jules,' he said.
'They're all I'm getting, everything is going to have to happen
in the prethumous era.' Everything he said was important. He
constantly told me that I was going to have to remember it all.
He thought that as I still had a whole life ahead of me, I should
make use of his wisdom.

Jimmy also talked to Kaitlin, but their conversations were never as serious. They were about her man trouble. And about clothes. Kaitlin spent a fortune on clothes and each week showcased her new acquisitions in a fashion parade for Jimmy. Anything he didn't like, she would return to the shops. Jimmy enjoyed these fashion shows. Kaitlin was his sister but she was a pretty girl and Jimmy always loved looking at girls, especially pretty ones.

To my mother he gave mainly practical jobs. He would ask her to cook turnips one more time, that sort of thing. A few days ago he felt like eating cherry pie, with cherries from our own tree. My mother baked her finest cherry pie ever.

'Aren't I a lucky beggar, still being in my prethumous period when the cherries ripened?' Jimmy said.

My mother believed it was God's work.

He managed only a few mouthfuls; Kaitlin and I had the rest.

Sometimes Jimmy summoned my mother to his bedside and asked her to tell particular stories about his childhood which he wanted to hear again. She retold them.

There were some people he wanted to see, and speak to, the rest absolutely not. He wanted a U2 LP back, which he had once lent to a cousin. I had to call the cousin and tell him it was urgent because Jimmy could die at any moment.

'That LP is going to have to be here within the next twelve hours, that's your deadline.' It was Jimmy's idea to use that phrase. We both roared with laughter at the word 'deadline'.

As I said, the two of us laughed a lot during those last weeks. We don't any more. Never will again. That's why laughter was so important then. And why I have had to write it all down. I am worried I will forget things.

Part Two

The Casa da Criança

Chapter Eleven

I am high above the clouds, and flying south. The lady who sold me the ticket was very sweet and helpful. I went to the cocktail bar at Schiphol Plaza first, to build up some courage. Then I took a Valium and went in search of a ticket desk. I think I may have told the lady at the desk that I was Chair of the Society for the Preservation and Protection of Families, that Jimmy was dead, that I needed to get away, that I had a husband and two children. I showed her their passport photos in my wallet: I said that they would be waiting for me, and that most of us stay in the same boat for ever, but that, from time to time, you just have to get away to stop your brain from exploding. I got the impression she understood what I meant because she gave me a friendly smile. She called a male colleague, who came over to lend a hand. I thought it was nice that the two of them were going to see if they could help me together. On the other hand, they could easily afford to since it wasn't exactly busy.

The man asked where I wanted to go. I laughed because I still hadn't really thought about it. Which is a bit strange when you are at Schiphol airport, I guess.

There aren't many travellers who reply: Dubai or New York? Or: was it Zurich or Sydney I just came from? Everyone knows their destination. That's why airports make me so happy. Where else would you find such clarity?

I think I didn't answer, because they asked me again if I knew where I wanted to go.

'Where is the weather good?'

The woman said there were lots of places with good weather.

'It can't be too far away,' I said. Should anything happen to the children, I'd need to be able to get home quickly.

She listed some: 'Spain, Italy, Greece . . .'

I looked doubtful. I had been to all of those before.

'Portugal?' The man didn't want to be left out.

Portugal. I rolled the word round my mind. I didn't know it. It started with a p. P for penis, that could be a good sign. But also p for Paul – I was less sure about that one.

'Is there a particular place in Portugal you had in mind?' I asked the woman.

At the p for place I smiled briefly. The man and woman exchanged glances.

'Faro is popular.'

Suddenly I knew why I liked this woman so much. She was helping me. She accompanied me through my p sequence, and she didn't leave it all to me.

'Faro. Something happened there. A disaster, a plane crash, a Dutch company, and lots of people killed, right?'

The man and woman nodded solemnly.

'Excellent,' I said. 'It's less likely for something to go wrong there again then. Am I right?'

This was something they could neither confirm nor deny.

Yeah, yeah, I get it: officially you're not supposed to say anything, but we all know that in the wake of such little incidents, the safety precautions are usually stepped up a bit. If, in the near future, another Boeing were to head towards the runway vertically rather than horizontally, it would be the end of the Algarve as we know it, nobody would want to go there any more. Let's stop agonizing about it – you've persuaded me, well done, my compliments.

'Would you like a single or a return?'

The plane comes in to land.

Once I'd got through customs, I rang home. They weren't in. I called Paul on his mobile. He was somewhere noisy.

'Where are you?' he asked briskly.

'At Schiphol.' My speech was a bit slurred because of the Valium and alcohol, hopefully it wasn't too noticeable.

'Still?' I heard Isabel ask if it was me.

'Where are you?' I asked.

'At McDonald's.'

'Can I talk to Mummy?' I heard Isabel beg.

'I'd rather not, Paul,' I said quickly. Hearing her voice would probably have made me want to come home straight away.

'It's not Mummy, it's someone else,' Paul said to Isabel. 'Go and get Jim for me, will you? His food is getting cold.'

'How are they?' I asked.

'What do you want me to say? Jim has ordered a Happy Meal, Isabel chips and a milkshake. They're trying to stay strong, but they're confused.'

'And you?'

'I'm having an absolutely fantastic day. My wife has pushed off, I've no idea where she's going or when she'll be back, and I'm left to deal with everything on my own.'

'You know, I was thinking Angela's mother might like to help out with looking after the children. She could use the money, her husband is in prison . . .'

'Is that why you're calling? About extra babysitting?'

'I miss you.' It sounded whiny, insincere, but it was true. I really did miss them. I hadn't expected it. Not so soon.

'Sod off. If you *were* missing us, you'd be home by now. What on earth have you been doing all day? Have you been drinking somewhere, or what?'

'Paul, please . . .'

'You're calling the wrong person, Julia. Find someone who *does* understand you – not that anyone springs to mind.'

The connection broke. For several minutes I just stared at my mobile. He didn't call back, there weren't any missed calls either, no text messages, nothing at all. This was what I had wanted: to be left in peace, complete peace, no demands from anyone. It was going to take a bit of getting used to, I suppose.

To tell the truth: I thought it would be better than this.

By the time we land, Faro is shrouded in darkness. I switch on my mobile – the time needs to be adjusted. I hear a beep: a text from Paul? Maybe he regrets our row; maybe he understands I really had no choice, and wants to wish me a good journey, after all. I open the message.

Where is the Vacu Vin?

Kitchen drawers, second from the top, I text back. How are the children?

No reply. Paul was so angry, I hope he isn't taking it out on them. They can't help it.

I didn't speak to anyone on the plane, except the staff. I went to the toilet twice. The second time I removed my wedding ring – it came off easily with the liquid soap. Once I was back in my seat I put it in one of the side pockets of my handbag; I mustn't forget to put it in a safe place later. In a trance I collect my bag from the conveyor belt, walk outside, and look for a taxi. The driver speaks reasonably good English. I tell him I want to go to a hotel as quickly as possible, at least three stars, more is fine too.

'Hotel Eva?' he suggests.

Sounds good.

'Right by the harbour, very beautiful, four stars, excellent quality.'

'Let's go.'

He drives me to the hotel. I give him a tip. He carries my bag into the lobby and starts speaking very quickly in fluent Portuguese to the man at the desk. I look around me. On the wall hangs a piece of cast iron, on which two sailing boats and a sun are painted, the sort of thing you'd find in a Dutch parish hall from the 1970s. The bar is lit by spotlights, there are peach-coloured armchairs, peach-coloured sofas and peach-coloured curtains. A pianist is playing for two men and a dog.

There are still rooms available. The taxi driver leaves. I show my passport and book a double room for

one night, adding that I might stay longer. I don't need
help with my bag. I go up to my room, which is on the
fourth floor, and unlock the door. OK, spacious and
clean. I fling my bag into a corner, kick off my shoes
and lie on my back on the bed. I stare at the ceiling.
You could hear a pin drop. Shall I switch on the
television? No, I must enjoy this, savour the moment.
For the first time in ages, I am alone, truly alone. Paul,
Isabel, Jim, my parents, Kaitlin: none of them know I
am in the Hotel Eva. They don't even know I am in
Portugal. I take out my mobile and make a point of
switching it off. Now nobody can contact me. I think I
deserve something from the minibar. I have persevered.
I have done it. I have escaped.

Chapter Twelve

The next morning I wake up with my clothes still on, and a dry mouth. Automatically I reach for my phone and switch it on. Half past seven. A text message from Paul: children tried to call you. You were unobtainable. Jim in tears.

I ring them straight away. No reply. Of course not, it is half past eight there, they'll be on their way to school. They'll have taken the bikes, and Isabel probably made the packed lunches.

I want to call Paul on his mobile to ask if Jim is OK, but something stops me. He'd only be nasty, try to get even with me. I just can't cope with that right now.

I usually wave them goodbye. When I watch them setting off with their little backpacks, fresh-faced and chirping away merrily, I feel like a normal, good mother. I stand in the doorway, probably still in my dressing gown, and no make-up. In my head I look a bit like Marilyn Monroe in that famous photograph where she leans out of the window. The one where she wears a cream-coloured bathrobe, neatly covering her low neckline, and she holds her left hand against her cheek. Her hair is fairly short and wavy, her smile sweet with a touch of melancholy, and her expression is serene. She once said that it was one of her favourite photos because it looks as if she has just been saying goodbye to her children. I would do my best to look like that too: serene and sweet. Only sometimes, when the children had turned the corner of the street, my bathrobe would fall open – I couldn't tell you why.

Jim had been in tears.

Marilyn never had the chance to wave her children goodbye. I do, but I am not making good use of it. I am at the Hotel Eva, in Faro. Alone.

I realize I mustn't think too much about Isabel and Jim. I should go and do something else. I get up, and walk over to the bathroom to have a pee. As I take off my clothes and drop them on the floor, I realize I haven't uttered a single word yet. I look in the mirror and address myself: 'Good morning, Julia, your big adventure has begun. You don't look particularly radiant today, but we are about to do something about that. Why don't you go and have a shower, slip into some clean clothes and then go and have breakfast? What do you think?'

I nod to myself approvingly.

If only Kaitlin could be here now. That would be fun. She'd know how to cheer me up. Kaitlin and I once went on holiday together to Corsica. Two voluptuous teenagers from Amsterdam on an island full of horny men – it is a miracle we managed to get away unscathed. Once we were home again I wrote down our adventures. I thought it would be good practice; I wanted to become a writer. A writer, or a famous actress, one or the other. I showed the stories to Jimmy. He loved them. He fell ill only a few months later.

Jimmy's favourite story was 'The Key Man'. Just before he died he wanted to hear it one last time. Key Man was a creepy little Frenchman in his late forties, who spied on Kaitlin and me when we were sunbathing on the beach. He would jump out from behind the rocks, wearing only a pair of minuscule red Speedos. He always had a bunch of keys on a piece of white string hanging from his Speedos. Whenever we heard the jingle-jangle of keys, we knew he was on his way over. As soon as he spotted us, and was sure that we had spotted him, he would take off his Speedos, without holding up his towel. This happened not just once, but on several occasions. He seemed to find it very exciting.

'Shut your eyes!' Kaitlin would yell at me. 'The pants are down.' And after a few minutes: 'OK, you can look again.'

Each day the scrawny little man repeated the same ritual and each day he moved slightly closer to us to perform his peep show. After a few days we'd had enough. Key Man had positioned himself just a couple of metres from where we lay. The little red thing had already been up and down three times. He was constantly leering at us. Sure, we were topless, but that still didn't mean he had an excuse.

'Watch this,' Kaitlin said. The beaches on Corsica consist of fine pebbles – they aren't sandy like Zandvoort. As soon as Key Man had closed his eyes, she stood up. She grabbed her damp towel and tiptoed over to where he was lying. With a fierce movement she shook out her towel: a perfectly aimed shower of Corsican pebbles flew straight into his face.

Key Man jumped up with a shriek, Kaitlin laughed defiantly, turned round, carefully spread out her towel again, and lay down on her back. I set the egg timer. After ten minutes we rolled over onto our fronts.

I feel like calling my sister. I think I will in a moment, but first I must have a shower. I imagine Isabel going on holiday with one of her friends a few years from now. Who will look after her then, would she be sensible enough? She comes across as a smart and independent girl, but the world is full of mad people. Isabel is strong, I tell myself, she's not the victim type, she can stand up for herself. When I get home I'll send her to kickboxing classes, better be safe than sorry.

I get into the shower. Alone. At home I always shower on my own too, but somehow it's different in a hotel room. It calls for a man, a stranger – not your husband, in any case – someone who comes and stands next to you under the water jet, and massages soap into your breasts, or better still, someone who pulls you out from under the shower and throws you back onto the bed, grunting that he hasn't finished with you yet.

I dry myself and then, wrapped in a towel, I walk over to the window to open the curtains. The sun is shining: it is a beautiful day; the world is my oyster.

I pick up my mobile and call Kaitlin. She is somewhere in Africa – where exactly, I can't remember. The phone rings five times, then she answers.

'Hey, Jules,' she says sleepily.

'Hi. Sorry I'm calling you so early. Were you already awake?'

'Sort of.'

'I've got something to tell you. I'm in Portugal. In Faro.'

'Oh, that's nice,' she says, sounding unimpressed.

'Well, Faro itself isn't much to speak of, but there are still some good spots to be discovered in the Alentejo.'

'The Alentejo?'

She yawns. 'North of the Algarve. Less touristy. But you're with the kids of course.'

'I'm on my own,' I say proudly. 'Paul is at home with the children.'

'Have you two fallen out?' asks Kaitlin. Suddenly she sounds a lot more alert.

'No. Well, yeah, a little, because Paul just doesn't get it. He'd never go anywhere without his family.'

'I wouldn't have thought it was your kind of thing either.'

Even my very own sister doesn't see me as anything other than a diligent wife and mother any more. As if I wouldn't dare do anything on my own. It's high time my image was updated.

'How long are you staying?' Kaitlin asks.

'No idea. For as long as it's fun. I can really understand now why you're always going away on your own, Kaitlin. It's good to be away – far away from everything and everyone.'

'Portugal is not exactly far away, Jules,' she says jokingly. 'When did you arrive?'

'Last night.'

She bursts out laughing. I ignore her.

'I was just thinking about Corsica,' I say. 'Can't you come and join me? We'll hot up the Algarve together.'

'I'd like to, but I'm in Kenya.'

'If money is an issue I can pay for your flight, no problem.'

'Has Dad finally given you a pay rise?' She doesn't wait for an answer. 'Sorry Jules, I'm with a group, I can't really just slip out.'

I try to hide my disappointment. 'Well, if you change your mind, you know where to find me. I'm going out clubbing tonight, is there anywhere you can recommend?'

'In the Algarve? You haven't got much choice. Go to The Strip.'

'The Strip,' I repeat. 'Sounds exciting.'

'It's the entertainment district of Albufeira. Lots of drunken Englishmen, that kind of thing.'

After Kaitlin's enthusiastic description, I feel like having a drink myself.

'Hey, Jules, they're calling me, I've got to hang up. Everything all right with Mum and Dad?'

'Yeah, don't worry about it.'

'Great. Have a good holiday. Ciao!'

Suddenly I am in a hurry. I've got to get dressed, find the breakfast room, grab something to eat. Then I want to get out of Faro and find a nice place on the coast to do what I've come for: have fun. I get my bag and unzip it. On the top I see something I didn't put there. It is a small, square, flat parcel, gift-wrapped, and with an envelope attached to it. For Mummy, it says in Isabel's handwriting.

I open the envelope.

Dear Mummy,
  Have a lovely time. When we are on holiday you always miss this the most. That is why we are giving it to you.
  Kisses Isabel and Jim
  J I M xxx xxx xxxx

The second Jim is in his own writing, with ten kisses after it and I know straight away what has happened: Isabel signed on Jim's behalf; Jim got angry, snatched the letter from her hands and, despite his sister's opposition – 'I've already done it, Jim!' – he signed his name again. With an extra ten kisses.

I feel the parcel, and instantly know what is inside it. She has bought me a packet of liquorice, I bet it's my favourite kind, I know my Isabel. I remove the wrapping paper, sit on the edge of my bed and stare at the little blue packet. Coin-shaped liquorice, made by Klene, the right brand.

My hands are shaking. I am really not feeling well. I must take something to calm my nerves. From tomorrow I am going to cut back on the tranquillizers. I take two Valium tablets, and remove a beer from the minibar. I quickly gulp down the contents of the can and let out an enormous burp. Jimmy, Kaitlin and I used to have burping competitions. Kaitlin usually won.

The liquorice is lying on the bed. Without thinking, I pick it up and tear it open. I burp again, not quite so loudly this time. I love liquorice, I love Isabel, and I love Jim. They are good kids. Nicer than I am, much nicer. I take a liquorice coin. The last thing I ate was a roll on the plane. Suddenly I have an idea. I take the piece of liquorice out of my mouth, dab it dry on the bedspread, and put it back in the packet. I'll keep the sweets for when I get home. It can be my way of showing the children how much I love them.

I will show them the packet and then I will tell them how, each day, I longed to have one, but that I restrained myself because I wanted to share them with Isabel and Jim. It would have been a brilliant plan if I hadn't just been so stupid as to rip open the bag. Now it is too late, I can't really prove that I didn't have any, and I can't tape up the packet, that would be too obvious.

I hear a chuckle. For a moment I think it is coming from the corridor, but it's right next to me.

– Hey, Jules. Do you realize how long you've been sitting there in just a towel, with an open packet of liquorice in your hand?

Jimmy. He's come to Portugal with me. How nice.

– I thought this was meant to be your big escape. What are you playing at?

– It's harder than I thought.

– So was dying.

My breath stops short. I know where he's heading with this. I don't want to talk about it. Not now, not ever.

– Don't be such a jerk, Jimmy. I'm trying, can't you see?

– All I can see is that you're washing down huge numbers of pills with masses of alcohol.

I close my eyes. When I open them again, I see Jimmy, slouched in one of the chairs of my hotel room. He is leaning his back against one armrest with his legs dangling over the other. It is the young, dashing Jimmy, the one the girls were lining up for until he first became ill. After that, fewer and fewer girls came to our door and the ones that did come he sent away. There weren't many people left he'd agree to see, apart from Mum, Kaitlin and me. And Patrick.

– You should stop worrying so much about your children. They're flexible, they'll be OK. No one is indispensable.

He, of all people, should know.

100

– You're still attached to them through a thousand invisible threads, Jules. Your body has left, but your head is still there. You're trying to make them happy from a distance. It's not going to work. You might as well be at home in that case.

He is right. Everyone can fly to Portugal. This is just the beginning. Now I have to follow it through. I have to cut them loose and choose *me*. It won't be easy, it'll hurt but it's got to be done. That was the point.

I stand up, letting the towel slide to the floor, and walk over to the window to open it. I draw in a deep breath, then turn the packet of liquorice upside down and scatter the sweets onto the courtyard of the Hotel Eva. When the packet is empty, I let go of it. It blows away. I shut the window and look around me.

My handbag is on the chair where Jimmy was. I get it and take out my wallet. There they are. Two little faces behind a piece of clear plastic, so beautiful, so innocent. I am often more moved by photos of them than by their real appearance. For a long time I thought I was the only person to feel that way, until one day I was standing in the playground with my neighbour. The school photographer had been. The children came running out of the building with the results, and dutifully handed them over to us. Both my neighbour and I ripped open the plastic sleeves impatiently, and within moments our faces were overcome with tenderness.

'What are yours like?' my neighbour wanted to know.

'Nice. Especially Jim. Isabel is not quite as good this time, but I'm definitely taking them. What about you?'

'Gorgeous. Just look at my youngest.'

We exchanged photographs, confirmed each other's feelings, passed them back, and returned to our silent reverie.

The neighbour's children – she has three – were lingering around her and pulling her coat. 'Can we go home, Mum? We're hungry.'

'Just leave me in peace for a moment, will you?' she snapped. I'd never heard my neighbour snap before. 'In the photo they're so cute, don't you think?' she whispered. 'And so fabulously quiet.'

After this admission she didn't look me in the face again, took her bike, tucked the photos into her pannier, lifted her youngest into the bicycle seat and cycled off, her two eldest pedalling on their own bikes, one on either side.

I remove the passport photos from behind the plastic bit in my wallet. It's better to remove them from sight, otherwise I'll be reminded of them every time I pay for something.

'Forgive me, Isabel,' I say quietly. 'Forgive me, Jim.'

One at a time I rip up the photographs into minuscule pieces, first my daughter, then my son. I place the remnants on the table. I take a little walk round the room. It's painful to see the shreds lying there, but I don't want to throw them in the waste-paper basket. That would be taking it too far, it might bring bad luck. They are my children, I brought them into this world, they belong with me. I open the minibar. No alcohol now. A small bottle of water, natural spring water. With my right hand I gather the remnants on the table and push them into my left hand, which I hold flat against the edge of the table. I bite into the little pile, take a mouthful of water and swallow. I notice that one of the shreds left on my hand shows a corner of Jim's smiling mouth. Quickly I put the rest in my mouth and wash it down with more water. Done. I carefully fold up Isabel's note and put it in the bottom of my bag.

Chapter Thirteen

The breakfast area is on the top floor and offers a view over the harbour, where dozens of little boats lie moored. It is quiet – most of the guests have been and gone. I am sitting, with my sunglasses on, at a small table, sipping my coffee. I am not really hungry, but I have a bit of fruit and a croissant all the same. Well, a croissant: it looks like a croissant but it actually tastes like a stodgy white bun. I ought to complain. That is what the new Julia is supposed to do. Kick up a fuss. You call this a croissant, do you? You must be joking! Has your cook actually been to France, or has he just glanced at it from the air? This is a plaited dough ball, which tastes of nothing. I demand to speak to the chef. Drag him away from his stove. No, I have a better idea, I want to see the manager. Tell him to meet me in room 411. Do you even know who I am? I'm Julia Roberts. Yes, I know, I seem taller on screen, I get that all the time, but let's not go into that now. My agent booked me into this hotel, he's not heard the last of it yet either, of that you can be sure. Hotel Eva, four stars – pull the other one. Tell the chimp who runs this place it won't be more than two next time.

I finish my breakfast in less than five minutes.

'Was everything to your liking?' the waiter asks routinely.

'The croissant was a touch dry.'

He notes my comment.

I take the lift down to reception, and ask for local tourist information. The woman behind the desk motions me to a rack of brochures. I take a bundle and return to my room.

I lay them all out on the floor. I am in the Algarve – the catchwords jump off the pages: sun, sea, vast sandy beaches, stunning rock formations, beautiful nature reserves and picturesque villages. I fumble around inside my bag. When I was at Schiphol I picked up a guidebook at the last minute.

Under the heading 'Hospitality' I find information about the Portuguese as a nation. In general, the Portuguese are well brought up and set great store by their appearance. No matter whether they are rich or poor, they always look well groomed, and that goes for their children too. They are generous, friendly and welcoming towards foreigners. The Portuguese are calmer and more reserved than the Spaniards and Italians. They are patriotic and respect is highly important to them. About 47 per cent of men have a moustache.

I let the information sink in. It makes quite a claim, this piece of print. It turns out that the Portuguese are probably the nicest people in Europe, perhaps even the nicest people on earth. Why didn't I know this before? They are in the EU; how can we stop these pure creatures from being ruined by us?

All I have to do now is choose a picturesque village. I don't want to stay in Faro, I want to lie among stunning rock formations and go deep brown. My eye falls on a brochure about Carvoeiro. It looks lovely in the photos. The sea is as blue as Kaitlin's eyes. The small, crescent-shaped beach is enclosed by massive yellow rocks on both sides. There are a few strategically placed fishing boats lying on the sand. They could be museum pieces but perhaps they're still in use – I wouldn't want to bet my life on it. Straight from the golden yellow sand you walk into a square, which seems to be the hub of the local catering industry. From the square the streets of Carvoeiro lead up a hill, branching out like a fan. Rows of houses fan out in terraces like an amphitheatre, repeating the crescent shape of the cliffs that protect the beach, so that Carvoeiro with its bay makes an almost complete circle. I read about the 'unique selling point' of Carvoeiro and its surroundings: no high-rise blocks. I fall in love with the place. I want to go there.

There is a man ahead of me in the queue at the reception desk of Hotel Eva. He is a tall, slim, black man, closer in colour to Will Smith than to Eddie Murphy. Will is wearing a soft-yellow tailor-made suit. If bling hadn't been invented yet, he would have done it. Everything he wears, gleams. His rings – he's got three on his fingers and one on his right thumb – his watch, his bracelet, his chain necklace, and the small clip holding together a wodge of 500-euro notes: everything is made of gold, even the cover of the mobile phone which he is pressing against his ear. Holding the money between his forefinger and thumb, he dangles it in front of the receptionist's eyes; she patiently lets him finish his telephone conversation.

Will is conducting a business call, with lots of *yeahs* and *rights* and *sures*. He sounds American and tells the person on the other end – a man, I assume – that he's checked out of the hotel. In actual fact this isn't true. Hotel Eva, staff and guests alike, are quivering in anticipation, like a bunch of frightened chinchillas, of what is to come next. The entire hotel is holding its breath until such time as Will is ready to hang up and get on with what he says he is doing: checking himself out of the hotel. His royal highness seems to be in no hurry whatsoever; he's got a few more things to say to his partner yet. Meanwhile, there are nine people in the queue behind him – a family, two couples and myself – all waiting our turn, but it doesn't bother him. Or perhaps he hasn't even noticed.

I watch the scene with growing fascination. How can he pull it off? One, because he is good-looking. Two, because he is, or appears to be, rich. Three, because he is a man. Four, because he is not troubled by guilt, shame, or any other feelings of discomfort.

Lift me over your shoulder and take me with you, Will. I don't care where you got the money from, you're probably deeply involved in drug trafficking (I like the little diamond in your ear lobe, by the way), it doesn't trouble me; in fact, it makes you all the more exciting. It is too late to change the world, let's enjoy ourselves. Follow me to room 411, take me on the bed, against the wall, on the washbasin and on the floor, and after that teach me all your tricks.

Will clicks his phone off.

'Did you use the minibar this morning?' the receptionist asks.

'No idea.'

This throws her into confusion. She was clearly expecting a simple 'yes' or 'no'. 'Er, I do need to know. Did you have anything from the minibar today?'

Her fingers are ready to hit the keyboard of her computer.

Even I can see it is unwise to ask Will the same question twice.

'It's your job to check that. I'm a guest here.' Will is fiddling with his money. His mobile phone is lying on the desk.

A sigh passes through the line of waiting people. How much longer is this going to take? The receptionist calls over a colleague, who, after some deliberation, goes off to Will's room to check if he has helped himself to a box of peanuts before breakfast this morning.

Will looks around with an air of boredom. It isn't just his colour, he really does look like Will Smith, he could easily be a close relative, or the man himself even. His eyes rest on me. I feel a twinge in my stomach. I am a woman; I am alone. He is a man; he is alone. Could it be that something is happening between us, at this very instant?

I smile at him, brushing my hand through my hair. Jesus, I am flirting.

Will raises his eyebrows. Oh my God, I am making a fool of myself. He finds me ridiculous, too old. He probably has as many girlfriends as he has rings on his fingers. Why am I being so pushy? And anyway, my last experience with a black man – with Clark at the funfair – was hardly a smash hit.

'Are you leaving Portugal, or just Faro today?' Is that really my voice? Yes, I am speaking to him. I have asked him a question. I can still do it. I haven't completely lost my touch.

'No idea,' he says.

Of course, why give a normal reply. That wouldn't be cool. Thanks, Will, I've got nothing more to say.

'What about you?' he asks, looking me straight in the eyes.

Oh my God, he's good-looking. I'm overawed. I have to hold on tight to stop myself from fainting. Luckily I'm not wearing high heels, or I'd be sprawled out on the marble floor now, with the back of my head lying in a slowly expanding pool of blood.

I wonder if I should act mysterious as well. I think I probably should. Jimmy always insisted that that is what men want: mystery. The less they know about you, the more they want from you.

'I'm passing through,' I say after, I hope, a long and somewhat weary silence.

'Where are you going?'

I shrug my shoulders.

Activity is resumed at reception. Will has been found innocent of opening his minibar this morning. The receptionist can finish her task. Will's phone rings. He keeps it short this time. He has spent five nights at Hotel Eva, I learn. I wonder how many of those were spent alone. Again, a sudden twinge in my stomach.

Will pays cash. He puts away the rest of the money in his inside pocket, pulls up the handle of his suit-case, gives it a little shove with his knee and turns round.

– Do something, hisses Jimmy.

– Like what?

– You want that guy, don't you? So do something. Ask for his number, I don't know.

I look around me, panic-stricken. He is almost at the door.

Stretching her arm out, the receptionist opens her mouth. Immediately I see why: Will has left his shiny mobile behind on the desk. Before she can get to it, I lash out and put my claw on it.

'Hey mister!' I shout. 'You're forgetting something.'

He turns round.

– Don't go to him, let him come to you. It's like it is with dogs: you've got to make them crawl, work for you. Only then do they know who is boss.

I prove him right. Will calmly stands his suitcase on its side and walks towards me in slow motion.

'Here you are,' I say. Our hands touch when I give him the phone. I nearly faint. It's like the Nokia advertisement: *Connecting people*. Those two little hands moving together when you switch on the phone, so pure, so beautiful. I am also reminded of Nike: *Just do it*. Commercial slogans have helped me more in life than the Bible. At Schiphol I passed a brilliant advert, with Tiger Woods, the golf champion: *Every great accomplishment is at first impossible. Go on. Be a Tiger. Is it enough for you to improve your game? Or is it your goal to change the game itself? Go on. Be a Tiger.* Those aren't just slogans, they're vital questions about life and death. And they instantly make you want to become a tiger yourself, you just can't help it.

Prince Will looks a bit like Tiger too, from a distance.

'Where are you from?' Will asks.

'Amsterdam.'

This brings a smile to his face.

'What's your name?'

'Julia.'

He smiles again, a bit more broadly this time. I don't understand why, people don't usually find my name amusing. Will puts the mobile in his inside pocket and briefly rests his hand on my shoulder.

Electricity: I can feel at least 180 volts. Does he feel it too?

'Nice meeting you, Julia,' he says.

'Likewise.'

There isn't much left for us to say now. He knows that, and so do I. If we want to take it further one of us will have to make a move pretty quickly.

Just do it.

'If you happen to be staying for a bit longer in the Algarve, I'm on my way to Carvoeiro. It's a small place, close to Lagoa,' I say, emphasizing the word 'small'. I leave out the fact that Carvoeiro is also known for its picturesque character. I don't know what the English word for picturesque is and Will doesn't strike me as the kind of person who would care much, anyway.

He nods his head. Is he taking in the information, or have his thoughts already moved on to other things, like a lucrative deal with some 'motherfucker' or other, who is waiting for him in the coffee shop round the corner? I feel crap, I no longer know how to play the game. Once I was a desirable pro, now I'm just a sad amateur.

I take a deep breath. 'Maybe we'll meet again,' I say. I do my best to sound indifferent, but I feel as if the success of this trip now depends entirely on his answer.

'Maybe,' he repeats.

And that is it. He turns round and walks away from me, to his suitcase, to the door, through the door and off he goes.

The woman at the reception desk looks at me expectantly. I let someone else go first; I need a moment to recover myself. I walk over to the bar and sink into the nearest peach-coloured sofa.

Let's recapitulate for a moment. This isn't Corsica. Then I had to fight them off. I was sixteen years old. I'm thirty-six now, in other words, twenty years older. You can go on trying to mask it till you're blue in the face, but it is never going to be enough. Time isn't kind to women. A few lines here, a few kilos there, the first grey hairs. And then the fear. That you won't notice what others realized ages ago, that you are way past that so-called frivolous minidress. That they are whispering: Liz Hurley from behind, Liz Taylor from the front. That you permanently look a fool without knowing it.

I have drawn up my wish list for the plastic surgeon. It is getting longer by the day. I just haven't got round to it yet. You have to find endless ethical justifications before you can have anything done. If you dye your hair blonde, nobody will mind, if you change your cup size you get cross-examined. I feel so sorry for celebrities. Journalists always ask them if they have had 'anything' done yet, and if so, what? When? And was it really necessary?

Sometimes I feel so old. Inside as well as out. As if I have been through too much at too young an age. As if after Jimmy's death, all the colours of the spectrum faded overnight. It was terrible that he died, but also so intense, so special. I have not experienced anything like it since, not even when the children were born. Maybe I am trying to find what I lost then. A rainbow, a light so bright that it hurts your eyes.

Jimmy joins my stream of thoughts.

– Exactly! You've got it. This is what we had agreed.

– I know. I haven't forgotten my promise. That's why I'm here. Perhaps there's hope yet.

– Dammit, there better had be. Go on, Jules, go and

grab that guy, the one who was here just now. Prove it. Prove that you're alive. You can do it. You can still do it all.

I stare at the door Will has just gone out of.

– I don't even know his name. He's not like you, he's a real person made of flesh and blood, he has a will of his own.

– Excuses. Go on. Be a Tiger.

Jimmy hasn't forgotten how to be bossy.

– Hey, Mr Omniscient, if you really want to help, give me his name and number, will you?

No reply. He's gone. Apparently he's got a will of his own too. I'll have to manage by myself.

Chapter Fourteen

'I need a car, and accommodation in Carvoeiro. I don't mind what it costs,' I tell the receptionist firmly. Will has inspired me.

Immediately she jumps to attention, calls a taxi to take me to the nearest car-hire firm and gives me the addresses of several villas that are to let. There is one she singles out as being her absolute first choice. She knows the landlord, he is very reliable. 'But it does fall within the highest price bracket,' she says rather pointedly.

I nod as if, in any case, I wouldn't be happy with anything less.

The Casa da Criança is situated in Sesmarias, on the outskirts of Carvoeiro. According to the receptionist, it's a villa of the very highest class with everything you could possibly need or want. It is enclosed by a wall all the way round, 'architect-designed', it offers panoramic views of the sea as well as the surrounding country-side, it has six rooms, a large kitchen fully fitted with all the latest equipment, three bathrooms, two jacuzzis (one indoor, one outdoor), a sauna, a washroom with washing machine and dryer, a heated swimming pool with 'poolman', three terraces, a tennis court, and a daily cleaner, if required. All of this on a plot measuring one and a half hectares, including the tennis court, a putting green, and a garden featuring fig, almond, pepper, orange and palm trees.

'Shall I find out for you what the weekly rent is?' she asks.

'No, don't bother. I just want to know how soon I can move in.'

I go up in her estimation by the second. She reaches for the phone. Casa da Criança is available. Had I thought yet about how long I'd like to stay?

Two weeks to begin with, and then we can think again.

She takes care of all the arrangements, gives me the name and address of the landlord – an Englishman – and directions to his house.

'You're an angel,' I say. 'Thanks.'

Most places in travel guides are terribly disappointing when you visit them in real life. Carvoeiro is an exception to the rule. It's a sweet little village, well organized, friendly, and a bit touristy but not too much: I have made a good choice. I've parked my hired jeep in the main square, I have got out and I'm looking at the sea. Paul, Isabel and Jim would love it here too. The children would immediately run off to the sea; Paul would tell me to straighten the car because it's not parked exactly between the lines.

I take my shoes off and step onto the sand. The bay is small, with big rocks to right and left. A little boy of about six is climbing up the rocks. Who is with him? I scan the beach. There is a woman sitting on the beach twenty metres away from me. She is talking, rather loudly, to her husband, and it sounds as if they're having a row. He is standing on the sand, digging his hands into his pockets, and staring straight ahead with a grumpy expression. He is wearing a knitted turtleneck jumper: a peculiar choice in this weather. The woman is sitting on a rug, wearing a bleached T-shirt, a cream skirt, and army-style boots without laces. A little dog hovers around the couple. The man walks off in the direction of the square. The puppy runs along with him.

Suddenly the woman seems preoccupied with her mobile phone. Neither of them is paying attention to the little boy. I climb up onto the rocks and begin a conversation with him. He speaks German and he is called Leon. I ask Leon where his mother is. He points to the woman with the army boots. So it is her. Leon tells me that there are starfish and mussels further along on the beach. That is where he is heading. He carries on climbing – he is a real sweetie. I tell him to be careful.

The woman has got up. She walks over to the other side of the beach, removing herself even further from her son. She holds her phone in front of her with her arm outstretched. Presumably she is using the camera function.

I keep an eye on Leon; someone should, I feel. With one eye I watch the child and with the other I look at the sea. After a few minutes the boy waves at me frantically. He has found something; he wants me to come over and see. I climb up to where he is. It is a starfish. We both think it is absolutely beautiful. I stroke his head and return to where I was standing before. Leon's mother is walking towards us now.

I want to reassure her, tell her everything is fine, but I can't make eye contact with her. She is still preoccupied with her phone. She doesn't call her son until she is right by the rocks. She can't see him from where she is. I notice she has a tongue piercing.

'He's over there,' I say. 'He's looking for mussels. I'll keep an eye on him.'

She nods. 'Just make sure he doesn't go too near the sea, there's a dangerous current out there. I almost drowned in it myself as a child.' She makes a vague gesture in the direction of the sea to the other side of the rocks. Leon is getting quite close to it. 'I was swept along. Terrible. That's why I want him to be extra careful. Will you tell him?'

Of course I will.

'Is my husband with him?'

I shake my head.

'And the little dog?'

'It followed your husband to the square.'

She turns round and walks away.

A little later, when the family are reunited, I can come down the rocks without having to worry. I saunter over to the ice-cream parlour and order a cone with two scoops. In the middle of the square stands a circular stone bench. It is occupied by a couple, who seem completely absorbed in each other, and a little old man, who looks like something out of a Portuguese travel guide. He has a hunched back, hollow cheeks, he wears a flat, light grey cap and he is holding a stick. I install myself beside the little man and lick my ice cream. It's a shame I don't know any Portuguese, otherwise I would say something friendly to him. He doesn't look lonely and vulnerable, even though he is sitting outside on a bench, all by himself. Whenever I am in a hot country, I am struck by how much more comfortable the elderly are inside their wrinkled skins.

They are also much better at getting themselves about without the help of walking frames on wheels and mobility scooters. Holland has the largest density of walking frames on wheels in the world. My mother-in-law lives in a neighbourhood where you can't move for those bloody contraptions. The average person living in the Amsterdam *Oud-Zuid* quarter is seventy-five years old, has had at least one hip replacement, and won't leave his or her home without one of those useless folding things on swivel wheels.

The ice cream is delicious. My phone rings. It is Paul. I answer the call.

'Your daughter wants to speak to you,' he says.

Isabel comes to the phone. 'Mum, is that you?' she says, catching her breath.

'Hello, darling, is everything all right?'

'Yes.'

'You seem very breathless.' Apart from that she sounds normal. Not distraught, not desperate. Maybe it isn't as bad as I thought. Of course she can manage without me for a little while. It is important that she does. I might have got breast cancer, I might have died. All in all, this is a positive thing. When I return I'll be a more fun mother.

'I just cycled really fast. Where are you, Mum?'

I hesitate for a moment. Paul doesn't know where I am yet. Somehow, I like that idea. 'In Portugal,' I say. It's a pretty big country, after all.

'Is it nice?'

'Yes, quite.' I don't want to sound too enthusiastic.

'Do you have the Internet?'

'No.'

'You should get it, Mum. Then we can chat.'

So far I haven't spotted any Internet cafés, not that

I've been looking. I haven't been to the villa yet. Perhaps it will have a computer.

'When are you coming home?' she presses.

'Sweetheart, I've only just arrived. How is Jim?'

'He's gone to football.'

Of course, it is Wednesday afternoon. He'll be coming home soon and then he'll want to tell everyone how many times he scored, and how well he passed the ball.

'Why hasn't Daddy gone with him?'

'He went with Denzel and Denzel's mum. Daddy was too tired.'

There is no one now to cheer him from the sideline. This is the result of my decision.

'Do you want Daddy?' Isabel asks.

'No, it's all right.'

'Oh, he wants you though. Here he is, Mum.'

Before I can say anything, Paul comes on the phone. He also wants to know where I am.

'Portugal,' I say. My ice cream is melting rapidly so I lick it.

'The children are really struggling,' he says. 'We had quite a drama when they couldn't reach you this morning. I've agreed with them that they can call you three times a day. Mornings, lunchtimes and before they go to bed.'

'Lunchtimes? But they're at school then . . .'

'I'm buying Isabel a mobile phone. And I think you and I should be in touch at the end of each day so that we can quickly run through everything together.'

It seems I have no say in the matter. 'Is three calls not a bit much for the children?'

'That way their suffering will be kept to a minimum.'

On the other hand, it could go the other way if they

are constantly being reminded of the painful situation. Of the fact that their mother is not around, a mother who keeps saying, 'Not today: I am not coming home yet.' I wonder if that won't upset them even more. And what about me? Being in touch three, no, four times a day? A thousand invisible threads and a more or less permanent telephone connection.

'What's your address there?' asks Paul.

'Haven't got one yet. I'm still looking.' Next he'll decide that the children are coming to see me this weekend.

'Let me know as soon as possible, OK?'

He hangs up.

I finish my ice cream. Suddenly it doesn't taste as good any more. Imagine you eat an ice cream and you can't taste it at all: the example I gave to Isabel and Jim.

I hear a series of short bleeps next to me. It sounds like a pager. I didn't know those things still existed. The old man digs into his pocket and, indeed, produces one. He presses a button. The bleeps stop. He nods in satisfaction, and then looks at me as if to say: here we go again. I smile at him and lick my fingers clean. He says something I don't understand, puts the thing back in his pocket, and stands up. Leaning on his stick, he hobbles away. I have to go too. The Casa da Criança awaits.

First to the landlord to collect the keys. When I park my jeep outside his modest villa, two enormous, barking dogs come storming towards the fence. The receptionist at the hotel had warned me about them. That is to say, she told me I would recognize his house by the dogs, French mastiffs: brown, with large heads and loose folds of skin hanging down over drooling mouths. Tom Hanks once played opposite a dog like that in the film *Turner & Hooch*. (Hanks was Turner, the dog was called Hooch.) The pair jump up against the fence – they are halfway over it.

'Calm down, boys, I'm a friend,' I try. They are not impressed. On the contrary, they become even fiercer. I take a step backwards.

A lean man of about sixty appears behind the mastiffs. He is completely dressed in white: shorts, polo shirt and sun hat. The only thing missing is a golf club or a racket. In perfect English he tells his dogs to lie down. They obey him – well, not quite, but they stop barking. Briefly.

'Hello love, you're the Dutch girl, aren't you?' I melt instantly.

'I'm Eddie,' he says.

We shake hands across the fence.

'Julia.'

'Well, well. That's a lovely name for a lovely young lady.'

He takes the keys out of his pocket and hands them to me. Would I like him to come along with me, and explain how everything works? It is a tempting offer but I decline. I want to explore my new accommodation on my own.

Eddie gives me a piece of paper with the alarm code plus his phone number, and assures me that I can always drop round, or phone him or his wife, Doris, if I should have any problems. Did someone tell me about needing to pay a week's rent in advance?

No problem, I have plenty of cash; I stopped at a cash machine earlier. What do I owe him?

'Two thousand eight hundred euros,' says the landlord.

I turn pale. I thought it would be about half that and that I had left a generous margin. 'Sorry,' I stammer. 'I don't have that much on me.' I remove my sunglasses and look at him appealingly. Hopefully he sees that I am trustworthy. 'I can manage fifteen hundred and bring you the rest tomorrow.'

'No problem,' says Eddie.

I get out my money and begin to count.

'Are you on holiday all by yourself?'

That's right.

He wants to know if anyone will be joining me. It is a very big house for a woman alone, he thinks. I hesitate for a moment. Then it dawns on me that here in Portugal I can be whoever I want to be. I ask Eddie if he can keep a secret. He says he can. I tell him that I am an actress. A famous one – in the Netherlands, at least – and that I have come to get some peace and quiet.

'A famous actress – who would have guessed that? Do you have a husband too?' Eddie wants to know all the ins and outs.

'I do have a husband,' I confirm, 'but we're going through a bit of a rough patch at the moment.'

'Oh dear,' says Eddie. 'Do you have children?'

I should have seen that question coming.

He will think I am a bad woman if I tell him I have a daughter and a son; he won't understand. I don't want him to know; I don't want anyone to know. I don't want to become known by the people here as 'the woman who left her children'.

'That's a painful issue, Eddie,' I whisper.

He apologizes at once.

'It doesn't matter,' I say. 'It's just that we . . . how shall I put it? We can't have any. That's the problem. And I—'

122

I can't go on. It's as if I'm betraying my children for the first time.

'There, now,' says Eddie. 'I understand. No need to say anything further. My sister-in-law . . .'

He embarks on an elaborate story involving his wife's youngest sister and the many miscarriages she had to endure before giving birth to triplets, of whom two were stillborn and the third died after only one day.

I nod. Very sad indeed.

'Eventually she adopted children,' Eddie explains. 'And she's blissfully happy these days.'

'My husband doesn't want to adopt,' I say. 'Hence our row.' I heave a sigh.

Eddie sees I want to bring the conversation to an end. He gives me a sympathetic nod and repeats that I can ring at any time.

'Here are fifteen hundred to be going on with.' I give him the pile of banknotes through the fence. He takes the money and, without counting, goes on to explain how to get to the house.

The Casa da Criança is only a few hundred metres away, just past the next curve in the road. It's an ultra-modern villa; he hopes it will be to my satisfaction. I hop into my jeep and give him an enthusiastic wave. The mastiffs spring into action again.

I drive off, curious to see the Valhalla that is about to appear before me. After the curve I see two villas lying a fair distance apart. One is a charming white Moorish house, surrounded by an English garden; the other is a grotesque building in primary colours, which can best be described as a bucket of Duplo, plonked upside down. The phrases 'ultra-modern' and 'architect-designed' instantly seem very negative. Surely I've come to the wrong place?

I go up to the charming villa first. This time I am greeted by only one barking dog. A king poodle with a little bit of Labrador mixed in: a Labradoodle. You can tell from its coat. When I was a girl I always longed to have a dog, but instead I was given a dog encyclopaedia. That's how I know all the different breeds.

Casa Encantador, it says on the ceramic nameplate attached to the gate.

There is nothing for it, I'll have to go on to the bucket of Duplo. It looks rather desolate. No dogs, that's a point in its favour, but the rest just makes me want to cry. Casa da Criança is constructed of large cubes, which stick up into the air and rest only partially on top of each other. Some are a faded red, others baby-boy blue, mint green or desert yellow; the colour of the roof wavers between fuchsia-purple and Paris Hilton pink. And that's with my sunglasses still on. The garden really is full of different trees, surrounded by a tapestry of pitch-black gravel. There is no traditional Portuguese ceramic nameplate. Instead there are some rusty-looking cast-iron letters, which have been screwed onto the fence in a slapdash manner – presumably with the idea of making it look playful, but reminding me of a typical Dutch kindergarten.

I don't even bother to get out of the car, and drive straight back to Eddie. The hysterical dogs come rushing out again, Eddie following in the trail of their saliva. He laughs, looking pleasantly surprised: he wasn't expecting to see me again quite so soon. What he hasn't noticed yet is that my mood has dropped by about twenty degrees in the last three minutes.

I leap out of my jeep.

'Look who's here again, it's the famous actress. Hello,

Julia.' Then he sees the thunder in my face. 'What's wrong, love?'

I take off my sunglasses. 'I've just given you fifteen hundred euros, haven't I?'

He nods.

'And I owe you . . .'

'Thirteen hundred.'

'Exactly. A total of almost three thousand euros to sleep in that . . . that . . .' I fumble for words. 'How dare you ask that much?'

'Casa da Criança was designed by Tomás Taveira,' Eddie says coolly. 'Taveira is a highly reputable architect. He's responsible for the new marina at Albufeira, for instance.'

'And for Disneyland, by any chance? I've never seen anything so hideous in my life, Eddie.'

Eddie remains polite. 'Taveira is keen on using colour, certainly. If you have time, you should go and look at the marina, you'll recognize his style. He's a great artist.'

I look at him in desperation. He means it.

'Casa da Criança was an experimental project for Taveira, he designed it for a foreign investor, just before he got the commission for the marina.'

The story is getting better by the minute. I am stuck, for at least two weeks, in a finger exercise by Tomás Taveira.

'I noticed another villa, which looks really sweet. Casa Encanta something-or-other. You couldn't let that to me instead, could you?'

He shakes his head. 'Casa Encantador is permanently occupied. By Dutch people as it happens, you might like to meet them. They're a nice couple, only . . .' He falters.

'Only what?'

'They've got a big family. A girl and three little boys. Their youngest was born not long ago. Doris thinks he cries a lot, they told her it's because he suffers from colic. A food or sun allergy – they haven't quite worked it out yet.'

Something tells me I should take the next plane to New Zealand. My phone rings. That'll be from the home front again. I grab Eddie's hand through the railings. 'Whatever you do, please don't tell those people there's a famous Dutch actress staying at the Casa da Criança. Before you know it they'll be onto a tabloid paper, and the next day there'll be a paparazzo aiming his telephoto lens at me from the front garden. I wish to remain anonymous here. Do you understand?'

He nods.

I answer my phone. It's Paul. 'Your car is due for its MOT. I'm taking it into the garage tomorrow. Where do you keep the registration document?'

'Cabinet in the hall. Left drawer.'

'Thanks.'

I have no choice, I'll have to go to my new residence. Who knows, perhaps it's better on the inside. I drive back at a snail's pace. When I pass the villa where the Dutch family stay, I look the other way. I get out at the Casa da Criança, open the iron gates, get back into the car and drive on to the grounds. I park my jeep on the gravel and enter the house, looking for the living room. Thank goodness, Tomás has kept his paws off the interior. The room is decorated in a fairly neutral style, with cream colours and furniture that has been treated with some white staining to give it an antique look. There is a marble floor.

My phone rings. Paul again. I don't feel like answering. The ringing stops, only to start again after a few seconds.

'Hello?' I can't hide my slight irritation.

'Jim got concussed,' my husband says point blank.

'What?'

'He was hit on the head by a ball. Very hard. He was sick afterwards.'

This is what I have always been afraid of. That something might happen to Jim. The way it did with Jimmy.

'How is he? Where is he now?' I ask, panicked.

'Denzel's mother took him to casualty. He's home now. I've got to wake him up every hour.'

'Why?'

'Doctor's orders. To check he's OK.'

'And if he isn't?'

'I don't know, Julia, I'm not a doctor, am I?'

'Shall I come home?' I say it without thinking. I want to be with my son.

'That's up to you.'

'Is his life in danger?'

Paul sighs. 'He's at home, Julia, he's resting. In theory it should sort itself out, so long as he takes it easy. I'll check on him every hour and—'

'Can I speak to him on the phone?' I interrupt him.

'He's asleep right now. I'm not going to wake him.'

'How long do you have to keep doing that, the waking-up business?'

'Till tomorrow morning.'

I start doing the sums in my head. Even if I manage to book a flight, it will be at least eight hours or so before I can be home. If all goes well the greatest danger should be over by then. And then what? What do I do once I'm home? Give Jim a kiss, and push off again the next day? That means breaking his heart all over again. 'Paul, just be honest, please. Is it serious, does he seem very ill?'

'I don't know. He was looking pale and he had a headache. I gave him paracetamol and then he fell asleep. I've got to go up now and see how he is. I'm checking every half-hour, just in case. I'll speak to you later.'

Paul will keep a very good eye on him. I am absolutely sure of that. Flying back on the spur of the moment might be overreacting. It is only concussion. I remember Kaitlin had one when she was small. She had fallen off a fence. She was up bouncing on her bed again after only two hours because she was so bored. My mother got angry; she was terrified a blood vessel might burst in the aftermath, with fatal consequences. Nothing happened. Kids are strong. Most of them are. So is Jim.

– I wasn't.

– Yes, Jimmy, you too. You were very strong. You managed to hang on for such a long time. Right up to the last minute. You were indestructible.

He smiles omnisciently. I massage my neck. I think I can feel a migraine coming on. Valium, that's what I need. Valium, paracetamol, and preferably a *vino tinto*. There's no vino in the house, though. Let's start with the Valium. I take my handbag and pop down three tablets. After fifteen minutes I doze off on the sofa.

An hour and a half later I wake up with a start. Jim!

I call home. Paul picks up. Everything is under control, nothing to report, the patient is asleep. He even had a little soup an hour ago.

'Are you going to come home?' Paul asks.

'No,' I say tentatively. 'There's not much point now.'

'OK,' says Paul, and puts down the phone. We're not getting on at all well – the atmosphere between us remains icy. I don't know how to handle it.

The villa is dark and quite chilly, but then it is only February. I switch on a few lights. I want to light the fire, but I can't see any wood. Or any matches for that matter. Tomorrow I'll go shopping, tomorrow is going to be a better day. Let's see: I've been away for a day and a half now. What's happened so far? Not much, in fact. There is more to escaping than just taking yourself to a different place. The whole idea is to have more fun than you would have done if you had stayed at home.

OK, tomorrow night I will go to The Strip in Albufeira. I will use the day to stock up on food and drink, get a new outfit and perhaps have my hair fixed somewhere. And then I will be ready to let things rip. The prospect perks me up a bit. I get up and open the curtains. As the sun is setting, the sky over the sea turns crimson. The view is breathtaking.

Chapter Fifteen

I am walking around at The Strip. It's as if I am pushing an invisible walking frame with wheels. Nobody notices me. Am I imagining things or are they really avoiding me? Everyone is at least ten to fifteen years younger than I am and enjoying themselves, or so it seems. Girls in crop tops, with provocative texts stretched across the width of their breasts, saunter arm in arm along the street, shrieking with laughter, and smoking one cigarette after another. Every three minutes they apply a slick of gloss to their lips, while the boys nonchalantly wear their caps back to front and their trousers at half mast.

I am wearing a floral dress with a denim jacket, and flip-flops. I feel like a fish out of water. Where am I supposed to go? Where can I have fun? Where can I find people who feel the same as I? What is the ritual when you go clubbing these days? I very rarely go out, and if I do it is usually to have a civilized meal somewhere, or a drink in a café. That's about it. How do today's youngsters unwind? They get tanked up, you hear people say that. Maybe I should do that first.

*   *   *

A remote corner of a quiet bar. A glass of beer. Make that half a litre, will you? I take a big swig, breathe in deeply, and gulp down some more. Just give yourself a chance, I tell myself. You're a party animal, a tiger. In the early hours of the morning you'll be the one that has to be asked – politely but urgently – to please leave, so that they can let in the cleaners.

I can feel the beer sloshing around in my tummy and decide to have a Bacardi and Coke next. The staff are not paying much attention to me, nor are the rest of the customers for that matter.

I have switched off my mobile. Paul called three times today with stupid practical questions. I don't know what has got into him, he seems to have decided that he can pretend I haven't left, that I am just working late at the office. Jim is fine, nothing worrying happened in the night. He slept well and went to school in the morning. At circle time he told the class about his concussion. The other kids were deeply impressed.

'At least now they all know you have a brain, Jim,' I joked on the phone.

Isabel wanted to know if I had managed to get Internet access. She keeps going online but she never spots me on MSN.

'I haven't had time yet, madam.' I feel I have failed again. I wonder if that will ever pass.

'OK, speak to you in the morning,' Isabel said. I didn't have the courage to tell her that I was intending to go clubbing, and that it might get late.

I pay for the beers. 'Where can I find the best disco around here?' I ask the bartender.

He rinses out another glass and doesn't even bother to look up. 'Kadoc,' he says.

*   *   *

I leave the place to go in search of Kadoc. It is easy to find, everyone knows it. I hand in my coat at the cloakroom and force my way in. Kadoc has a number of rooms, each with a different style of music. I go into the one where, despite the deafening racket, I can still make out some kind of tune. A swaying horde, flashing lights, clouds of smoke, scantily clad girls and boys with open shirts: things are looking up. I join the crowd and allow myself to be engulfed by it. I am dancing.

Paul doesn't like discos. He doesn't like parties much either. 'Parties just serve to make us forget that we are lonely, unhappy and doomed to die. In other words, they just turn us into animals,' he once told me. He was quoting a French author whom he mentions quite often. I keep forgetting his name. I am not so much of a reader myself.

'But in that case,' I replied, 'we should be pleased there are parties, shouldn't we? All the more reason to go to them.' There is nothing I would rather do than forget I am lonely, unhappy and doomed to die.

Paul sees things differently. He prefers to read books which show that humankind is lonely, etc., etc. He likes to watch DVDs about wars: the Second World War, the Vietnam War, the war in Iraq, the Eighty Years' War, the Spanish Civil War, the Balkan Wars, the list is endless. Whenever he's seen one, he switches off the television with a look in his eyes that shows his worst fears about mankind have been confirmed again.

I avoid such films for precisely that reason. I don't see the need to relive other people's tragic experiences. I never sailed to the US as a chained slave; I never lay in a trench; nor has my head ever been carpet-bombed, nor have I looked down a gun barrel. No one has ever

132

forced me to be a slave: I have not been humiliated, raped, suppressed or tortured. Come to think of it, I suppose that – in the context of the history of mankind – I have missed an awful lot.

There are loads of beautiful people in Kadoc. Beautiful, young people. Their liveliness is contagious. My cheeks are glowing. I laugh and sing along with the music – if I know it, and there are words to sing along with, that is. I dance and look, and look and dance. Every so often I see a Very Cute Boy, and try to lure him over with my eyes, just like the old days. The difference with the old days, however, is that it is not working because the Very Cute Boy, in his turn, has his eyes fixed on a Very Cute Girl, fifteen years my junior. I am determined not to give up too soon, and take my time to explore the dance floor. It seems a little sad, though, that I am not connecting with anyone. I wonder how Kaitlin goes about it when she is away. I should have asked her for tips. Let's get a drink from the bar first. There are always people sitting there: it'll be easier to get talking to someone.

It is very crowded at the bar, and all the stools are taken. With much difficulty I manage to order a Bacardi and Coke. I take a couple of big gulps and enjoy the burning sensation in my throat.

'Are you alone?' I hear someone say next to me.

Surprised, I look to my side. I can't see anyone.

'Are you alone?' I hear again.

Is someone trying to make fun of me?

'Hello!'

It's coming from below. I look around me. Right behind me stands a man, the crown of his head only coming up to my hip. In each hand he holds a pint of beer. I am looking at a midget, a German midget. You hear people talk about low points in their lives – I'd never imagined it could happen in such a literal sense. I can't help it: I burst out laughing.

The mini man walks off, the beer spilling over the edge of the glasses. For a second I wonder if I should go after him to apologize. But why should I? He made a move, he didn't stand a chance, I was upfront with him. Why should we always be so careful about everything?

After two more Bacardi and Cokes I go dancing again.

I don't care if I pick up anyone tonight or not. I am at Kadoc, this is party land, I am having fun, I can get sloshed, I can do anything. I am a free agent.

It is at that point that I spot The Portuguese Guy. Or rather: The Portuguese Guy spots me. He is a Very Young Portuguese Guy. His dark hair is parted down the middle by a straight line. You can tell he has made an effort with his appearance. He didn't quite manage to camouflage the spots on his forehead. On the other hand the birthmark on his cheek makes up for a lot. Cheeky expression, not wildly attractive, but a good average player. The friend who is with him doesn't interest me. We establish eye contact. He comes and dances a bit closer to me – I let him advance. Not much later the Very Young Portuguese Guy and I are dancing together. Because I am wearing heels I am slightly taller than him.

'What's your name?' I have to shout into his ear.

'Nuno,' comes the answer.

Nuno doesn't ask for my name. But he does make me an indecent proposal: would I like to kiss him?

'Me? Kiss you? Now? Here? This minute?'

'Why not?'

'Why should I?'

'Because.'

'Do you know how old I am?'

'What difference does that make?'

'How old are you?'

'Seventeen,' he says with some pride. 'Well, how about it?'

Nuno's hands are already on my hips. They feel delicious, he tells me. I can't imagine how a boy his age can possibly derive pleasure from kneading my love handles, but each to his own.

His friend taps him on the shoulder and makes a gesture.

'We've got to leave!' shouts Nuno. 'What's it to be?'

Yes, what is it to be?

He bends over towards me and presses his lips on mine. I let it happen. I open my mouth a little; he forces his tongue in and rotates it wildly. At the same time his right hand slides down over one of my breasts and squeezes it. Seventeen years old and totally shameless. I take his wrist and firmly remove his hand. He gets the message. His tongue swims around a few seconds longer.

It is not particularly sexy, or enjoyable, and yet it is crucial. I am kissing a minor, I am crossing a boundary. That's what I am here for. To live. To have new, crazy experiences. The hot-blooded fellow presses me against his body while his friend watches impatiently. I can feel his erection. If I wanted, I could go to bed with him. He doesn't have a micropenis, that's for sure!

'What do you want?' he whispers in my ear. His breath reeks of beer.

Again I feel his erection against my erogenous

zone. Christ, times have changed. Or is it me that has changed?

'I'm a mother. I could be your mother.' I feel he is entitled to this information before we do anything else.

'What do you want, Mummy?' he asks. 'I want milk. Warm milk from Mummy.'

This lad is bonkers. I push him away again.

Nuno is not impressed and asks if I'll be back tomorrow. His friend is pulling him by the arm now.

'No idea,' I answer.

He sticks his hand up and disappears into the crowd. I feel an immediate craving for another Bacardi and Coke.

The rest of the night I have lots more to drink – too much – and become increasingly uninhibited on the dance floor; I feel myself growing more attractive by the minute although I am probably not because when I try to chat up a Fairly Attractive Portuguese of about twenty-five, at four in the morning, he looks at me with something like repulsion. Maybe my make-up has begun to leak. I urgently need to go to the Ladies. It's busy in there. We all have small bladders and there are never enough toilets. I am about to go to the Gents when, suddenly, I hear my name.

'Hey, Julia!'

For a moment I think I must have imagined it, but someone in front of the mirror really is calling out my name. Our eyes meet in the mirror. I don't recognize her. She turns round.

'How crazy to see you here, don't you remember me? It's me, Lotus.'

136

Lotus, Lotus . . . I can't think of anyone I know called Lotus.

'My name used to be Marion,' she helps.

Oh, Marion, of course, Kaitlin's friend. Haven't seen her in ages. Her hair looks different. Longer and blonder. And she is so slim. Slim and toned. She can't possibly have children.

'Hey, Marion, I mean Lotus, how are you?' The sentence doesn't roll off my tongue. It's several hours since I last said anything.

Lotus pours out a barrage of words: how funny to bump into me here, it's so totally unexpected, she had heard from Kaitlin that I had got married and had two kids, a girl and a boy, exactly as it should be, and that I had settled into domestic bliss. 'Kaitlin always says, "She lives in Amsterdam, that's the only thing that's still wild about Julia,"' she concludes, laughing.

I don't know what to answer.

'You look a bit pale, are you all right?' Lotus asks.

'I've had a little too much to drink.'

'Are you on your own?'

'Yes.'

'Do you have a secret life and keep it from your sister? And your husband and children, where are they, have you left them on their own in the hotel room?'

I find Lotus very sharp for this ungodly hour. Too sharp.

'My family are miles away and I'm alone,' I say. 'And nobody seems to believe that I could possibly have fun on my own. Even though I can.' Suddenly I want to cry. Cry my heart out on Lotus's shoulder. At the same time I feel sick. And I need to pee.

'What have you been drinking?' Lotus asks. She opens her handbag and rummages around.

137

'Mainly Bacardi and Coke.'

'Do you want something to pick you up?'

I gaze at her with glassy eyes.

'A white pick-me-up,' she explains. She takes me to a corner of the toilets, and pushes her hand under my nose. There is some powder on the ball of her hand.

'Is that cocaine?' I ask, a little too loudly.

'Sst!' she says. 'Do you want it or not?'

Drug addicts, alcoholics and smokers are such gregarious people. They always want you to inject, sniff, drink or smoke whatever it is, with them. They want to share what they have. Which is to their credit. Surely a little cocaine at the age of thirty-six can do no harm. I inhale the stuff.

'You'll feel a lot better in a minute, just wait.' Lotus gives me an encouraging pat on the back.

'Thank you,' I say, confused.

When I eventually lower myself onto the toilet I realize just how dizzy I am. For a moment I sit absolutely still with my eyes shut. This is OK. Slowly but steadily my urge to be sick passes. I would love to stay on the toilet a lot longer, if only things would stop spinning so much. The spinning has got to stop. I blink a few times. Ping! All of a sudden, it's as if a strip light pops on inside my head. I feel lucid. Super lucid. Must be the cocaine, what else can it be? I stand up, pull up my knickers and walk out of the toilets.

I feel surprisingly steady on my legs and make for the big room. I spot Lotus at the edge of the dance floor, chatting to a boy. I must go over to her. She smiles when she sees me and brings her face close to my ear. 'Do you like it?'

'You bet, I'm feeling much better. Thanks.'

'If you want to feel even better, I have something else for you.'

What a special girl she is, this Lotus. She's so kind to me, even though I hardly know her.

She takes my hand and presses something into it.

'It's just a half. I don't suppose you've ever had one before?'

'What is it?'

'XTC. If you take that, you'll become mellow all over.'

I daren't open my hand.

'For ten euros, it's yours. Don't drink any more Bacardi and Coke once you've taken it. Just water, lots of water. Pretend you have to cough and then pop it into your mouth quickly – they watch you in this place.'

'I take Valium during the day,' I say to Lotus, who seems to be an expert. 'Can you mix XTC with Valium and cocaine?'

'Sure.'

I take a deep breath in, pretend I have to cough and swallow the little half. Lotus offers me a sip from the water bottle that belongs to the boy she was chatting to. All this time he hasn't said a word, but keeps staring at Lotus as if she were some astonishing sight.

I give Lotus ten euros. How long before I notice anything?

She can't hear me any more because the boy has pulled her towards him. I expect him to kiss her but he has different plans. He licks her cheeks, moving his tongue energetically from left to right. Lotus undergoes it with a faint smile. When he pauses for a moment, she licks him back. She starts on his chin and works her way up via his mouth and nose to his forehead, and then down again. They carry on like this for a while, interrupting the lickathon only to take sips of water. They no longer pay any attention to me, but don't seem bothered by my presence either. How curious. Perhaps it is a new trend. Once you are over twenty, it is hard to keep up with what is hip and what isn't.

I go back to the dance floor. It doesn't take long for Lotus's half-tablet to take effect. The strip light in my head is becoming dimmer, everything around me has turned pink, as if Tomás Taveira is at work inside my brain, and I don't even mind. I think Tomás is sweet, I wish he was here, then I could tell him. I'd say that he is a cutie, and that all he does is try and make beautiful things for people, and that there will always be grump-bags like me who have to run everything into the ground. Tomorrow I am going to write a note to Tomás, that's for sure.

My mouth is dry – I must drink some water. On my way to the bar I see the midget sitting in a corner. I must be getting double vision, because there's another one right next to him. I blink a few times. There are still two, they look the same, only one is wearing a Hawaiian shirt, and the other a striped T-shirt. They are staring ahead in silence. If I remember rightly it was the stripy T-shirt who was trying to chat me up. I go over to him.

'Sorry I laughed at you earlier,' I say. 'I hope you don't mind me speaking English – I'm afraid my German isn't very good.'

He doesn't mind, he replies in a German accent that sounds terribly sweet. In fact, everything about him is sweet, and that also applies to the one next to him. Look at them, sitting side by side in Kadoc. Two droll gnomes.

'Are you still angry with me?'

'No, don't worry.'

'Can I buy you both a drink?'

'Beer, please.'

I get two pints and a bottle of water for myself. 'May I join you?'

He doesn't see why not.

'Are you two related?' I ask.

'Yes.'

'Brothers? Cousins?'

'Brothers.'

'How unfortunate for your parents.' Immediately I put my hand over my mouth. 'Sorry, I didn't mean it like that.'

It doesn't matter, they are used to it. Their parents are also short. The one with the Hawaiian shirt says there was a one in four chance that they would be normal. Their parents had risked it twice.

'Let's raise our glasses,' I say. 'Short, tall, fat, thin: who cares? We're all human. We all want the same things.' I begin to sing: 'A little bit of freedom, a little bit of sunshine for this earth on which we live.'

It is the only German song I know. Oh yes, and the one about ninety-nine balloons, but I can't quite remember that now. While I am singing, I suddenly wonder if their genitals will be a normal size. I imagine they will. After all, it's all soft tissue.

The couple put on a doubtful face. Maybe I am not singing in tune. Maybe they aren't so keen on German songs. I find it difficult to read them.

'*Skol!*' I finally shout. We all take a sip.

'By the way, I'm Julia. And you?'

My midget is called Wolfgang, and the one in the Hawaiian shirt is Heinz.

'Wolfgang? As in *Amadeus*?' I ask.

He nods.

'That's my favourite film! It's fantastic. Great! *Wunderbar!*' I throw in a bit of German to please the little fellows.

Wolfgang has never seen *Amadeus*, and neither has Heinz. I can't believe it.

'What madness! *Amadeus* is the best film ever. It's an absolute must-see!'

The midgets prefer James Bond. They also like *Lord of the Rings*.

I can't sit still any longer. I jump up out of my seat and skip around.

'I know what we could do. Let's go to a video-rental store and borrow the DVD of *Amadeus*, and then we can watch it at my villa.'

'Your villa?' asks Wolfgang.

'Yes man, I've got a villa here. You can easily fit a hundred . . .' I almost say Lilliputians, but manage to stop myself just in time.

'. . . people in it.'

Wolfgang and Heinz look at me hesitantly.

'You'd like us to come with you to your villa?' Wolfgang asks. 'Now?'

'Yes, I would! And then we'll go and have fun. I've got a very large bed. And two jacuzzis. And a swimming pool. Do you know what the name of my villa is? Casa da Criança. I've no idea what it means, but it's a splendid house. On the inside.'

'Where's your husband?' Heinz wants to know.

'He's somewhere else. Not here. I'm alone, completely alone.'

All of a sudden the Lilliputians become active. They empty their beer glasses and stand up.

142

'Are you the only . . . I mean . . . do you know any other small people in the area?' I ask Heinz.

He shakes his head.

'Is there no meeting place, a society, or something like that?'

'No,' says Heinz. 'Why?'

'Promise not to get angry?'

They promise.

'I think you're awfully sweet.' To demonstrate how sweet I find them, I kiss them both on the forehead. 'I can imagine life is very difficult for you and so I'm going to cuddle you to death in a moment. What I'd really like to do is take another five midgets with me to the Casa da Criança and spoil them all as much as I'm going to spoil you. And you could pamper me too. We'd all pamper each other from top to toe and then I'd wake up the next morning and feel like a true princess.'

Heinz whispers something in Wolfgang's ear. This upsets me. Surely we can be open and honest with each other. We are friends.

'Well, what do you think? Are you coming?' I ask.

They whisper a little more.

'My brother thinks disabled people turn you on,' Wolfgang says. 'And that's why you've invited us.'

I must be hallucinating. Am I really about to be turned down by a pair of midgets? I try to keep a straight face. 'Dear Wolfgang, dear Heinz, cross my heart: I have never fantasized about sex with disabled people. Not because I won't allow myself to, you mustn't think that – it just hasn't happened so far. Do you believe me?'

Wolfgang nods but Heinz remains a bit suspicious.

'Shall we go, then?'

'OK,' says Wolfgang after a quick glance at his brother.

143

'Smashing! Let's take my car. I have a very sexy jeep. Hang on one moment, I'll be right back.'

I want to find Lotus. She is on the dance floor with her boy, dancing very slowly. I go over to her and give her a little nose lick. So as not to offend her boyfriend I give him one too. I hope they are impressed by how quickly I am assimilating to the nightlife here.

'That little pill of yours,' I shout in her ear, 'isn't half bad. Can I have the rest too?' I press a ten-euro note into her hand.

'Sorry, it's all I've got left. I'll let you have it, but only if you pay me twenty.'

As if the Chair of the Society for the Preservation and Protection of Families would find that a problem. I look in my purse: I only have a fifty-euro note. Lotus has no change and the boy is not up to handling a financial transaction. I can't be bothered to go to the bar. Fifty euros it is then, for half a tablet of XTC. Here we go: cough, and in goes the little bugger.

I put my purse back in my bag, take out my mobile and switch it back on. After thirty seconds my missed calls show up on the screen. There are seven altogether, seven times Paul. He has left no messages. If something really important had happened, he would have done. It's too late to call back, I'll do it tomorrow.

Wolfgang and Heinz are patiently waiting for me. I fetch my denim jacket from the cloakroom. We go outside and breathe in the crisp night air. I look up.

'Wow, look at the stars! Aren't they just amazing!'

Wolfgang and Heinz are more interested in my jeep. They walk all the way round it, admiring its splendour.

'Where exactly are you staying?'

'At the campsite of Albufeira.'

'In a tent?'

They both nod.

The midgets climb into my jeep – it is quite an undertaking for them. We zoom off to my villa. Wolfgang is sitting next to me; Heinz is in the back. At a hundred and eighty kilometres an hour we'll be there in no time. I turn on the radio and we arrive at Sesmarias in high spirits. The men seem impressed when I open the gates to my villa and switch on the outside lights for the pool.

'Welcome to the Casa da Criança!' I say proudly. 'Shall we dive in? The pool is heated.'

Wolfgang and Heinz don't want to. I do. I take off my sandals and denim jacket, and jump in. I feel the blood freeze in my veins – it is as if I have jumped into a tub of ice water. Jesus Christ, Eddie must have turned the thermostat right down to its lowest setting. I vaguely remember something about covering the pool with a sheet of plastic at night. I forgot.

I swim over to the thermometer. The water is 15 degrees centigrade. I put on a brave face. 'Come on, boys, come and join me, it's lovely. You don't know what you're missing.'

'We want to go inside,' says Heinz. 'We're cold.'

They do know how to moan, those midgets.

I heave myself out of the pool. With blue lips and a dripping wet dress I walk to the front door. 'Would you mind getting me my jacket and shoes, sweetheart?' I ask Wolfgang. He hesitates for a moment, then walks back to get my things. Strange that he waits to be asked. They are a bit boorish, anyway, these midgets of mine. I mean: who paid for all the rounds? Julia. Who has invited them back to a luxury villa? Julia. A little gratitude would not be out of place.

145

Small people must feel so stretched by all they have to do to hold their own ground that social behaviour is not high on their list of priorities. That must be the explanation. It would be an extraordinary coincidence if I had found the two worst-mannered midgets in the world to spend the night with at my villa.

Casa da Criança gets the seal of approval from Wolfgang and Heinz. While the men explore the villa, I take off my wet clothes in the bathroom, rub myself warm with a towel and slip on a cream-coloured bathrobe.

I find my new friends in the kitchen. They are looking for beer.

'Sorry, I've only got wine. And milk.'

They don't like wine.

We search through all the cupboards and discover a bottle of vodka, which is still three-quarters full. They will have some of that, they say. I can't find the glasses quickly enough, so fill two coffee cups instead. I have water.

We toast.

'What shall we do, boys?' I ask after ten minutes. Heinz has already refilled his own and Wolfgang's cup once, without asking. The couple say little – actually, they say nothing. It is up to me to keep the conversation going, to keep everyone's spirits up – it's quite a challenge to be a good hostess.

Wolfgang shrugs his shoulders. He looks cute in his stripy T-shirt; like a little zebra.

'You're wearing a nice shirt,' I say. 'It looks very soft, as if you've got animal skin on. May I have a feel?'

He lets me. I stroke Wolfgang's chest. I was right, it is very soft: it makes my hand glow. I carry on stroking him, I can't stop.

146

Heinz helps himself to another vodka. Wolfgang declines. Heinz is looking a bit annoyed, perhaps he feels ignored by me. His shirt is white with red flowers. I stop stroking, go over to Heinz and bend down to smell his shirt. I sniff his collar. 'I knew it,' I say, delighted. 'Your shirt smells delicious, is it Anaïs Anaïs?'

One day, tenderness will win over the world.

That promise saddens me. Because it isn't true. You would like it to be true, and when you see that nymph-like girl who never gets any older and blows into her open hand so sweetly, you would almost think it was possible, but then the eight o'clock news comes on and all your fantasies about tenderness are crushed.

'Let's be tender,' I say to Wolfgang and Heinz. 'Let's start spreading tenderness across the world. I'll ring Tomás Taveira, let's all build a pyramid of tenderness together.'

Heinz and Wolfgang begin to whisper again. I am getting the impression that they are not desperate to help me build a pyramid of tenderness.

'Do you have something to eat for us?' asks Heinz.

Unbelievable, what a pair. They are lucky I am in such a generous mood. And that I have been out to get milk, bread and eggs this afternoon. I inspect the spice rack in the kitchen. There is cinnamon. Excellent.

'Fancy some French toast, boys?'

They don't know what that is. It's a bit like pancakes, I explain, made with slices of bread. Wolfgang nods enthusiastically; Heinz shows he can smile after all.

I open all the drawers, find an apron and put it on. It would be a shame to get my bathrobe dirty. The midgets offer no help. I am beginning to think they are rather spoilt. Shaking my head, I pour the milk into a bowl.

While I am busy cooking, my guests become less and less talkative, and they weren't exactly saying a lot before. By the time I want to show off the first golden-brown slice of toast, they're both asleep: Wolfgang resting his chin on his chest, and Heinz with his on the table. It's a quarter past four by the kitchen clock.

'Dinner!' I gently rouse Wolfgang. Heinz also wakes up and has a good stretch, and a yawn. I put a plate of French toast on the table.

'I need to have a piss first,' says Heinz.

'Don't forget to wash your hands afterwards, will you?' I say it without thinking.

He gives me a funny look.

Wolfgang gets three plates from the cupboard.

There is no sugar, just sugar lumps. We will have to make do. I do my best to make it cosy – after all, I don't have guests in my villa every day. The French toast can't be bad. Heinz has three slices and Wolfgang two. I don't feel hungry at all. Wolfgang and I clear away the plates, while Heinz polishes off what is left. Everything is gone, I am pleased.

At a quarter to five the kitchen is tidy. We have run out of things to say to each other and we have finished eating. All Heinz can do is yawn. The party has peaked.

'I'm going to bed.'

The midgets stand up simultaneously.

I see that I can't send them home now. 'Boys, there are plenty of rooms upstairs, go and choose yourself a nice one.'

Heinz shakes his head. 'We're sleeping with you. You promised.'

'Yes,' Wolfgang agrees. 'You were going to pamper us.'

'Isn't that what I've just been doing?' The pink light in my head is slowly turning green and yellow. I'm beginning to find the midgets less irresistible and cute. They're so bloody hard to please. It's easier to bring home a pack of famished Rottweilers than two men coming up to one metre and thirty centimetres.

'We want to sleep in your bed,' Heinz repeats.

'Forget it.'

'Why not?'

'Because I'm exhausted.'

Heinz starts to whisper in his brother's ear again.

'What's the matter?' I ask in an irritated voice.

'Heinz thinks you're discriminating against him,' replies Wolfgang. 'He says that you don't want to sleep with us because we're short.'

'Can't Heinz speak for himself?'

'You've really disappointed him.'

They want to come into bed with me. There is plenty of room, I suppose. I assess the brothers with a critical eye. Would they be strong enough? Would they be able to overpower me if they conspired against me? I don't want to be raped by those two idiots.

'Well?' Wolfgang asks.

I feel I have been asked before. I can't remember what I said then. I am no longer able to think straight, I am about to keel over. 'All right, you can come into my bed. But just to fall asleep. OK?'

We go up to the master bedroom of the Casa da Criança. Wolfgang goes to the toilet, Heinz takes his clothes off. I am praying he will keep his underpants on.

I am still in my bathrobe with nothing underneath. I

grab the biggest pair of knickers and widest T-shirt I can find, and go to the bathroom. When I return, the bedroom is pitch dark. 'Hey, I can't see a thing,' I protest.

Someone switches on a light.

Wolfgang and Heinz are lying side by side, glancing hopefully in my direction. They are stripped to the waist. They have got very hairy chests. When I see them there, I find them quite sweet again.

'You've been warned, yeah?' I say briskly. 'No messing about.' I get into bed. At last I'm lying down. Thank God for that. My poor feet. 'Goodnight, boys.' I turn onto my side and switch off the bedside lamp.

'What did I tell you? We're not even going to get a goodnight kiss,' Heinz grumbles.

I sit up with a jolt. 'Now, you listen to me, dammit! Stop it! Who do you think you are? Ungrateful *Schweinhund*. Do you really want a goodnight kiss? Here . . .'

I switch on the lamp, bend over to Wolfgang and press my lips hard onto his.

'There! Was that good? Do you want more?'

He looks at me anxiously.

I meant to take Valium when I was in the bathroom, shame I didn't. 'Just say what you'd like me to do: do you want a tug, or a quick blow job, perhaps?'

I am not doing very well. It is all becoming a bit too much. The alcohol, the pills, the midgets. I wish I was at home. I wish I was lying safely next to Paul. The only ones who should get a goodnight kiss from me are Isabel and Jim – no one else.

'Don't get upset now,' says Wolfgang.

'Just leave me alone then!' I shout. 'You have no idea.'

Wolfgang strokes my back awkwardly.

'Just what do you expect?' I ask.

'Nothing – nothing at all.' Wolfgang tries to soothe me. 'Go to sleep.'

I lie down again. Heinz gets out of the bed. He is stark naked. Stocky and naked. His member is normal. It is semi-hard. I don't want to see it but I do. He mutters something inaudible and leaves the bedroom.

'Would you like me to go as well?' asks Wolfgang.

'Are you wearing your underpants?'

'Of course.'

'Stay, if you like,' I whimper.

The light goes off again.

There is complete silence: neither of us dares to move a muscle. I worry that I'll never be able to fall asleep. But I do. I dream about two midgets standing over me and jacking off, and giving each other a high five afterwards.

I hear a sound in the distance. A piercing, familiar sound. It won't stop, it goes on and on, please let it stop. It keeps going: it's my phone. Someone is trying to call me. With my eyes shut I fumble around on the bed table until I find it.

'Hello,' I say hoarsely.

'Hi Mummy, it's Jim.' I hear my son's sing-song voice.

At once I am wide awake. I look to my side and see Wolfgang. He has slept right through the noise. His mouth is hanging open and there is a wet patch on the pillow.

'Hi, sweetheart. How are you?' I whisper. Wolfgang must on no account be woken up – I don't want Jim to hear a male voice. As I pull myself up, Wolfgang turns

151

over. His hand lands on my belly. I just manage to suppress a shriek of horror.

'Fine. Mum, Dad says that this afternoon after school I can . . .'

Carefully I lift Wolfgang's hand and put it down next to my body. I slip out of bed.

'. . . and Isabel too. Isn't that great?'

'Wonderful, darling.' I tiptoe out of the room. One of the bedroom doors has been left ajar. I assume that is where Heinz is lying.

'When are you coming home?' Jim asks.

'I don't know yet, Jim. I've only been here two days.' I walk down the stairs. At each step my head thumps. I haven't felt so hung-over in ages. I am never going to drink again, and Lotus can keep her pills from now on. 'Are you doing anything nice today?'

'I just told you,' he says indignantly.

'Sorry, sweetie, I'm still a bit sleepy. It's an hour earlier here.'

'Here's Isabel.'

'Everything OK with your brain?'

He's already gone. I look at the kitchen clock. Quarter past seven, so it is a quarter past eight there. This is what it is going to be like every morning. I hope Paul gets them to ring a bit later at weekends.

'Hi, Mum!' Isabel is sounding cheerful.

'Hello, my girl.'

'Daddy has bought me a mobile phone.'

'So I heard.'

'It's cool, you can even make little films with it. And take photographs. I'm going to record something every day. Do you have email now?'

'No. Not yet. Why?'

'So that I can send you my clips, of course.'

'Of course.'

'I've got to go to school now.'

'OK. Have a good day. Give Daddy a kiss.'

'He's standing next to me, here he is. Bye, Mum.'

There is no escape, Paul comes on next. 'Where were you last night?' he asks sternly.

'I was out.'

'Yes, I'm aware of that – I couldn't contact you.'

'My phone was in my bag,' I say defensively. 'I didn't hear it ring.'

'It wasn't switched on. I got your voicemail. I tried you seven times. Seven times! You obviously didn't even check your phone. Imagine if something had happened . . .'

'Nothing did happen, Paul!'

'We had an agreement, Julia.'

'Excuse me, *you* made that agreement. You never asked me anything.'

'Not so loud please!' Heinz appears at the top of the stairs; he's still naked. 'I can't sleep!'

I point to the phone and put my index finger over my lips.

'I can hear something. What is it?'

'Nothing,' I say quickly.

'Is there someone with you?'

Go away, I signal to Heinz. He scowls at me from the top of the stairs, then disappears.

The door of his bedroom slams shut with a bang.

'Now I understand why you weren't available. Madam has already found herself company.'

'Oh, come on now, Paul. There's no one here, believe me.'

'Do you want to know how your family are doing? Does that interest you at all?'

'I've just spoken to the children.'

'And that's you having done your duty, you mean?'

'That's not what I mean.' I'm trying to stay calm. 'I've just woken up, it's not even half past seven yet over here.'

Paul sighs. 'I'm not doing this to get at you, Julia. I'm doing it for the kids, for us . . .'

The rest of his words are drowned by the noise of a drill.

'What was that?' I ask when it stops.

'They've started the demolition work,' he says, irritated.

Of course, that dreadful business was going to start this week, I had completely forgotten about it. They are knocking down a block of derelict houses in our street and putting up new ones. It looks as if I planned my departure rather well. I am about to say that I find three phone calls a day a bit much when the drill starts again. Maybe this isn't such a good moment. I will bring it up another time. Once I am clear-headed, well rested, and not hung-over any more. Christ, I can't believe how awful I am feeling.

'This is impossible. Let's speak later, OK? Bye, Paul!'

I go up to my bedroom. Wolfgang has slept straight through it all. I take a few stomach settlers, some Valium and get back into bed.

When I wake up again, I smell coffee. Wolfgang has gone. It is a quarter to eleven. I must get up: Isabel's lunch break starts in fifteen minutes. Hopefully my guests are having breakfast; the sooner they go, the better.

I walk into the bathroom. Wolfgang is sitting in the jacuzzi.

'Good morning!' he says with a broad smile. He certainly seems more cheerful when his brother isn't around.

'Oh, hi there,' I return unenthusiastically.

'I could get used to this, how long can we stay here?'

For a moment I'm lost for words. 'Stay?' I manage to say after a few seconds. 'You're not staying, you're leaving!'

Wolfgang emerges from the bubbles. 'My brother was right,' he concludes. 'You have no feelings for us.'

'Of course I have,' I lie. I should say *had*. I genuinely had feelings: they were chemically induced, but that doesn't make them less real.

'Why don't you take off your shirt then, and come and join me.'

I sigh. 'Wolfgang, I want you both to leave.'

'We're staying.' He submerges himself in the water again.

Don't tell me I'm going to have to call in extra help to evict two midgets from the Casa da Criança! Nervously I chew my lip. 'My husband's coming home today.'

'And you want us to believe that?'

'I don't want any trouble,' I quickly go on. 'He's quite a bit older than me, and very jealous. He's been away playing golf for a few days. I'm not sure exactly what time he'll be here. Please, get dressed, take your brother and go back to your campsite.'

'Heinz is also keen to stay. You're not going to find it easy to get rid of him. And anyway, how are we supposed to get back to our campsite from here?'

'I don't know.' Half a night in my villa and already they are completely dependent. 'I'll see if I can get you a taxi. Just get out of that bath now, my husband could be arriving any moment.'

155

I go to the bedroom and pick up my mobile. Instead of the taxi firm, I call Eddie.

'Eddie, Julia here.'

'Hello, love.'

Good, he has forgiven me my rant against Tomás Taveira.

'I have a slightly unusual request, Eddie.'

'Julia, I'm almost sixty, I can cope with unusual requests.'

'A couple of colleagues have come to pay me a surprise visit. Actors. *Method actors*, you know. We're having a bit of fun, improvising. We're in the middle of a scene and we urgently need a jealous husband. Do you think you . . . I hardly dare ask this . . .'

'Do I think what?'

'Do you think you could play that part for us? It's important that you're in your role from the moment you arrive, could you do that? My two colleagues are pretending to be my lovers. As soon as you see them, you go wild with rage and chase them out of the house.'

'Is that all?'

'Yes. And ideally we'd like you to come straight away. We're in the middle of the scene, you see. I'm pretending to phone a taxi because I'm expecting my supposed husband to walk through the door any minute.'

Eddie puts his hand over the phone, I hear muffled voices – presumably he is talking to Doris.

'No problem,' he says. 'Let me just repeat what it is you want me to do: I am your husband, I come into the room, I see your lovers – there are two, right?'

'Yep.'

'And I chase them out of the house.' He says it in a deep, angry voice.

156

'Fantastic, you're a natural, I can tell.'

'Shall I bring the dogs?'

'No, no: no need. You're returning from the golf course.'

'Oh, in that case, I'll go and get my golf clubs.' He laughs. 'Good thing I've got the keys to the villa, hey? It'll be just as if I am the real lord of the manor that way.'

'Absolutely,' I say. 'Just one more thing: you may be taken aback when you see my colleagues for the first time, but that shouldn't be a problem. They're used to that. It'll make your reaction all the more convincing, OK?'

'You're beginning to talk gibberish, love. I'm coming to rescue you.' Eddie puts the phone down.

Please let Heinz be dressed, I pray. Let Wolfgang have finished his bubble bath. Let Eddie play his role well. Let this nightmare be over.

'Darling, I'm home!'

Eddie comes in with a golf bag over his shoulder and wearing a chequered cap. I rush to kiss him on the cheek.

'Hello, dearest,' I say.

He winks at me. 'Goodness me, have I had a good time on the golf course. Absolutely marvellous,' he says just a little too loudly. He puts his bag down in a corner of the entrance hall. 'I'm starving. I think I'll go and have a look in the kitchen to see if my wifey has left me something delicious in the fridge.'

He gives me a little pat on the bottom. 'Wait!' I shout in a pretend-panicky voice. 'We've got guests.'

'Guests?' shouts Eddie. 'You didn't tell me that.'

'Unexpected guests,' I say.

'Unexpected guests? But we never have unexpected guests!' Eddie is practically screaming.

At that moment Wolfgang and Heinz enter the scene. Heinz is holding a cup of coffee in his hand, and is still naked; Wolfgang only has a towel round him. Three jaws all drop at the same moment.

'Darling, I'm sorry.' I grab Eddie's arm and shake it to force him back into his role. 'I should have told you. These are friends of mine. Friends from the past. We spent all of last night reminiscing about the good old days. We had too much to drink. They stayed the night.'

Eddie has recovered from the shock. 'Stayed the night?' he thunders. He clearly struggles with inventing his own lines.

'Nothing happened, I swear.'

'She's right.' Heinz cuts into the conversation. 'She was keen, she begged for it, but we didn't fancy the idea. She's too old for us. We can do better than a pair of drooping tits, a fat bum and a wrinkled face.' He takes a sip of his coffee and smirks at me.

Eddie seems at a loss.

'Julia,' he says. 'Julia.'

Improvise, please, let him improvise.

'Do you call these your friends?' he finally manages to say.

'Yes, I mean, no. They've taken advantage of my hospitality. I wanted them to leave, but they insisted on staying.' I stare at the ground.

'Shame on you!' Eddie takes off his chequered cap and throws it to Heinz. He puts his coffee down, picks up the cap and covers his genitals with it.

'Get out!' shouts Eddie. At last. 'Do you hear me? Get out. You have insulted and embarrassed my wife. Get out!' He opens the front door.

'Without clothes?' Eddie whispers in my ear.

Why not. Wolfgang and Heinz move slowly backwards. They are going the wrong way. Eddie is really getting into the swing of it now. He takes his mobile out of his pocket.

'I'm calling the police. The police in Portugal don't like people who trespass.'

The brothers change direction. I run up to the bedroom, grab their clothes and return to the hall. The midgets are standing with their bare feet on the gravel. Eddie brandishes a golf club menacingly.

'And don't you ever dare come back here!'

I throw their clothes outside, the midgets pick them up and take to their heels. Together we watch them run off into the distance.

'Was I good?' asks Eddie. 'Or is there more to come? Are they coming back again?'

'No, they won't. We always continue the scene.'

He nods understandingly. Wolfgang and Heinz are still running. They pass the Casa Encantador, they are at the curve, they vanish out of sight. The next moment we hear Eddie's dogs bark furiously. I pull a face.

'One of them still has my cap. They'll bring that back, won't they?' Eddie asks, worried. 'I won it at a tournament in 1996. It's my lucky cap.'

I don't answer him. A fat bum, drooping tits and wrinkles. I have made a mental note for myself. Short people and drunkards tell the truth.

159

Chapter Sixteen

I am on my way into the centre of Carvoeiro. Isabel just called. She had some great news. She wasn't really supposed to tell me yet, but Daddy had promised that if she and Jim were very good, the three of them could come out and visit me. And that, probably, I would then go back home with them. I nearly dropped the phone when she told me. Has Paul completely lost the plot?

I park the jeep in the square, sit down on the bench and look at the sea. The sun is shining in my face. I close my eyes and take a few deep breaths. I hear a soft, soothing voice next to me.

– Relax, Julia. Try and manage without Valium today. See if you can manage under your own steam. This is Portugal, there is no stress here: you don't have to fit in with anyone else; Holland is far away and nobody knows where you are. Just remember that if you don't want it, they can't find you.

Jimmy! I am so glad he is still there. He understands me. He knows why I need to be on my own. My mobile beeps. A text message from Paul: what is your address?

I delete the message without replying. This isn't

going to work: Paul isn't giving me any breathing space, I am constantly reminded of home, I am never going to be able to break free this way and get round to my own needs.

An old man with a stick comes shuffling towards me. It is the same one as last time – the one with the pager. He sits down beside me. I give him a friendly nod, he nods back. I don't think he recognizes me.

Another beep. Paul again: will call tonight at ten o'clock your time. Make sure your phone is on.

This is the problem. He can get in touch with me. I am gone, but he can still find me. Every time I receive a message from Holland, I feel a pang of guilt. Every time I speak to the children, I am paralysed with doubt: am I doing the right thing? Should I persevere or stop? Should I go home?

Dammit, I have only just left: of course I should persevere. There are too many unresolved matters, which I can't sort out when I am there. At home I get swamped, I am the sponge that absorbs all the problems of everyone around me, and I always want to put everything right immediately. Paul and I have become locked into our own separate ways; there is a gap between us these days, and I am afraid that we'll end up just as my parents did: completely alienated from each other. Can you narrow a gap by running away? Will I be able to explain it to Paul when I come home? Will I be able to sleep again and love him – truly love him?

I must remain practical. That has always been my biggest strength. The main thing is that he should be able to reach me in case of an emergency. God forbid that anything happens to the children, but if it does, it is important that Paul can find me quickly.

I look to my side. The old man seems to be happily leaning on his stick. That's it. He has the solution to my problem in his pocket. I tap him on the shoulder. 'Pager? Pageros? Bleeper?' I try, pointing to his trouser pocket.

He still doesn't seem to recognize me and gives me a puzzled look. How do I know what he keeps in his pocket? After some hesitation he takes out the gadget. I smile broadly and reach for my purse.

'How much? *Quanta costa?*'

He shakes his head. No, it is not for sale.

'Where can I buy pageros?' I ask. The old man begins a long story in Portuguese, of which I can't understand a word.

This is going to take for ever. I make my way to the girl in the ice-cream parlour. Does she speak English? Yes, she does. Would she mind asking the old man on the bench where he bought his pager? Of course. The travel guide was right: the Portuguese are lovely to foreigners. The girl acts as interpreter. It turns out that the pager was a gift from the old man's daughter, and that she in turn had got it from the hospital where she works.

I see.

'Could you please tell him that I want to buy it? I'm willing to pay a hundred euros,' I say rashly.

The girl's eyes grow wide. She translates my request. The man does not want to part with his pager.

'How much then?' I ask the girl. By now I'm ready to make out a blank cheque.

Another round of negotiations.

'Two hundred and fifty euros,' she says cautiously. Presumably that's six months' pay at the ice-cream parlour.

I count out the money. The little device changes hands. I ask what the number is, and try out the pager with my mobile: it is working fine. We shake on it and go our separate ways.

Carrying my shoes in one hand and my mobile in the other, I step onto the beach. One more phone call. Paul answers almost immediately.

'Hello, how are things?' I do my best to sound cheerful.

'Why do you never reply to my text messages?' His voice is cold. It is the same voice that has often told me how much he loves me. The same voice that used to whisper naughty propositions in my ear, long ago, when he was in the mood for sex. I am the one who is responsible for the change in tone. I had better face it. Best to keep it short.

'Do you have pen and paper ready?'

'Yes,' he answers reluctantly.

'I'm going to give you a number. It's the number for a pager. If there is an emergency, you can bleep me and then I'll call you back straight away.'

'Bleep me? What the hell are you talking about?'

'I'm getting rid of my mobile.'

'Why?'

'Because this just isn't working. I'm not getting any peace.'

'You're not getting any peace. And what do you think I'm getting, with two kids around me the whole time?'

'I know. I'm sorry. Can you please make a note of the number?'

'You were going to give me the address.'

I was afraid this might happen. I don't answer.

'I'm your husband, Julia, why can't you tell me where you are?'

Instead of answering the question, I reel off the number. I have no idea if he is writing it down, I don't even know if he can hear me because the drill in our street starts up again.

'Paul!' I shout. 'If anything important happens, please bleep me. I'll send you a text message, and after that I'm turning off my phone. Bye!'

My fingers are trembling when I bring the conversation to an end. Just to be sure, I text the number not only to Paul, but also to Kaitlin and to Isabel. Three people have it: that should do.

I was planning to chuck my Nokia out to sea – it seemed such an appropriate and symbolic gesture – but now that I am standing here I can't bring myself to. It is a fairly recent model, it would be a pity. I open the phone and remove the SIM card. I put it down on the sand and return the mobile to my bag. I take off my clothes. In my thong, and clutching the SIM card in my hand, I run into the water.

I don't care that there are no other swimmers, I don't feel how cold it is, all I sense is joy. After twenty metres or so, I plunge forward into the water. I swim a little further, doing the front crawl and clenching my fist. As the next big wave comes rolling towards me, I close my eyes and dive underwater. I open up my hand and let go of the SIM card: I am free.

When I resurface, I see Jimmy sitting on the beach next to my clothes. He's wearing Eddie's lucky cap, his oxygen bottle is standing beside him – what a nut he is. I wave wildly.

'I did it, Jimmy, I did it! The old Julia is coming

back, I promise. I am going to do everything I said I would.'

He applauds.

'Will you keep an eye on my clothes for a moment?'

I turn round and swim further into the sea.

A few days before Jimmy died, he summoned me to his bed. 'I want to read you something.'

He got out a book from underneath his bed. It was *The Plague*, by Albert Camus. I only knew the title. Jimmy opened it. 'This passage is about a little boy who dies of the plague.'

I remember thinking: how predictable. But then Jimmy started reading. It wasn't a nice bite-size chunk of suffering that makes you feel better. That is the only good thing about suffering: that it can pep you up. If you are in a room full of people and a wheelchair comes in, the entire company instantly feels better. Happier, even. People do it without meaning to, it's a knee-jerk reaction.

The boy's death struggle in Camus did not make me feel better, on the contrary. The descriptions were so detailed and evocative that they sent shivers down my spine. It went on and on, page after page; I was secretly hoping Jimmy would stop, because it all seemed such a struggle – not just the boy's death but also Jimmy's reading it out loud. He was gasping for air. It sounded as if he was trying to get to the top of Mont Blanc, stopping every two minutes for a puff from his oxygen bottle.

I'll read it myself, I said during his third inhalation pause, but he wouldn't have it, he wanted me to hear the whole thing, right up to the moment when the boy was at his last gasp. If I remember rightly that happened several times in a row, because every time it seemed to be over, the child would start breathing again. The doctor looked on helplessly. There was nothing he could do.

'Listen,' said Jimmy. He was almost completely breathless now. 'The story continues . . .'

A brief respiratory pause.

'. . . Tarrou, the doctor's assistant, runs into the boy's father.'

Another pause: slightly longer.

'The father asks if his son has suffered much . . .'

A pause of three seconds. I had automatically started to count.

'. . . do you know what Tarrou says next?' I shook my head as slowly as I could, to allow Jimmy to draw in some air.

'He says: "No."'

A long pause. At least five seconds.

'He's lying. He's lying to the child's father.' Jimmy pressed the mask over his mouth and inhaled.

I looked at him hesitantly. Was that good or bad? My brother had become such a strict and principled person, everything was either black or white with him; there no longer seemed to be a middle course. He put the mask away again.

'You, my posthumous spokeswoman, must do exactly the same. You must tell Mum and Kaitlin that I didn't suffer. That you could see that when you found me.' Jimmy could barely speak now – he gasped out the words.

At last, I plucked up the courage to say something. 'What if they find you before I do?'

'They won't, because you'll take care of that.'

'How?'

'Just get up early each morning, Jules,' he said with a faint grin. 'And check if I'm still alive.'

*　　*　　*

At half past nine, on the day the doctor was due – the day after the night Jimmy had died – when Mum, Kaitlin and I were gathered round his bed, Jimmy was looking perfectly peaceful. That had been my doing.

I took Mum's hand and assured her that Jimmy hadn't suffered, you could tell from the expression on his face. No sooner had I spoken than his oxygen bottle spontaneously tumbled over and rolled across the room. Mum and Kaitlin turned as white as Jimmy. I started to giggle. 'That's Jimmy. It's his special sign. He promised he would let me know if there was a hereafter. This is it, I'm telling you.'

I could see that Mum felt comforted by what I'd said. She nodded, folded her hands and said, 'Girls, it's all right. My son is with the Lord. He's no longer in pain, he has been received with joy. Let us thank the Lord.'

I couldn't tell you how many times my mother thanked the Lord, but He was the very last one I wished to thank. I'd rather have spat in His face, oh, how I would've liked to have done that! I was angry with Him, livid. I thought He was a son of a bitch, no, a prick, and I didn't even believe that He existed – that was quite an achievement, you had to hand it to Him: that someone who doesn't exist can wind you up like that.

Part Three

Romeo

Chapter Seventeen

I am standing naked in front of the mirror in the master bedroom. Over the last few weeks I have partied so much that I have almost forgotten I am lonely, miserable and doomed to die. I bumped into Lotus again. She told me she had recently come out of a long-standing, boring relationship. A week after she split up with him, she got her breasts done. And then she flew to Portugal. She is staying with an acquaintance. She never wears knickers when she goes out: it adds to the thrill. She has a different boyfriend every night.

I have extended the lease of the Casa da Criança by a month. Funnily enough I have become attached to Tomás Taveira's finger exercise. I have developed a daily routine, almost without noticing. I now know my way round Sesmarias and environs. The Intermarché and the Continente have become just as familiar as Albert Heijn and Super de Boer. There's a big Lidl in Albufeira. I always think of Paul when I drive past it. My father's pass also lets me into the Makro opposite the Algarve Shopping Centre.

Eddie and I regularly stop for a chat at the gate. He always asks after my husband and his lucky cap; I keep saying that I have called the midgets at least a hundred times but they never reply.

'Unreliable people,' Eddie thinks. I usually try and steer the conversation to his dogs next. They recognize me and don't bark for quite as long when they see me now – at least that's what Eddie and I tell each other.

Meanwhile, I have met my staff. First the pool man: I'd been indulging in wild fantasies about him. I hoped he'd be a Portuguese macho, with whom I'd get up to some very naughty things in and around the pool. I asked Eddie if he knew his name but he didn't. He said he called him the Scarecrow.

'What does he look like?'

'Like a typical Moor: dark skin, Mexican moustache, barely taller than those actor friends of yours,' he summarized. 'Last year he was charged with petty theft and extortion, and jailed for several months.'

I was looking forward to meeting him enormously.

The Scarecrow had an unsympathetic personality and a shy manner. I overcame my aversion, and studied the art of pool maintenance. I watched how he vacuum-cleaned the bottom of the pool, operated the pump and filter systems in the machine room, and maintained the correct pH and chlorine levels. As soon as I felt confident enough to take over, I suggested he came less often. His presence made me nervous and, besides, I found him hideous to look at. I really don't like eyesores. The rolled-up sheet of plastic next to the pool is another case in point.

As well as the Scarecrow I have come to know the cleaning lady. Stella is a small woman, unflappable and pithy. Almost everyone here is small. At 1.70 m, I feel like a giantess. She arrives, changes into slippers, ties on a blue apron and systematically works her way through the villa. Stella is the first Portuguese person I can understand a little bit. When I told Eddie, he explained that it's because she's Russian. She speaks slowly and clearly, unlike the local population, who swallow half their words and turn the rest into mumbo-jumbo with their incomprehensible pronunciation. Thanks to Stella, I am learning a few new words every week: dishcloth (*rodilha*), mop (*esfregão*), bucket (*balde*), that kind of thing. Stella has two little boys. They live in Russia with their gran, her mother. She showed me a photograph. Two boys with short blond hair, wearing tailor-made suits and ties. I managed to stop myself just in time from telling her that we are both in the same boat. That my kids are in a different country too. That, like her, I miss them, and that I see their little faces every day, even though I don't have their photos with me. That I know what it feels like: as if something has been amputated. That I have noticed alcohol has a numbing effect.

'I write,' Stella told me, unsolicited. 'When I'm sad, I get out pen and paper. Then I write down everything and weep.'

My pager never bleeps. I carry it with me wherever I go and check it every few hours. Since I no longer speak to the children, I wrote them a note:

Dear Isabella and Jim,
    How are you? This is Mummy. I am still in Portugal. It is a beautiful country and the people are friendly. The weather is nearly always good. It gets dark early here, earlier than in Holland. Sometimes I go for a stroll near the house where I am staying, and then I look up at the moon and

173

think of you because you can see the same moon. Will you think of me if you see the moon tonight?

I got rid of my mobile so that I can rest even better. I hope you are well. I am glad Daddy is at home to look after you. Are you working hard at school? Is your brain no longer concussed, Jim? Sorry, Isabel, but I still haven't found anywhere to go on the Internet.

Remember I told you about the wall around my heart? It is getting thinner. Isn't that great news? It hasn't completely gone though, so I am having to stay a little while yet. I promise I'll write a lot.

Thinking of you all the time and missing you. See you soon!

Lots of xxxs and hugs from Mummy.

PS: If you want to send me post, the address is: Julia de Groot, Posta restante, 8400 Lagoa, Portugal.
PPS: Give Daddy a kiss too, of course.

Lotus and I make a good team. We consume plenty of mind-expanding drugs, we laugh, we dance, she has stopped asking about my family. The only thing I am still waiting for is a result: the men who want to chat me up are fat, ugly and drunk. The men I want to chat up find me fat, ugly and drunk. To put it bluntly: I still haven't had sex with a substantial penis. In fact, I haven't had any sex. Not with any penis. It is beginning to worry me.

The curtains are drawn: bright daylight pours into the room relentlessly. I promised Jimmy the old Julia would come back. I promised Jimmy too much: that is one thing that is clear. I still feel haunted by Heinz's words. When I take an objective look at myself I have to agree with him. This body is past its best. It is too late to become Playmate of the month. I don't have a girl's body, I don't even have a woman's body, come to think of it. What I have is a mother's body. I had a flat belly once, but now it is a golf course. There used to be a gap between the insides of my legs, but now they're stuck together. What used to be my waist is a bulging line from my armpits down to my hips. Apparently, Cher had her lower ribs removed, so that she looks slimmer. I can understand that. If I think away my lower ribs, it would make a difference too. Not that all my problems would be solved, but it would be a nice little start.

– My, we're being positive again!

Jimmy looks at me via the mirror. He's wearing only white. He could be a doctor.

– Sorry, I know. But you have to say so yourself: I look a total mess.

– Details.

– So far, I haven't had much luck with my details, Jimmy. I'm not shunning temptation; temptation is shunning me.

– Do something about it.

– What do you mean?

– Do I have to spell it out?

– Yes please.

– If your right eye causes you to sin, pluck it out. If your fat bothers you, have it sucked away. You've got the time, you've got the cash, all you need is a good surgeon.

– Are you serious?

– Don't pretend you've never given it a thought.

He's right. I am not going to have another opportunity like this soon. Nobody will notice, nobody's going to ask questions, I can do as I please. Lotus had her breasts done at a clinic in Belgium – apparently it is considerably cheaper there than in Holland. She had nothing but praise for them.

Chapter Eighteen

Tap Air takes me to Brussels. I have only got hand luggage and feel that I am a woman of the world. I have become such a globetrotter.

The clinic is in the centre of Brussels, on a narrow street with tall buildings. The doctor who does my registration interview is in his forties. He is handsome: he has dark hair with a few streaks of grey, and it is ruffled. Grey suits men, whereas with women you tend to think, for God's sake, woman, get yourself to a hairdresser. The doctor could be a sculptor: there is something vaguely artistic about him. He sees you and he doesn't, his thoughts are all over the place, one of those types. He shakes my hand hastily, and sits down at his desk with his pen poised. I am ready to take my clothes off, but the doctor wants to talk first. Fine by me.

'What can I do for you?' he says with a Flemish accent.

I take off my sunglasses and unwrap the scarf covering my head. 'As you can see, decay has set in. My face, my body, it's getting worse by the day. I want you to be completely honest with me: is it too late to patch things up?'

He puts his pen down. 'How old are you?'

'Almost thirty-seven.'

'Any children?'

I can be honest here. I tell him that my youngest is six years old. He sits up and scrutinizes me from head to foot. 'I can't see anything inordinate.'

'Do you mean that?' I adjust my hair a little.

'Well, yes, I'll need to assess the situation a bit more closely, of course – we'll do that in a moment. Tell me first: what bothers you the most?'

'Everything.'

The doctor sinks back into his chair.

'It's all equally awful. I have wrinkles. They used not be there. They're on my forehead, in between my eyebrows, above my lip. Here, on my cheek, there's a really long one, it's getting deeper and deeper. The corners of my mouth are a mess, my skin is growing slack. Under my chin as well.'

As I talk, the doctor takes notes.

'As for my body, it was never ideal. Well, I wasn't a model or anything, but it used to be in proportion, if you know what I mean?'

He does.

'I've given it a lot of thought and I want to give you carte blanche. You can do as you think fit. I want you to transform me into a dream woman. The woman every man would like to have.'

'Do you have anyone in particular in mind?' he asks with a frown.

You bet! I had lots of time to fantasize about it on the plane. 'I want Marilyn Monroe's voluptuousness, Paris Hilton's youthfulness, Pamela Anderson's breasts, and Meg Ryan's face.'

'Your hair isn't blonde,' the doctor observes.

178

'It will be,' I promise. Blondes have more fun, everyone knows that.

The doctor leans across. 'Just to prevent any misunderstandings, I won't be doing the actual surgery myself. I'm only in charge of admissions.'

'That's fine by me. As long as I can have your best surgeon and the very latest technology. I want to feel twenty-eight when I walk out of here. Eighteen wouldn't be realistic, but twenty-eight ought to be possible, don't you think?'

He writes something else and puts his pen down. 'You may get undressed behind the screen. You can keep your briefs on.'

'I thought you'd never ask.' I wink at him. He looks frightened: I don't suppose he often gets a wink from a patient.

I have bought a new lingerie set in soft spring tones, specially for the occasion. A moment later I am standing, barefoot, in front of his desk. The doctor gets up from behind his desk and looks at me from all angles. He feels my skin, prods it, lifts a fold of flab and looks under it. It tickles. I can barely control the urge to giggle.

'Do you think you might need to remove some ribs? Feel free, I'm not particularly attached to them.'

He shakes his head.

'A leg extension, then?'

The other day I saw something on TV about Chinese women who are having their legs extended en masse. It is a bit of a carry-on – they saw your bones in two and insert pins – but if it works you can easily grab an extra ten centimetres. Seems wonderful to me. I'd no longer have to wear high heels the whole time.

'Mrs, er . . .' the doctor says, standing up.

'De Groot,' I help him out.

'Mrs de Groot, those are very big interventions which we don't do at this clinic. To be honest, it beats me why you should even consider such things.'

'I want to be more attractive, Doctor. I want men to turn their heads when I walk past.'

'Are you married?'

I nod.

'What does your husband think?' He gestures for me to sit down. My breasts are still bare. If he's going to be a psychiatrist, I am off.

'My husband has got nothing to do with this,' I say stiffly. 'If you're not interested in helping me, I can find another clinic. No problem.' I reach for my bag and get ready to leave.

The penny drops.

'Please, stay,' the doctor says with a honeyed tongue. 'Of course we're keen to help. We just want to make sure that you don't rush into anything before fully realizing all the implications. You're talking about drastic changes. These can affect yourself as well as your surroundings. It is my duty to warn you about this.'

Drastic changes: I can't think of anything I'd like more. It is the doctor's job to gratify my yearning instantly. Goodbye Big Mama, roll on Hot Babe.

'Consider it a challenge, Doctor. I'm allowing you full discretion. Money won't be an issue.'

'Would you mind standing up again for a moment?' he asks.

Here we go again.

This time he puts on his specs. He looks me over carefully. He feels my breasts. It is a long time since anyone touched them like that. I try to ignore the tingling sensation.

'It's quite nippy here, don't you think?'

I get no answer – he's completely absorbed in my body. He takes out his notepad and starts writing.

'You may put your clothes back on,' he says finally.

When we sit at his desk again, I look at him expectantly.

'I've got good news for you, Mrs . . .'

'De Groot,' I say again.

'*Excusez-moi*. Mrs de Groot, you have an elastic skin with a perfect structure, which I would expect to recover beautifully upon treatment.'

'What are we going to do?'

'I suggest that we apply liposculpture. We can remove the excess fat from your upper arms, your hips, the inside of your thighs, the outsides and flanks of your upper legs, your abdomen, the area around your waist, and on your back, where the bra straps sit.'

He describes it as a perfectly straightforward routine job. Which, to him, of course, it is. To me it is a dream: you lie down on a table, and someone comes in with a vacuum hose and sucks away years of accumulated crap from underneath your skin.

'And my bottom?'

'Would you mind getting up again?'

He comes and stands next to me. 'The shape itself is good.' His hand slides around the curve of my buttocks: I can almost feel it. 'Your buttocks are round, I'm not going to change anything there. But, if you like, I could take away a little from the areas below and above.'

I nod enthusiastically. Never knew the shape of my bottom was good. I am so glad that is official now.

'Should we need to, we could correct your abdominal wall surgically, once we've done the liposculpture. Do you play any sports?'

181

'Should I?' I put on a doubtful face.

'It would certainly help. Especially with the abdominal muscles.'

'Hmmm. I'll give it some thought.'

'And now your breasts . . .'

My heart races with anticipation.

'What cup size did you have in mind?'

It is as if I have been granted an audience with the Creator.

'A small D?' I suggest.

'Exactly what I was thinking,' he says. 'I believe that Pamela Anderson takes a slightly bigger size, but this would be more in tune with your body. I recommend that you have your breasts lifted at the same time.'

'Please lift anything that can be lifted as you go along. You have my full permission, darling.'

We're partners in crime now. I just called him darling. Dr Shivers smiles.

'And my face?'

'I take it you have no objection if we enlarge your upper lip a fraction? I don't think eyelid enhancement will be necessary. Not at this stage. We might do a mini-lipo to deal with your double chin.'

Go for it, girl, have the mini-lipo as well. If it's got to be done, it's got to be done.

'I'd also like to inject some filler in a couple of places. Temporary, to begin with. If you like the result, we could replace it with something more permanent.'

'I thought I needed a facelift.'

'No way,' the doctor says resolutely. 'You're far too young for that kind of thing and, anyway, we don't do them half as often nowadays. A facelift tightens the face, whereas applying fillers softens the lines: it rounds your features. A round face is a young face. As you grow older, your skin loses volume and strength – we can compensate for this by injecting filler.'

I hang on his every word. This man knows his onions.

'Some Botox for your furrow and forehead, and that should do it, I think.'

'No nose job?'

'I really don't see why you should want to change a lovely nose like that.'

I'd like to throw my arms around him. 'And my laughter lines? What are you going to do about those?'

Laughter lines, saddlebags, jodhpurs, love handles, waist rolls, turkey neck, hamster cheeks, beer belly – as you age, your body suddenly acquires all these new parts, which are known by the most unsavoury names.

'We'll inject some filler into those.'

I lean back, contented.

'Do you work?' asks the doctor.

'Er . . . I'm on leave. A sabbatical, so to speak.'

'Is there anyone to help you? Do you have children?'

It's a pity that Dr Shivers is growing demented at such a premature age. I nod.

'You'll need to get extra help to look after them. If you really want to go through with the whole thing, you'll have to take it easy for a month.'

'I've got help. And I want the full package.'

The doctor gives me a long, piercing look. He still doesn't trust me completely.

'You can tot up the lot to a nice round figure, and book me in. I'll be getting a discount, I assume?' I look at him mischievously.

He scribbles something on a piece of paper. The damage comes to fifteen thousand euros. It isn't even that much, considering I am getting a brand-new body

– including breasts – but I pretend I am horrified and begin to calculate. I have spent almost twelve thousand euros on my villa, the jeep costs three hundred euros a week and I gave Paul ten thousand. I am getting through it more quickly than I'd anticipated, but, hey, I've still got fifty thousand left: it should be fine.

Cheerily we say goodbye.

Chapter Nineteen

Even if you are a woman, there are some things you've
got to bear like a man: childbirth, a hangover, abortion,
that sort of thing. And plastic surgery, as I discovered
recently. No doubt those Belgian surgeons were fully
qualified professionals but they attacked me like wild
animals. The liposculpture, in particular, brought back
memories of the third Cod War.

The surgeon who dealt with me was the very image
of a comic character: thin as a rake – I imagine he'd
sucked away his own fat, down to the very last cell.
When he did his thing with his felt-tip pen, before the
start of the show, I thought that by mistake I had ended
up with a tattoo artist. He scribbled half a road map
onto my skin, complete with dotted and continuous
lines, zebra crossings, and restricted zones.

I am sure it'll all be fine in the end, I remember
thinking, dazed from the Valium the nurse had given
me on top of my usual portion. I became semi-
conscious and dropped off. Towards the end of the
procedure I came to. It felt as if someone was prodding
me in my lower back, near my coccyx, with a hard,
rod-shaped object. It wasn't just what it felt like, it was
actually what they were doing, I realized. The rod

moved up and down underneath the skin, occasionally hitting against a bone.

A voice asked if I could stand up.

I managed, but only just.

I was prodded some more. I was about to say it was getting rather uncomfortable, but I couldn't. I dozed off again – just in time, somebody managed to keep me upright. The second time I came round, I felt several pairs of hands lifting me into a tight-fitting suit. Supported by two shadows, I sleepwalked out of the treatment room. I was allowed to lie down on a bed somewhere, to recover. I was leaking from everywhere. The shadows explained it was a mixture of anaesthetic fluid and blood. It needed to come out: that was good. Then the shadows left.

Next to my bed was a screen and behind it was someone else who had probably been sucked empty. She could hear me groan and began chatting away through the screen. On which areas had I received treatment? How many litres had they removed? She had only had her saddlebags and banana rolls done this time round. Her thighs, belly and arms had already been dealt with. Last time they had taken two litres; this time almost three, she told me eagerly. You're better off without it than with, girl. It hadn't been half as bad as she had expected: she was feeling as fit as a fiddle.

'I didn't ask how many litres,' I said timidly.

'Oh, but you should,' she said, 'go on, ask quickly before they chuck it away.'

The thought of my fat being washed down a sink made me feel even more nauseous than I already was. I was left to recover for an hour or so. Then the shadows returned and told me I could go home. They'd do my face at the end of the week, and then my breasts. I had booked a room in the nearest hotel, and called for a taxi to take me there.

The driver looked doubtful when he saw me on the pavement outside the clinic. I probably looked as if I could be sick at any moment, which wasn't far from the truth. At Dr Shivers's recommendation, I was wearing an unflattering jogging suit over my wetsuit. Something comfortable and dark, he'd said, so that the wet patches from the leaking wouldn't show too much.

I covered the passenger seat with the little plastic sheet I had been provided with by the clinic. The driver looked even more disapproving than before.

'It's not far, I'll be OK,' I said.

He answered in French.

'*Pas de problème. Ce n'est pas loin,*' I said. '*Deux kilomètres.*'

He took me along. Fifty metres from the hotel I had to throw up after all.

'*Arrête la voiture!*' I shouted, but it was already too late. I managed to catch most of it with my hands – the rest ended up in the taxi and on my bag. I wiped my mouth and hands with a sanitary pad that I happened to be carrying with me – I was supposed to press it down onto the areas where I was leaking. I apologized to the driver and gave him a generous tip. He remained angry and refused to carry my holdall into the hotel.

I didn't leave my room for two whole days. Not only was I bruised all over, but certain areas of my body became so swollen because of the build-up of fluid that overnight I really changed into an old woman. Or rather, a dead body that has been lying in water for too long. Blue, bloated and ghastly, I didn't fit into my clothes any more, they had become too small: I was further from being a size eight than ever. I tried to keep my spirits up; things could only get better from now on.

In for a penny, in for a pound: once Dr Shivers had reassured me that all was going to be fine and that I just needed to be patient, I let the butchers have a field day with my face. That turned out to be another instant success: I looked as if I had spent at least five rounds in the boxing ring with Muhammad Ali's daughter, blindfolded and with my hands tied behind my back.

No pain, no gain: I couldn't have looked more hideous. I was beyond desperation and allowed my breasts to be cut open in order to have a couple of pear-shaped prostheses shoved in. I stayed in the same hotel throughout the whole thing. Everyone knew me, I was a curiosity on crutches: every day I would have another part of my body in a bandage.

I drag myself to the clinic and back for the umpteenth check-up. Dr Shivers's tone has become much more forward since our first meeting. Didn't he tell me so? I am a lucky devil: my skin responds fantastically to all aspects of the treatment. And look at those breasts, so round and expressive. He circles around me admiringly, and gives a playful tap against my lifted nipples. Of course, with a comparatively young body like mine, he can do anything: you can still really make something of it. The majority of women who step into his office are in their fifties or sixties; little advantage can be gained by them. Yes, he still treats them – you have to keep the pot boiling – but it is a waste of time and effort.

'I'd like to ask you something on behalf of the clinic.

If you have no objection, we'd like to use your "before" and "after" photos for our website. We'd make sure nobody could recognize you, of course.'

I had almost forgotten: just before the great suction event, they took pictures of me with a digital camera. I was naked, apart from a little blue cap. I couldn't have looked less appealing, and was about to have iodine rubbed all over me. There I was, shivering on a little mat, waiting to be photographed before being painted orange. It was like some kind of tribal ritual.

'What do you think? We're asking you because you'd make a perfect showpiece for the clinic.'

He's trying to humour me. He wants a free advertisement.

'This showpiece comes with a price tag,' I reply.

'Unfortunately, I can't offer you money,' he says. 'But we can offer you free treatment.'

'I think I've just had everything done.'

'That's true,' he admits. 'Except for . . .' The doctor pauses.

I am getting curious.

'Do you have children?' he asks. 'Or did I already ask you that?'

'Two.'

'That's right. I remember. What do you say to some genital reshaping, courtesy of the clinic?'

'Some what?'

'Labia reduction,' he whispers.

I am uncomfortable with the thought that Dr Shivers knows the size of my labia. 'Would you be wanting to put photos of that on the website too?'

'Not without your permission. No one has allowed us to do so yet,' he says with a sigh. 'Though we achieve splendid results with this procedure.'

He opens a drawer and produces two polaroids of a vagina. The first one shows the labia spread open, like a bat in mid-air. Underneath the right side there is a hand in a plastic glove, holding up a ruler. It is difficult to make out the measurement, but I think that the width of this genital lip roughly equals the length of Paul's penis. The second photo shows a sealed-up vagina. The woman no longer has real labia: just two discreet little ridges.

'Is there nothing sacred left?' This is circumcision, this is genital mutilation!' I exclaim.

The doctor gives me a bewildered look. OK, it may sound funny coming from someone whose mouth is stuffed with Restylane, but I feel I ought to speak up.

'This client was suffering major inconvenience. She couldn't wear tight jeans any more. Now she has a designer vagina.' The doctor puts the photos back into his drawer.

'Ha! That sums up the whole Western world. This is 9/11 in a nutshell. A designer vagina: the phrase says it all. Our women mutilate themselves so that they can seduce. So that they can wear tight jeans. It's madness. It's not them that's crazy, it's us.'

I sound just like Paul. Why have I suddenly taken over that moral tone from him?

'I bet this woman no longer needed to find a man, just admit it . . .'

The doctor hesitates. His memory is failing him again. 'Will you let us use your photographs, then?' he asks, changing the subject.

'Oh, all right.'

'And would you like to have that labia job done?'

'Yes please.'

Chapter Twenty

It is at least four weeks – roughly when I am able to lift up my arms again – before I feel as pleased with myself as the doctor does. The last few bruises turned green, then yellow and now they are back to their original skin colour. The felt-tip markings have finally gone. My labia – or what remains of them, I think they amputated one by mistake – no longer look like tiny pieces of rolled meat: the lumpy bits have disappeared and I can flop onto the sofa without fear.

I visit the hairdresser and go home to Carvoeira as a blonde. The initial despair has been replaced by a feeling of ecstasy. My favourite pursuit is to spin around endlessly in front of the wall of mirrors inside my walk-in cupboard. I pose in *Playboy* fashion, in high heels, wearing nothing but a bra and knickers. I try out the most obscene poses, and I can only conclude: here stands every man's wet dream.

Amsterdam seems further away each day. A few weeks after I had sent off my letter to the children there was an envelope from Holland waiting for me at the post office in Lagoa. I picked it up, threw it in a drawer in my bedroom and kept putting off opening it. I was too busy, I told myself, with settling in, taking care of the pool, talking to Eddie, my trip to Brussels.

Today I have finally run out of excuses. After my morning session in front of the mirror, I open the drawer, take out the envelope, go and sit down on the bed and tear it open. There are two sheets of paper: Isabel has typed her letter on the computer, Jim's is written by hand.

Hello Mummy,

How are you?

I had to give a talk today and I did it on Portugal. The teacher gave me a B. B = satisfactory to good, remember?

I looked up Lagoa on the map. Are you staying in a hotel or at a campsite? Daddy says he doesn't know. Do you go to the beach a lot? I bet you'll be really tanned when you come home. Have you got the Internet yet? I went onto Google and found a hotel with Internet access. It is called Vale D'el Rei and it is in Lagoa. Perhaps we could arrange a time to be on MSN together. I can do any night after supper. Do you still have my address? IsabellaCaramella@hotmail.com

Everything else is fine at the moment. Daddy has become even stricter since you left. Can't you come home a bit sooner ;-) ? Jim and I play outside a lot. They have knocked down those houses, Daddy doesn't want us to go too near to the site, but we secretly made a den there. Don't tell Daddy, will you?

When are you coming home?

Kisses from your daughter,

Isabel de Groot

PS: There is also a letter from Jim in the envelope. I hope you can read it. He wanted to make a drawing at first. I told him that people abroad prefer to receive letters.

Hello Mummy,
   This is Jim. Daddy bought me a box of K'nex! It is great. It is nearly my birthday. It would be very nice if you could come to my party.
   XXXXX jim

My heart is in my mouth. It isn't true, it can't be: that letter has been lying there for weeks. I have lost track of the date, I haven't got a diary; when I was in Brussels, I nearly missed one of my clinic appointments. What day is it today? I don't have a newspaper, no calendar, my mobile doesn't work. I must find Eddie. Nothing ever throws Eddie, least of all a scatterbrained actress from Holland.

I slip on my bathrobe. I fly down the stairs and run outside on my red high-heeled shoes, straight to his *casa*. The dogs leap against the fence, and shortly afterwards Eddie appears in the doorway. It flits through my mind that I have never actually caught sight of Doris. Does she always stay inside? It occurs to me that she may not exist.

Eddie approaches me in a relaxed manner. 'Quiet, boys,' he reprimands the dogs. 'You know who this is: it's Julia. Lie down.'

Does he by any chance know what date it is? Of course he does. He tells me.

Is he absolutely sure?

'Absolutely. Is everything all right?'

Without a word, I turn round and run back. I try to contain myself, but I can't: as I run along, I begin to cry. Soon I am howling – howling hysterically, with loud yelps. When I get to the villa, I stumble along to the kitchen. I need a drink. A drink or pills, or both. In my hurry I trip over my bathrobe and tumble head first on the tiled bathroom floor. The fat deposit on my thigh, which might otherwise have softened the blow, has been sucked away. I fall with a nasty bang. Good, I deserved that. I hope my hip is broken. Or even better: shattered. I deserve to be in pain, lots of it. I sit up and hit myself in the face, two, three times, I shout that I'm a fucking bitch, I take off my bathrobe and pull on my hair, harder and harder, until I sit there with the tufts in my hands.

Then I curl up on the glazed tiles.

My son has turned seven and it has completely passed me by. I remember briefly thinking in the clinic that it was almost his birthday, and how strange it would be not to be there. But after that it just went out of my mind.

He invited me to his party. I never even replied. The very least I should have done was send him a postcard. I should have called him from a pay phone. He gave me plenty of advance notice. I forgot Jim's birthday, my own son's birthday. If Jim were Jimmy, he would cut me off for good.

After a while I go numb with cold. I pull myself up, and crawl over to the living room, kicking off my shoes on the way. I keep my Valium in one of the drawers of the sideboard. Three pills should do to relieve the worst of the pain. I crawl back to the kitchen and wash them down with the vodka left by the midgets.

I lie down again. Not for long this time. I crawl about the kitchen on all fours.

Every great accomplishment is at first impossible. Go on. Be a Tiger.

Where did I go wrong?

Is it enough for you to improve your game? Or is it your goal to change the game itself?

I wanted to change the game. I wanted to take charge. Draw up the rules. New rules. My rules. I was going to be my own boss again.

When faced with new questions, do you reply with old answers or new ones?

I have failed. It is my own fault.

I am a masochist, that's it: I am a master at seeking out pain. There was no need to write to my children. I left my family because I wanted to have time to myself, and yet I wrote to them. If I hadn't provoked Jim, he couldn't have invited me.

My heart is a dartboard, I allow everyone to just hit me with their arrows. Everybody hits the mark. Not because they're all such dead shots, well my mother is, but because they're standing so close to me. They can practically stick them in. Why do I let them? What is it with me?

The old man's pager is in my bag. It never bleeps. In the beginning I would check ten, twenty times a day, but after a while I stopped. If they really need me, they'll get in touch. So far, I have heard nothing. Clearly no one is missing me so much that they've needed to get me on the phone, or gone to the trouble of finding me here. It seems that everyone is managing fine without me. I am not only a masochist, I am a megalomaniac as well. They don't need me. It is all in my head, all my worries: I have been away for six weeks now, and nobody cares a hoot.

That's not what this journey is about. This isn't what I promised Jimmy. Pain always arrives spontaneously, he used to point out. Pleasure is something you have to seek out. It is hard work. Make sure that you get it. Every day. Try and have at least one peak a day, no matter how you do it. Have a fit of laughter or an orgasm, enjoy the smell of freshly cut grass, do something you're not allowed to, and get a kick out of it. Keep a record of your high points in a diary. Make sure it is not the same every day. When you're ill, or if someone dies – he said it with a grin – you can skip a day, then it is back to work. Eighteen hours after he died I began to write.

I stay on the floor for an hour and a half. Jimmy appears and tells me what to do. Low points, he says, are rather like high points. He had wanted to experience his end – the absolute low of his life – as a high, and it had worked.

– You've got to persevere, there's nothing to stop you now. You've cut yourself loose, you've undergone a metamorphosis, you're ready for it, all you need do now is reap the harvest.

I blow my nose on a dishcloth and pull myself together. Jim's birthday is over, I missed it: I should put it behind me, it is too late to put it right now. No use crying over spilt milk. I get into the jacuzzi in order to warm myself up. When the water comes up to my waist, the power is cut. The bathroom goes dark, the water supply stops. That's the third time this week. I'll need to replace the fuses. Whenever Stella uses the iron and the radio at the same time, the system gets overloaded. According to Eddie, it is the heated pool. That uses up so much power it sucks the system dry, as it were. I get out of the bath, shivering. I dry myself.

Such a beautiful body in such a beautiful house and in such a beautiful area, and yet so lonely.

Chapter Twenty-one

I have bought a black bikini: the bottoms are high cut, and it shows off my new body perfectly. The top only just contains my lifted breasts. I put it on this morning, underneath a short denim skirt and a green top. I am also wearing my kitten-heeled, open-toe sandals, with colourful beaded straps. And I have painted my toe-nails.

I am on my way to Praia Senhora da Rocha. It's a small beach enclosed by high yellow rocks, not far from Porches. Just before you get there you have to go down a steep, winding road. There is a derelict chapel on the cliff to the right, which sticks out quite a bit further into the sea than the one on the left. Stop thinking about Mum, now's not a good moment. There are usually tourists standing by the chapel, it's a popular vantage point. I am not a tourist, I skilfully manoeuvre my car down the winding road and park as closely to the Vilarhino restaurant as I can. I throw my bag over my shoulder and walk to the edge of the beach, to see who is there.

I spot him at once.

He is standing straddle-legged on the sand, holding a small wooden bat in his hand. He has long, slightly wavy, dark hair. He looks like Jim Morrison. Another Jim that died too soon. Don't think about Jimmy now, or about Jim.

Morrison is wearing a pair of dark blue shorts with a white flower pattern. A daring print, not all men could carry it off. But he can. He is slender and his chest is shaped like an hourglass. His nipples are small. He is neither too muscly, nor too thin, he is just right. His friend, who is nothing special to look at, is standing across from him, also equipped with a bat. They are hitting a small ball to each other. He can't be more than twenty-seven, at a guess – probably younger.

He is the most handsome guy on the whole beach, without a doubt.

I want him.

He is with a bunch of other people; Two empty towels are lying next to four guys and a girl, who every now and then shout out something to him. It's looking tricky. If the girl is his girlfriend it is going to be impossible.

I hollow my back and push out my breasts to make myself nice and tall, then I walk onto the beach, swaying my hips. We make eye contact. I keep my eyes fixed on him, and smile.

This could be your lucky day, my smile says.

I position my towel just a few metres from their group and put down my bag next to it. Slowly I take off my top and skirt, making sure that he sees exactly what I am doing. He watches me.

I turn gracefully onto my right side, so that my left hip sticks up like a wave. There are dozens of people on the little beach. Families, couples, groups of youths, I ignore them all. It's just him and me. From now on we are the only two people present.

I keep my eyes fixed on him. Not all the time, but enough to show him that I am serious: the game has commenced. He and his friend stop hitting the ball to each other. He plumps onto the sand, moves his towel a metre away from the others, and lies down on his side: his left side, so that he mirrors me and we can look each other in the eyes. I am wearing my sunglasses. He produces a pair from his bag too. Absolutely everything about him is cool, including his glasses, fan-tas-tic. He gets out a packet of cigarettes and lights one.

Pity I don't smoke, otherwise I could ask for a light. Occasionally he says something to his friends. The girl and he make no contact, a positive sign: they're probably not a couple, then.

After a couple of minutes the group begins to move. A few of the young men get up and walk down to the sea. The girl goes with them. He follows, but not immediately; first he finishes his cigarette. He is a loner, a nonconformist, or he wants people to think he is.

I sit up, and watch him run to the sea. He dives straight in, unlike his friends who take their time to get accustomed to the water. Not that I had expected anything else. Now that his hair has gone all wet and flat, it is harder to keep track of him among the other dark heads bobbing up and down on the sea.

If I want to start something with him, I had better strike soon.

I take off my sunglasses, put my skirt on top of my bag, and ask a girl on a nearby towel if she can keep an eye on my things for me. She nods in agreement.

It's incredibly hot. I would have gone in even without him.

I plunge straight in, just like him, and strike out,

away from the beach. Lovely. The sea – or the ocean, I should say – wins on all fronts from the pool at the Casa da Criança. This is swimming as it should be. Swimming into infinity. You paddle along completely unaware of how far above the sandy bottom you are, and of all the things that go on there. There might be a shark swimming below you, or a jellyfish, your feet could get entangled in seaweed: you simply don't know. The sea is exciting, unpredictable, and potentially lethal. That's why I love it. The sea gives and takes – not my own words but powerful ones all the same – let the sea give me this guy, and we'll remain friends for ever.

Morrison is still swimming, and quite close – if it is him: it's hard to tell, the sun is very bright. Yes, this guy has long hair, it's him. About fifty metres out from the beach there is a line of yellow buoys floating on the water.

'What are those things doing there?' I ask in English, pointing to the buoys. I know damn well why they are there, but that is not the point.

He looks at me hesitantly and doesn't answer.

'Do you speak English?' I ask.

He shakes his head.

I feel utterly disillusioned. He doesn't speak English. My Portuguese extends no further than bucket of suds and mop. I have left my *How & What* at the Casa da Criança. The language of love is universal, but we are not at that stage yet. We need some preliminary steps in between, careful explorations; I need to prise him away from his friends, but how do I do that without words?

I swim on a bit, and so does he. He doesn't speak English. What kind of a guy is this? Doesn't he watch TV, or listen to music? Hasn't he been to school? It is hard to believe. So cool, and not a word of English – it just doesn't fit.

Surely he thinks I am attractive? I mean: after all the stuff they have done to me, you can't possibly not find me fun and sexy? A shiver runs down my spine. Maybe I am to him what Key Man once was to Kaitlin and me. Maybe he finds me a creepy woman. After all, I am a few years older than him, and the fact that he doesn't speak English doesn't mean he is blind.

What do I do now? Get out of the water. That's the first step. Find my towel. Thank the girl for watching over my stuff. Stay calm. Pull myself together. I dry myself and lie down on my front. I peep in his direction. He has done the same, exactly the same: he has come out of the water and is lying on his front. Our eyes meet. I wonder what he is thinking? I would give anything to know what is going through his head. Ugh! She's still looking at me, or: stupid me, I had a chance and I blew it?

Please, let it be the latter, let there be hope still.

The sun burns on my shoulders. I take factor 20 out of my bag, sit up straight and begin putting it on. First my face, then my shoulders, my neck, and the exposed parts of my breasts.

He is also sitting up, with a cigarette in his mouth. He is fumbling around for his lighter.

Do something, I yell to him telepathically, think of something! Offer to put some sun cream on my back: anyone can see I can't reach there myself. Listen, sweetheart, if you want the same as I do – rough sex within the next hour, no strings attached – then you're going to have to help me. I made the first move, I can't do it on my own.

He looks, smokes and does nothing. There seems to

be an air of desperation about him, but that could be wishful thinking on my part.

What if it is all going to come to nothing now? I hadn't considered that possibility at all. I was confidently imagining I would leave the beach in triumph, with Morrison, as meek as a lamb, following in my wake. Perhaps I have left it too late, perhaps it's all over, perhaps I am condemned to a life with midgets and Portuguese drunkards.

I daren't look at Morrison any more. He has stretched out again, so have I, and that seems to be it: no more progress. When he gets up to join his friends for a second round of swimming I stay where I am. It would be too obvious to go into the water at exactly the same moment again. He can get lost: I am not going to make a fool of myself, I have some self-respect left. A couple of new visitors arrive on the beach, two guys, maybe I should set out on a new course. With a sigh I sit up. The one with the grey shorts and the Nike cap looks OK. Just about. If it wasn't for Morrison, I would give it a chance, but Morrison is still around and Mr Nike simply doesn't compare.

His friends emerge from the water. Where is my sweetheart? He is not there any more. They dry themselves, they don't lie down. I scan the beach and the sea – he is nowhere to be seen. His friends gather their things together. They are leaving! I stay calm on the outside, but inside I die a thousand deaths. Is that it, then? Will I never see him again, will there be no further chance to exchange a few personal details, like telephone numbers and email addresses, or arrange a date for tomorrow, same time, same place?

The girl and the young men saunter over towards the restaurant, carrying their shoes in their hands. One of them stays behind with Morrison's things – he is waiting for him, like me. Where did he go? I suddenly feel my heart pounding. Has he disappeared on purpose, is he hiding, so that his friends will have to leave without him, and he can join me at last? Is that his brilliant plan?

In that case, please let that friend of his hop it. Don't let him be so bloody altruistic. I revert to telepathic yelling again, this time to the little Portuguese guy, waiting stoically by Morrison's bag.

Go! He doesn't want you to wait, trust me. You can leave his things, I'll keep an eye on them. There are other forces at work – dark forces – you have no idea. You are intervening in something, you think you are doing your friend a favour, but you are doing the very opposite. Go! Vanish! Ksst!

The young man frowns, waits another two, three endless minutes, looks around one last time, picks up Morrison's rucksack, shoves the towel in and walks off.

The spot they occupied is empty. As if they had never been there.

Is there any need for Morrison to return to the beach now? Will Morrison manage without his things? Did that little moron take his shoes as well? Where have his friends gone? To the restaurant for a drink? Are they waiting for him by the car? So many burning questions to which I get no answers.

I have no choice but to be a powerless witness while my future with Morrison is crushed before my eyes. Where is he? I roll over onto my front. I don't recognize any of Morrison's friends among the people sitting outside the restaurant. Behind the restaurant there are some toilets and a shower block. Shall I go and have a look there? Just to make sure?

No. I must give up. It's over. I lost.

I pick up my sun cream again, feeling miserable. The doctor told me I should keep myself well protected, especially my face. What a waste of money it has been, all for nothing. Without meaning to, I keep staring at the people outside the restaurant. People are laughing and talking, while eating fresh fish and drinking wine. Waiters are holding up their fully loaded trays. Everyone is having fun except me.

Suddenly and as if by magic, I see him: my high for the day. He comes walking down the wooden steps on the right-hand side of the restaurant. He stops halfway, peers at the beach, then turns round and goes back up again to disappear from sight. All this takes place within a matter of barely two seconds, so quickly, in fact, that I wonder if I have dreamt it. But I haven't. The last thing I saw of him were his legs, which were sticking out of a pair of blue shorts with white flowers, on the steps next to the restaurant at Praia Senhora da Rocha.

The grieving process can begin.

A person has to eat.

That counts for me too, perhaps that could become today's highlight. A gastronomical high. Better than nothing. I shake the sand off my towel, put it in my bag and walk up to the restaurant. Vilarhino is packed, both inside and outside. I have to wait for a table to become available. After ten minutes a waiter seats me inside. No, I don't need the menu, just bring me a jug of water and a glass of white wine – make that half a litre. What is the fish of the day?

Perch.

The waiter says it, looking straight past me. It is too hot, there are too many customers, he is dying for his shift to be over.

That'll be fine, thanks.

I am feeling so low that I wish I had company. Lotus, Eddie – Jimmy, for all I care. I miss my mobile. I want to text someone, I want to have contact.

The waiter brings me my wine. He also presents me with a basket of bread and a tiny dish with tuna paste, goat's cheese and olives. I leave the bread and pour myself a drink.

The perch arrives promptly, just as I am polishing off the remains of my second glass of wine. It is a different waiter this time. His belly bulges out over his belt, he weighs at least thirty kilos more than he ought, but he has a friendly face. A tea towel is thrown over his shoulder.

'A beautiful fish for a beautiful lady.' With a flourish he puts down the plate with a generous piece of fish, three potatoes and a small helping of French beans.

'*Obrigada*,' I say.

The fish looks tasty. I pick up my knife and fork. No sooner have I tried the perch than the waiter returns to my table. He tops up my glass and looks at me expectantly. His fleshy cheeks go red. I believe he fancies me.

'Delicious bit of fish,' I say, before he can even ask. I nod enthusiastically and take a big mouthful to show him that I really mean it. I shouldn't have been so immoderate: I choke, the fish sticks in my throat. I try to dislodge it, it's as if there is a bone in it, I can't get it out, I'm beginning to feel short of breath, I grab my water and take a sip, that doesn't work either, I am unable to swallow, it's getting out of hand, I can feel myself going red, dammit, I'll choke to death in a moment: wouldn't that be just typical!

What happened to Julia?

She choked on a bit of perch in the fish restaurant at Praia Senhora da Rocha.

Oh my, how unfortunate. First the older brother, and now her. What were her last words?

Delicious bit of fish.

What were *his* last words again?

No one knows. He died alone. Before the doctor got there.

The waiter looks at me, panic-stricken. He can tell I am struggling but doesn't seem to have grasped how bad it is. He is too timid to take action. I point to my back, at last he understands: he puts his tray down on the table and pats me on the back, very gently at first, tenderly, almost. I keep pointing: harder, you've got to hit harder, come on now. I lift my arms up in the air, my children do that too when they choke on something, it's what they were taught at their nursery. The waiter hits me firmly with a flat hand between my shoulder blades. After a couple of slaps the bit of fish finally comes out. I cough it up and spit in every direction: white flakes land on my plate and on the table. Not a very nice sight for the other guests, I am aware of that; on the other hand, watching someone die right in front of you while you are tucking into your food is not ideal either.

I breathe in and out in gasps. Air, thank goodness, I am getting air. Still a little bit shaky, I pick up my napkin and wipe my mouth. I knock back my third glass of wine in two gulps.

The waiter takes away my plate. 'I'll bring you a new one.'

'No, don't worry. I've had enough.'

He shakes his head. 'I insist. I won't let you go. You need to have a proper meal.'

He goes away, returns with a cloth and wipes my table clean. 'May I offer you another carafe of white wine?'

Oh well, why not. I suppose we should celebrate that I am still alive.

A moment later he brings me my second perch and more wine. Again I get three potatoes and a small helping of heated-through French beans. He gives my table another wipe and puts the plate down.

'For the beautiful lady . . .' The beautiful fish gets no mention this time.

He lingers behind at my table even though I have thanked him. What now?

'I beg your pardon,' he says. 'There's a gentleman who's been waiting for a table for twenty minutes. He wants to know if he can join you. Please, don't feel under any pressure, I am only passing on his request, that's all.'

A single man waiting for a table. I wonder what it'll be this time: a hunchback, a cleft palate, or a serious case of psoriasis?

I tell you what, I'll let it be a surprise.

'Bring him over,' I say, as if it is an item from the menu.

The waiter nods. I detect a mixture of resignation and disappointment in the way he responds.

I have another glass of wine to boost my confidence, and tuck into my fish.

'Hi,' I hear next to me. 'Thanks for letting me sit with you. You really don't mind?'

I recognize that voice. I look up. Next to me stands a

tall black guy, light brown skin, with an abundance of
gold jewellery.

Halleluja.

Praise the Lord.

My kingdom has come.

Amen, brother, amen!

I am completely speechless, all I can do is nod, and
this time it's not because I have got something stuck in
my throat.

Will Smith pulls up a chair, puts his mobile on the
table and sits down.

Chapter Twenty-two

We shake hands across the table.

'I'm Julia.'

He smiles the same smile as in the lobby at the Hotel Eva.

'You can't be serious,' he says.

Why not? I never lie about my name. Just my age, occasionally.

'I'm Romeo.'

He is still holding my hand. It feels so nice.

'So, as I said, I'm Romeo,' he repeats,

Yes, yes, I got that. Nice name.

'And you're Julia.'

I nod. We've been over that. He gives me a meaningful look. Finally it dawns on me.

Romeo recites, *'What's in a name? That which we call a rose by any other name would smell as sweet.'*

'Wasn't that my line?' I remember.

'I take thee at thy word. Call me but love, and I'll be new baptized; henceforth I never will be Romeo.'

If we don't let go of each other now, this is going to end up being the longest handshake in history.

'We've met before,' I say, lifting my glass.

'Out of the question,' he answers. 'I'd remember.'

'A month or two ago, in the Hotel Eva.'

'It's possible, I did stay there,' he says, surprised. 'And we saw each other there?'

'You were checking out of the hotel. It was quite a performance. You kept everyone waiting, including me.'

He laughs like a little boy who has been caught in mischief but knows his mother won't get angry with him. 'I let you wait all that time. What was I doing?' He folds his hands together behind his neck, and leans backwards.

Jim Morrison is dead, Will Smith is alive. And his name is Romeo.

'You were mainly busy making phone calls.'

He looks as if he still can't quite believe it. He has completely forgotten our encounter. I made no impression whatsoever on him back then. But it is different now. Now he wants to join me at my table. I suspect he slipped that fat waiter a few dollar notes. He has made a special effort for me. Our roles have been reversed. Must send some flowers to Dr Shivers tomorrow.

The waiter hands Romeo the menu. He takes it and orders a glass of iced tea, without taking his eyes off me. 'Your English is good. Where are you from?'

'From Holland.'

'A Dutch girl, oh la la . . .' He raises his eyebrows knowingly. 'What are you eating?' he asks next.

'Fish of the day.'

'Any good?' He passes a critical eye over my plate.

Shall I tell him what happened to my first order? No, don't. Cultivate the mysterious Julia. He doesn't wait for my answer but calls the waiter, who comes rushing over immediately. He snaps his fingers and bows for Romeo, like a slave almost. I am sure the American has been handing out his dollars generously.

211

'Bring us your best fish. You can take this away.' Romeo makes a dismissive gesture in the direction of my plate. My fillet of perch is virtually untouched.

I take a sip of wine to mask my smile. There goes my plate again, back to the kitchen: Julia is through to the third round.

'Promise me you'll never order another dish of the day again, no matter where you are,' Romeo says solemnly. He behaves as if I have committed a crime.

'I'm not going to promise you anything.' We mustn't give in to this man too readily.

We look at each other and laugh. The die is cast. Our fate is sealed. Romeo and I are going to have sex. As soon as I give him the green light, we'll go for it. That is how it works between men and women.

I sigh with delight, empty my glass and pour myself another. It has taken a while, it has cost me a few pennies, but I have got what I wanted. I have got a bite. I have got the pick of the bunch. And I am going to have sex with him. The thought alone makes my mouth water, my groin go moist and my nipples go hard. How long has it been? Far too long. Romeo and I are going to shag each other like there is no tomorrow, we can start tonight, why not? He can make love to me passionately, he can bring me to a climax; today I am definitely going to have a high, a sexual high, and what a glorious one.

I feel an overwhelming urge to share this realization with my table companion. 'We're going to do it with each other, aren't we?' I say.

'Sorry?'

Is he joking, or does he really not understand?

'We will fuck,' I repeat. 'You me. Or I you. Whatever.' Romeo flinches a little. I have become reckless. My

212

four mouthfuls of perch are swimming around in a pool of alcohol.

'I mean: we're about to have a jolly time together, eating the best fish, drinking the best wine, the whole *enchilada*. You'll be telling me what you do, I'll be telling you what I do, la-di-dah, but it's all a bit of ritual nonsense, really. It's the preliminary round. Ultimately, we both want the same thing. I can pretend to be a good girl, I can play hard to get, but why should I?'

Without thinking, I am putting all my cards on the table.

'I've reached a point in my life where I don't feel like beating about the bush any more, I'm past that stage now. I want to fuck you, I wanted to the minute I saw you in Faro, and I know that you have a good penis. Not a small one, I mean. I've often been unlucky that way, to tell you the truth: always. I've done it once before with a black man, and the only reason I tried then was that I hoped he'd be well endowed. He wasn't. His name was Clark. Clark was a disaster. But you are not and today is my lucky day. You have a big surprise for me in your underpants, right?'

Romeo remains silent.

'What's the matter, did I shock you? Come on now, we're neither of us children any more. I know your sort, you're a man of the world. This is not the first indecent proposal you've had in your life. Probably not even the first one today.'

He opens his mouth in order to say something, but the waiter arrives with our food.

'Bon appétit,' he says.

I smile at Romeo. 'You were absolutely right, this looks infinitely better than today's special. Enjoy your meal.'

I take a sip of my wine and attack the food like a wolf. 'First class,' I say with my mouth full. Too late I realize this probably doesn't come across as very polite. I have been eating by myself for too long, I blame it on that. I quickly swallow my food. Romeo says nothing and leaves his cutlery untouched.

'Hey, what's up? Did I say something? Sorry if I seemed cheeky, but I thought that you—'

'You know who I am. Am I right?' he interrupts me.

'How do you mean?'

'You know who I am: you know what I do for a living.'

'Whatever it is, it must pay well,' I say with a snigger.

'Don't play games with me, Julia. It's obvious that you know.'

I leave my fork hanging in the air. Something tells me I won't be finishing this piece of fish either.

'My big surprise . . . is that why you let me sit at your table?' All the warmth has gone from his voice.

'Of course not,' I stammer. I am feeling uncomfortable. I am about to lose it again, this is just too ridiculous for words. If this were a film I would find it completely unbelievable.

'A lot of people find my work trite. You too, it appears. I thought you were different.' He throws his napkin on the table, and stands up.

I am feeling a bit faint. I haven't a clue what he is talking about: he is angry with me, he wants to leave. Whatever happens, I have got to stop him. 'Please sit down, Romeo,' I say. 'The entire restaurant is looking at us, we're behaving like a married couple.'

His lips are pursed, and the look in his eyes could turn a stream of swirling lava into a glacier.

'You've got to believe me: I have absolutely no idea

214

who you are, or what you do.' I touch his hand gently. He ignores me, picks up his mobile and slips it into his pocket.

The fat waiter appears from nowhere. 'Is there something wrong with your fish?' he asks.

'The fish is fine. Isn't it?' I look at Romeo. He doesn't reply.

'Another iced tea for you, sir?'

Romeo hesitates for a second, then he nods.

'And for you, madam?'

'I'll just have water, thanks.' I push my glass of wine away pointedly.

Romeo sinks back in his chair.

I give a sigh of relief. 'Your fish is getting cold,' I say to break the silence.

'I don't feel hungry any more.'

When the waiter brings our drinks our plates are ready to be taken away. Third time lucky.

For a couple of minutes Romeo and I sit facing each other in silence. Then I pluck up courage. 'You've aroused my curiosity.'

'Is that so?' He takes a sip of his iced tea.

'Absolutely. Are you going to tell me?'

'So you really don't know?'

I roll my eyes.

'OK, then.' He clears his throat. 'I work in the porn business in Los Angeles.'

'Are you a cameraman, a director, or . . . er . . .' I am asking the obvious and he knows it.

'I stand *in front of* the cameras, Julia.'

In front of the cameras. My Romeo recites Shakespeare and turns out to be a porn star. The canal was already brimful and now the banks are bursting. I see naked men and women, Romeo in the lead role: this needs to be censored, the next few images are not suitable for minors. Romeo has an enormous, oh my God, of course he has an enormous . . . presumably it's *gigantic*. And the things he does with it: he works his way through a series of women, thrusting it into them, one after the other – hard and deep – without mercy. They moan with pleasure. He jerks himself off over a pair of oversized lily-white breasts. He gets a freckled beauty with ginger hair to give him oral satisfaction. It's gross, it's delicious, it's crude, it's vulgar, it's wonderful. For God's sake, Julia, pull yourself together, it is his job, just a job, someone has to do it, why not him? Show this man some respect.

'Wow,' I say eventually.

A mildly amused smile appears on his face.

'Are you famous?'

He shrugs. 'I am, in my line of business. That's why I thought you knew me. There are plenty of DVDs which show me in action.'

'In action,' I repeat. Hopefully I don't sound too eager.

'Yes, in action,' he says drily. That was far too eager.

'So if I go into any video shop . . .'

'. . . you're bound to find me on a certain shelf.'

'You've got the right name for it, anyway.'

'That's not my name in the films,' he says curtly.

Which ones? I would like to ask. I would like to ask a thousand questions, but I don't feel brave enough. 'Do you mind talking about your work?'

'Do you mind talking about yours?'

I laugh. 'It's not that I don't like talking about it, it's that nobody is ever interested. I bet you won't be either.'

'Try me. I picture you in some exotic profession. I like exotics.'

I feel a sharp twinge in my lower belly. *Oh Romeo, Romeo! Wherefore art thou Romeo?* I want to be your exotic sweetheart. Just name the place and the time and I'll be there, legs apart. Whoa stop! I am going off at a tangent, I must get a grip on myself. 'I have a very dull job, I'm a bookkeeper,' I tell Romeo nicely.

'What kind of business?'

'Property. It's a family business. My father is my boss.'

'I see,' he responds.

I deliberately say nothing and watch him racking his brains about what to ask me next. It's so sweet.

'See, you've already run out of things to ask.'

'That's not true,' he shouts, offended. 'I was about to ask if you . . . er . . .'

I let him struggle a few more seconds, then I come to the rescue. 'If I'm a famous bookkeeper? You bet. World-famous in Amsterdam.'

His eyes light up.

'Amsterdam is a great city.'

Amsterdam is the only thing that is still wild about Julia.

'What are you thinking?' Romeo asks. 'You look as if you're in pain.'

This actor knows his profession. I slide my wine back towards myself and take a sip. 'Pain is the feeling underlying everything, isn't it?' I say casually.

– Very good.

Jimmy joins in the conversation uninvited.

– Show your serious side for a change, Jules. That'll make more of an impression than all those obsessive questions about sex.

Romeo gives me a quizzical look.

'Living is all about distracting yourself. As soon as

217

the distraction goes, the pain returns. You can see it even in babies. A baby has two modes: either he cries or he is quiet. He is quiet when he is being distracted: by food, by attention, because someone is rocking him, or hands him a toy, or when he is listening to his own prattle. Without this distraction, he'll begin to yell. Then he feels the underlying pain which he doesn't want to feel, but which is always there.'

'How do you know all this?' Romeo wants to know.

I immediately regret my exposé. Next he is going to ask me if I have children. 'I was a crybaby. I drove my mother up the wall.' It is a little white lie. According to the story, Kaitlin was the crybaby, she was the one who was difficult to distract. I was sweet – not as sweet as Jimmy – but good-natured, and quick to laugh.

'Forgive me for being so direct, Julia,' Romeo says slowly. 'You come across as lonely. As if you're experiencing a lot of pain.' He takes my hand.

Is this a porn star or a psychic?

I stare at the table. If I look up at him now, I'll burst into tears, I can't help it. 'This is precisely why I prefer talking about sex. Sex never hurts,' I say peevishly.

He now closes his other hand round mine as well.

'Then you've missed something, Julia. Then you've not yet made love as if it was for the very last time. That can hurt tremendously.'

I try to read the expression in his eyes. His face reveals nothing. His golden-speckled brown eyes look at me calmly. What is it with this man, what is he doing to me? My instinct tells me that he is a predator, that I am in danger, the greatest danger I have been in so far during my escape.

Chapter Twenty-three

We are sipping our coffee. We don't touch upon any other serious topics. Romeo walks me to my car. I have traded in the jeep for a Vauxhall Corsa. The four-wheel drive just soaked up petrol, it was costing me a fortune every week, I felt it was a waste of money: this one costs half as much to run. He points out his own car, a black Maserati. Perhaps I should have kept the jeep after all.

'Where are you staying?' I ask.

'In the Tivoli Almansor.'

I know it, it's a luxury four-star hotel in Carvoeiro. I went there for a meal once with Lotus. It is in a good location: the views are fabulous. The hotel is built against a big rock. Instead of going up from the reception area, you go down. You come in on the top floor, I think it's the fifth, the restaurant is few floors below that. 'Do you look out over the sea?'

'What do you think?' Romeo replies. He has become the man from Hotel Eva all over again: nothing but the very best.

I smile.

'Where do you sleep?' he demands to know.

'In a villa at Sesmarias. It's a very special house,

architect-designed. If you'd like to come round some-time . . .'

Romeo has taken out his mobile phone and is open-ing it up. My invitation stays hanging in the air. It is completely against the rules, but I carry on with my attempt.

'. . . I could cook you a meal, if you like.'

He looks up from the tiny screen.

'I make a good dish of the day.' That's enough self-humiliation.

'I'm sure you do.'

He doesn't say yes or no, this man is driving me completely round the bend. Less than half an hour ago he was all over me and now I constantly have to remind him of my existence.

'Tomorrow night?' I suggest.

He consults his electronic diary and shakes his head. He has already got a date then. How important can that be? His work is in Los Angeles. Romeo doesn't explain himself, neither does he suggest an alternative date, he just stares at the screen with a worried look on his face, as if he has only now realized that his diary is already fully booked.

'The day after tomorrow?'

He shakes his head again. What does this guy get up to every night, and, more importantly, with whom?

'Are you here on business? I thought you were having a holiday.'

'Both.'

'Pornography in the Algarve? And there I was, think-ing the Portuguese are such a prim lot. I haven't seen a single brothel so far. Plenty of opportunities for beauti-ful shots, though. Can I come and visit the set some time?' This really is my final attempt to make a future date, honest, I swear upon my kids' lives.

'I'm not filming.'

'What are you doing then?' I am determined to find out now.

He pulls something from his inside pocket and hands it to me. It is a business card.

Love Service
Call Romeo
919554667

'You must never ever give this number to anyone else,' he urges me. 'You've got to promise me. I'm highly selective when it comes to clients.'

'Clients?'

Suddenly it dawns on me. Romeo can be hired. His clients are all women. Lonely, desperate women. Women in big villas. Women who dine alone. Women like me.

'Is this why you came and sat at my table? Do you regard me as a potential client?' I fan myself with his card.

'I never said that. You wanted to know what I am doing here.'

'You just gave me your card. What happens if I call this number?'

'Then you can make an appointment with me.'

'A business appointment?'

'It may seem strange to you, Julia, but there are plenty of women who choose to. It cuts out the hassle, it's clear, it doesn't arouse false expectations. It's a

221

pleasant arrangement for both parties involved.'

'Parties? Jesus, Romeo, we've just eaten together, we've had an intense conversation, I find you special, I'd like to see you again. Are you saying that's not going to happen unless I fork out money?'

'I'm afraid so, yes,' he says slowly.

'Why?'

'It's my work. Suppose I wanted you to become my accountant, I'd have to pay you too, wouldn't I?'

'That's completely different.'

He folds away his mobile. 'You may not believe me, but I enjoyed meeting you.' He takes my hand and brings it up to his mouth. He kisses my fingers one by one, all the while keeping his eyes fixed on me.

I feel myself going weak.

'Julia,' he whispers through the gap between my index finger and thumb. 'What are we going to do now?'

It is the hand on which I normally wear my wedding ring. I have locked it away in the safe at my villa. I feel like a single woman: I am free, free to make my own decisions. I am standing beside my Vauxhall Corsa while a porn star, slash gigolo, slash psychic, slash God knows what else, licks my fingers. He is dishing out wise words as well as his business card – I must guard the latter with my life – he wants to see me again but only if we can come to some business arrangement, his business is called Love Service, I am one of the few lucky women – handpicked by Romeo – who can call on his service: one peep from me and I go straight into his personal organizer.

'In the films you have a stage name. Why do you use your real name for your Love Service?' I ask.

'Who says Romeo is my real name?'

'So you *did* see me as a client,' I say, outraged. 'You introduced yourself as Romeo.'

For the first time he looks embarrassed.

'How many names do you have, huh?'

'Enough.'

'I'd get pretty confused with so many identities,' I mutter.

'You've got them too. And that's why you've become so confused. All the roles you have to play have been lumped together into one box and that box is called Julia. Julia doesn't know who she is any more, Julia has lost the plot, Julia is a barrel of doubts.'

It's the oracle speaking again. And he is hitting the nail bang on the head.

'We didn't run into each other by chance, Julia, I don't believe there is such a thing as chance. You and I could mean something to each other.' Romeo nods in the direction of the business card.

I want to make him suffer just a little longer. 'And there I was, naively thinking that love can't be bought.'

'It says Love Service here,' he says amiably. 'Thanks to my service you will come to recognize the difference between true love and bought love. You will never again make the same mistake once you've learnt.'

What if some real chemistry develops between us? What if we suddenly fall in love? I am burning to ask him, but I manage to restrain myself: I am afraid of his reaction. I don't suppose men like him ever fall in love with women like me.

'Romeo, before I take my chance with your Love Service, I want to be absolutely clear about one thing. I'm paying you to have sex?'

He lets go of my fingers. 'That's correct. And to have

223

my company if you want it. Pure sex dates tend not to take up very much time.'

'Good. What's your schedule for the next few weeks?'

'I have three . . . er . . . four bookings left.'

'Sex or company?'

'Three sex dates, one sex and company. That's a total of about six working hours, excluding travel.'

'Fine. You can keep the dates you've already made, but otherwise I want you to be mine for a month.'

'How do you mean?' he asks, unsure.

Now that's what I like to see: he who pays the piper, calls the tune. 'You move in with me. You can quote me an overall price for the job, just make sure you deduct the hours you have to be with the other clients.'

'Of course,' he says in a thin voice.

'You don't take on any new jobs for the next six weeks, that way I will have the choice to extend my term of lease, should I wish to do so. And if I decide not to, I will compensate you for your time at a rate based on an average of two dates a week. Does that sound about right?'

He nods.

'You can start today. Just drive over to your hotel to collect your things. It's up to you whether or not you want to keep on your room at the Almansor. I'll explain to you where I live.' I throw back my head. 'You go and make an invoice, Romeo. Write it all down on a sheet of A4 and bring it along. You and I are going to do business together.'

'What if we can't agree on a price?' he asks. 'Then where do I take all my stuff? Wouldn't it be better if I give you a quick ring from the hotel beforehand to let you know my price?'

'I don't bargain over the phone.' I put Romeo's card

in my bag, take out my car key and unlock the Vauxhall. I sit down behind the wheel as gracefully as I can. 'Any questions?'

He shakes his head. I give directions to the Casa da Criança.

'See you in a moment.' I do a hill start and move off up the slope. The road really goes up very steeply. In my rear-view mirror I can see Romeo slowly walking over to his Maserati.

When I look in the mirror again, Jimmy is sitting on the back seat.

— You gave me a fright.

— Sorry Jules, I'm just trying to keep you on your toes. Though I'm beginning to think you don't need me as much any more.

— What do you make of Romeo?

— A bit of a weirdo. All the same: congratulations. You didn't manage it in Faro but now you have. OK, you're paying him, but still.

— Do you trust him?

— You trust him. You've asked him to move in with you.

— I want sex.

— He doesn't have to come and live with you for that.

— You'll think me a fool but I believe him. This is no coincidence. The mere fact that he calls himself Romeo . . . We'll have to spend more time with each other. I think he may be able to help me. He does something to me, he touches me, I could feel it the moment I saw him in the Hotel Eva . . .

— If you ask me, it's because you've been without a man for too long. Any bloke can just waltz past, feed you a few mushy lines and you're a gonner. Romeo, your Love Service: he's a nifty guy, unbelievable. And all those different names. I wonder if he keeps a stack of passports in his inside pocket. I wouldn't be surprised.

– You can be sarcastic all you want.

– It's your party, sweetheart. Do you still think about home from time to time?

– Only a minute ago.

There's some truth in it. I briefly thought of Isabel when Romeo mentioned the name of his hotel. Next to the reception desk in the Tivoli Almansor there is a small computer area, where you can sit down and go on the Internet. Lotus always goes there to check her email, she just pretends that she is one of the guests. The time she and I went to have a meal at the hotel, she made straight for the computers. I could have done the same, I could have gone on MSN to see if my daughter was online. I didn't. Suppose she had been online, what could I have said? I couldn't have made any promises about my homecoming; neither did I have any exciting news for her, I could hardly tell her about the midgets or my operations. Now that I have missed Jim's birthday, I have lost the courage to get in touch with them.

– Well?

– Nothing. Stop nagging me, Jimmy. I'm doing what you asked me to do. I am going to get some highs.

I look into my mirror. He is no longer sitting upright, he's lying on his back, examining his nails.

– That was the worst thing for me. I was a good-looking guy, wasn't I? There was very little left of that towards the end.

He says it with a heavy sigh.

– Are you jealous?

– Of the living? Are you kidding? All that worry, God no.

– I just said something to you: I am going to get some highs.

– Do you know what your problem is, Jules? You take people far too seriously. Make sure that they take you seriously. That's the only thing that counts.

Chapter Twenty-four

Romeo keeps his word. Within an hour I find him standing outside the Casa da Criança, with a pair of leather suitcases in his hands. 'Indeed . . . it's, er . . . a special house,' he says, as he looks up from the pale red façade to the fuchsia-purple roof.

'Feel free to say what you really think. At first I thought it was hideous too, but you get used to it. There comes a moment when you don't see it any more. Stranger still, in a funny way, you actually grow to like it.'

'Roughly how long did that take?' he asks as he enters the house.

'I don't think you'll be here quite long enough.'

He puts his suitcases down in the hall.

'Would you like a guided tour? It's a pretty big place, you could easily lose your way.'

'Later. For now I just want to stay very close to you, then I'll be safe, won't I?'

He comes and stands right in front of me, leaning both hands against the wall. I feel the concrete against my back, I feel trapped. He brings his face right up to mine. I can see the twinkle in his eyes. He is flirting with me. Mr Love Service is warming up rapidly. We haven't completed our negotiations yet; I must stay alert.

With a quick movement I dive under his right arm and walk across to the living room. 'Did you do your homework? You were going to put a few things on paper for me.'

'Well, well, you certainly are a true little business-woman.'

'I'm a bookkeeper, what do you expect? You could call it an occupational illness – I just like to have things in writing.'

Romeo takes a good look around the living room. He picks up a statuette from the sideboard, examines it from all angles and puts it down again.

'Maybe we should take a moment to go over it together, I didn't quite manage to solve it on my own. A month is a long time. Who says we'll last that long?'

'Would you like an advance payment? You can if you want.'

'I'm not just thinking about the money, Julia. We are about to embark upon a special adventure. Before I commit myself any further, I need to know more about you.'

That is the limit.

'You've got a nerve, Romeo, or whatever your name is. Who is taking the biggest risk here? I am bringing a man into my house who seems to have as many identities as pairs of pants. I am offering to pay him, while for all I know he could be a criminal on the run, and then he . . . you have the cheek to demand more information about *me*. That's taking it to the bloody limit!'

He ignores my outburst completely.

'Do you have a DVD player here?'

For a moment I am confused.

'I've brought you a DVD. So that you can see what you're letting yourself in for.'

'You're not serious.'

'Of course I am. You're Dutch: "*Kijken, kijken, niet kopen*: just looking, looking, not buying." I know you people.'

He actually spoke Dutch: it's a long time since I heard anyone say anything in my mother tongue. There are plenty of Dutch people roaming the Algarve, but I avoid them like the plague. Even my neighbours I have so far only waved to from a safe distance. I never stop for a chat, I refuse to: before you know it, you have to drop in daily at Casa Encantador to ask after little Junior's stomach cramps.

'Shall I put it on?' Romeo offers.

'Now?'

'When else? Tomorrow there won't be much point.' He gives me a knowing wink. Jimmy was right: he's nifty, this guy.

'Would you like to watch here or in the bedroom?'

'You might not be able to control yourself if we go up to the bedroom, Julia. We haven't got anything in writing yet: you don't want your accounts to get into a mess.'

Not to mention my hormones: they have been in disarray ever since a certain Romeo sat down at my table in Vilarhino. And now he walks around in my house as if he has lived here all his life.

He is tall, manly, and self-assured. He is wearing linen trousers and a white shirt with the top button open. The rest of the buttons are crying out to be undone, by him or by me, it doesn't matter which, as long as that shirt comes off and preferably a bit quickly, I want to see that broad chest, I want to get my nails into it, I want him to pull me towards him, I want to land on the floor, on him, under him, it could be quickly, it had better be quickly, my body is aching for him, it's hurting, it's really painful, I am suffering, I am an emergency, can't he see that? He is Romeo from Love Service, it is his job to provide a solution, he has got to save me, that is what he is paid to do, it is his speciality.

I walk to the Chinese cabinet with the television inside, and open it up.

Romeo gets the DVD. It is in a white case with no title, so that you can't see what sort of film it is. He comes and stands next to me, and puts the disc into the DVD player. I pick up the remote and put the television on. We go and sit together on the sofa.

'Would you like a drink?' I ask, while the standard spiel about only being for home use and copying being prohibited plays.

'No thanks,' he says.

'I'm having one, are you sure?' Slightly nervously I walk to the kitchen. It's as if I am about to watch Will Smith's latest film, actually with Will. I wonder what Romeo expects from me? Some compliments about his body, his acting skills, his sexual stamina? Are we going to watch the DVD right to the end? That would be funny. And I should say that the ending was an anticlimax: I must remember that, that's a good one.

I pour a glass of Barcardi nearly full, and for form's sake, add a little Diet Coke. My hands are shaking, a Valium wouldn't go amiss. Take a deep breath in, and out again. Think Zen, think sunset, think of your chakras. Get them all to relax. I take a big swig, fill up again with Bacardi, and go back to the living room.

Romeo has put the film on pause. When I am sitting alongside him again, he presses play.

I hear music, familiar music. It's the opening number of *The Sound of Music*. Strange.

Romeo leans forward.

Now I can see Julie Andrews. The hills are alive. Alive and kicking with the sound of music. They are beautiful, vast green hills and Julie has her qualities, but she is not horny, and the black man beside me is nowhere to be seen.

'Oops,' says Romeo. He picks up the remote.

I assume that he's going to fast-forward it a bit. I take it that *The Sound of Music* has been put in as a joke, to provide the naughty DVD with an innocent sauce, that after this we're going to see the real hills. The hills of Venus, with my plucky Romeo frolicking over them.

Romeo stops the film and looks at me sheepishly. 'Wrong DVD,' he says.

'You don't mean it.' How does he come by *The Sound of Music*, for God's sake? Oh, but that is his favourite film. Has been for years. He always has a copy with him, to play before he goes to sleep. It calms the Love Service down.

'I'm sorry, Julia, I picked it up too quickly. I've left the one I wanted to show you in the Tivoli Almansor, I'm afraid.'

'Have you checked out of the room?' He nods.

'It's the cleaner's lucky day.' Not mine. Or is it? I take my glass and glug it half empty. 'So,' I say, 'there's nothing else for it then.'

'What do you mean?'

'A live performance. Let's see what you can do, Romeo.' I wave him to his feet.

'No way,' he says indignantly.

'Oh come on now. *Kijken, kijken* otherwise there's no *kopen*. Do you need some music? There is a rack full of CDs over there, there's bound to be something you can use.'

Still unwilling, he stands up. 'I don't usually do this, OK? Just so that you know.'

'I don't normally use the Love Service. So far it's hardly impressive.'

For a moment I think that I have upset him. It's all right. He goes over to the CDs, chooses one and puts it on. It's *fado*, Portuguese crooning. I am sure that there's more appropriate music there, he is doing this to annoy me. A striptease to *fado* – go on, drive me mad.

Romeo stands in front of me. For the first minute he does absolutely nothing, he shuts his eyes, concentrating, then he starts to sway slowly in time to the music. First just his top half, then after some hesitation his hips are also moving, as if he can't resist. His eyes are still shut. I take a quick swig. It's lovely to be able to study him from top to bottom, unashamed. And to be in control. He is mine. I am on the point of buying him.

'That shirt could come off now, Romeo.'

He pretends not to hear me, but his hands are actually sliding upwards, and undoing the second button. He keeps swaying, slowly, sensually, while he moves on to the next button. And the next one. Really slowly.

'The rest in one go,' I order him. 'You can claim any expenses.'

His eyes open up a bit. He looks at me from underneath his thick curly eyelashes. He knows exactly how that look affects me.

I hold my breath. He grabs his shirt and tears it open, just as I had asked, the remaining buttons landing on the marble with little clinking sounds. His chest is partially visible, but by no means all of it.

I want to jump up and rip the shirt from his body, but I control myself. This is his audition, he's got to sweat it out. Romeo wriggles his shoulders and the shirt slides off onto the floor.

Suddenly he is half naked.

He is more muscly than I had expected. His chest is broad, bright and with a matt glow, what would he have rubbed into himself this morning? Will I be allowed to do that tomorrow morning? His hands are now by his belt. Holy Mother Mary, that's coming off quickly, he pulls it through all the loops in one move.

'Put your arms behind your back,' he says.

'Sorry?'

'I don't trust you. You still haven't paid a cent. I'm afraid that you won't be able to hold yourself back, that in a moment you'll take advantage of me . . .'

I can't tell if he is making a joke, or if it's a part of the game, I only know that I am going to do everything he asks me. He's got me wrapped around his finger: already, the roles have been swapped again. Is the *fado* still on? I can't hear it any more, I can't hear anything, he is the only thing I can see or hear.

'Can I first finish my drink?'

That is allowed.

He ties the belt tightly around my wrists. Only when he has finished do I realize that I am now in a vulnerable position. His next step could be a gag in my mouth, he could rob me, nobody knows he is here, not Eddie, not one of my Dutch neighbours, nobody at all. Stella won't be coming again until the day after tomorrow. My body could be cold by then. You only learn about boundaries when you look for them. Perhaps it was the

234

biggest mistake of my life to embark on the Love Service, perhaps it was the best thing I have ever done. I am in the twilight zone, all my senses are extra sensitive, I am super-conscious of everything around me, I can hear myself breathing, I can feel my heart beating, I am alive, the old Julia is coming back to life.

Romeo has taken his shoes off and put on another CD. The summer hit by Elvis and Junkie XL: that's more like it. My gigolo takes up his position again and starts to swing. And I am supposed to think he has never done this before? He twirls about, swinging his hips. The King is not dead, he undoes his trousers, lets them fall down and elegantly steps out of them. Snow-white briefs come into view.

A little less conversation, a little more action please.

Is this going to be it? Has he got some condoms? Of course he has.

Come on, come on. I am tired of talking.

He turns around. His buttocks are showing through his pants. A great butt. Very frustrating that I can't move my hands at all.

He hooks his thumbs under the sides of his briefs. Exasperatingly slowly, his thumbs move downwards. What I get to see is not so utterly amazing, it's two curves, separated by a cleft, as with everyone. But the fact that he shows them to me, that he is about to turn around, that he will be completely naked, that he dares do this when he scarcely knows me, means that my admiration for Love Service is growing by the minute, just like my readiness to hand over huge sums of money.

Romeo's briefs are on the floor. He steps out of them. There is a stark naked black man in my living room, with his back to me.

Satisfy me.

He does it.

The drum roll sounds.

He does a pirouette, on his toes, his arms twisting elegantly along. I can see that he has been to ballet lessons. It is the only explanation. His organ comes to me so quickly that I cannot see it properly. Romeo does another pirouette, a half one, slightly more slowly, and finishes up with his face towards his one-headed audience. He bows with a slight nod of the head, straightens his back and stands there like a shop-window dummy.

He is well hung, he is not stiff, but also not completely soft, there is a thick vein running its length. He is fantastic, they should make a mould from him, he should be in a catalogue.

'Bravo!' I shout. If I could have clapped, I would have done so.

'Is that for the act, or for this?' he asks, while he nonchalantly puts his right hand underneath his organ and lifts it up a bit.

I am speechless.

He smiles and steps towards me: the object of my desire is now reasonably close to my mouth. He routinely gives it a couple of tugs. 'This is what you want to buy, isn't it? It's about my merchandise, not me. Have a look and see if you like it.'

I comply with his request. His penis is fully erect now, I guess its overall length comes to at least twenty centimetres, if not more. Romeo is circumcised; the top is graced with a large and shiny, skinless glans. Underneath the penis hangs a well-filled scrotum. It all looks perfectly healthy and in good working order. It doesn't give off a pungent or unpleasant smell, there's nothing wrong with it, nothing at all. The decision is easily made.

'You can tie a ribbon round it, I'll take it,' I say. 'Could you please undo that belt round my wrists now?'

'Not yet,' says Romeo. He brings his organ even closer to my mouth. 'Want to try?'

He can sound so innocent. As if he is the little boy from next door who wants to share his ice cream with you.

I stick out my tongue. He quickly slides his glans over it and withdraws again.

'Hey! I hardly tasted anything.'

'Oh, all right then.'

He brings his penis close to my lips again. This time he pushes it further and deeper, he shoves it inside.

'Have a little suck,' he says indulgently.

So I do. Who is pleasuring whom now? It doesn't matter. I shut my eyes and enjoy the warm, full sensation in my mouth.

I don't think my lips have ever been so engorged before. What with all that Belgian filler that has just been injected into them, I'd better be careful or they might explode.

'There. That's enough.'

With complete composure Romeo removes his organ from my mouth. This is where you can tell the pro from the amateur. He picks up his briefs from the marble and slips them back on.

'You're not going to stop now, are you?' I stammer.

'My dear girl, I've hardly started.' He carries on getting dressed. In a moment that divine body will be completely covered up in clothes again, we can't have

237

that, I must stop him. I pull myself up, rather clumsily because my hands are still behind my back.

'Romeo . . .' I look up at him imploringly. Shall I kiss him? But how? It's not easy to kiss someone convincingly if you can't use your arms. Not easy at all – especially if the person in question is more than two heads taller than you. 'Release me. I want to feel you.'

Romeo clears his throat. 'First we were going to deal with the business side of things, Madam Accountant.'

Damn yes, why did I have to make such a fuss about that? That was then and this is now. I am not going to nitpick over a few cents. If need be, I'll prostitute myself in order to pay him. I'd better not tell him that, I am smart enough not to, I am an old hand at this game. 'Money is no object. Name your price and I'll pay you,' I hear myself say in a hoarse voice. 'Provided it is within reason, of course,' I add quietly.

'What do you consider within reason, Julia? You want me to stay for at least a month. That's a long time.'

Romeo grabs my wrists and undoes the belt. He is fully dressed, he is Romeo from Love Service, he is not the man I thought he was, the man in the restaurant who seemed genuinely interested in me.

'For a start I'll give you free board and lodging,' I say. 'Then there are these four other jobs which you'll do on the side. What do you get for those?'

Romeo has pulled his belt through the loops of his trousers and is doing it up. 'Each client has her own tariff, I can't go into specifics.'

'It's up to you to suggest a price: after all, you are the one who is providing a service. I'll tell you if I think it's too much.'

He sighs. 'Euros or dollars?'

'Euros.'

'Six thousand.'

Six thousand euros for a month of guaranteed sex-every-night with an expert. It's a lot of money.

'Six thousand, hmmm?' I repeat, to give myself more time.

'Per week. That comes to—'

'No way.' I go to the kitchen.

Romeo comes after me. 'If I charged you my normal hourly rate, it would work out far more expensive.'

'I don't care what rate you charge, I'm not going to fork out six thousand euros a week. I'd rather give money to help the hungry in Africa. I should do that anyway, I just keep forgetting. Would you like a drink?'

My lust has evaporated. It's because of all that talk about money, it dries you up. I wonder how men handle that side of things with prostitutes.

Romeo fancies a Bacardi and Coke too now.

I pour two glasses. We toast.

'To the hungry in Africa,' I say.

Romeo looks at me, bewildered. 'You're a strange woman, Julia.'

'Yep, I am.' I suppress a burp. 'A strange woman in a strange house. I live here all by myself. Nobody knows that I'm here. I wasn't expecting to say this, Romeo, but on second thoughts, I think that I might be one of those clients who is looking for company as well as sex. I'd like to talk to you the way we did at the restaurant. I'd like you to listen to me, to comfort me. Do you think you could do that? Or is that going to make it even more expensive?'

Romeo puts his glass down by the kitchen sink. He has hardly drunk from it; mine is already more than half empty again. 'How do you mean: nobody knows that you are here?' he asks.

'Well, you know,' I say with a shrug. 'My family, I've broken away from them, I've broken off all contact. Just like Merel.'

'Merel breaks off all contact,' wrote Leni Saris. I used to love reading her books when I was a girl. That sentence has stuck in my mind ever since. Somehow, I must have known that one day I would do the same.

'Merel?' Romeo mouths the name to try it out. 'Who is Merel?'

'Oh, she is a character from a book. She is in love with her sister's fiancé, which is why she leaves the country. All is well in the end, though, because it turns out he was in love with her also.'

True love was always rewarded with a happy ending in Leni Saris. She never got married herself, perhaps that is why she believed in it.

'Why did you do it?' asks Romeo.

'That's not important. I'm free now, I'm not accountable to anyone – except Jimmy maybe. Would you like another Bacardi and Coke? You're not drinking fast enough.'

'No, thank you. Who is Jimmy?'

I top my glass up. Today is a bit of a funny day, anyway. 'He is my brother. He's dead. Has been for ages, but recently he has been coming to see me a lot. Have you ever had that? Have you ever been followed around by a dead person? You might think I was glad of the company but actually I don't get much out of it. In one sense he is there but in another he isn't, if you see what I mean. Sometimes I just think I'm imagining it all. It's because I'm alone: you start seeing things. Are you real? I should touch you to find out, but touching you costs money.'

I have been spending so much money recently, Paul would have a heart attack if he knew.

'I know Eddie exists, I'm less sure about his wife. Eddie owns this villa. He claims to have a wife, he calls her Doris.'

I continue in a whisper, 'I've never seen her. Even though I've been here for two months or so, now. Don't you think that's a bit odd? Eddie is a nice guy, he thinks I'm a famous actress, just remember that when you meet him. My cleaning lady's name is Stella, thanks to her this place is so tidy. The only other guests I've had so far are two German midgets, Wolfgang and Heinz . . .'

Romeo puckers his brows.

'. . . forget it.'

They've got Eddie's cap, which is why I think they must exist. There are times when I wonder about my mental health. I am fine about the way I look now, but I am increasingly unsure about my inner self. Am I normal? Am I nice? Am I a good person? Is that actually what I want to be: normal, nice and good? Apparently not. I wouldn't have left otherwise. I wouldn't have broken off my relationships so abruptly.

'I've let them down,' I say under my breath, more to myself than to Romeo.

'Who?'

'My husband and children. I've deserted them . . .'

It is the first time I say this out loud since leaving, even Lotus doesn't really know. Romeo is the first to be officially told.

'. . . they know that I'm in Portugal, that's all. I'm not in touch with them any more.'

I take another gulp.

'They were calling so often, it was driving me insane. They are fine, you know, I'm pretty sure they are. If they weren't, they'd let me know. They can reach me, I've made sure they can: I bought a pager from a little old man. Shall I show you it?' As I head to the living room to get my bag, I notice that I am a bit unstable on my legs.

'Don't bother, I believe you,' Romeo says.

I hesitate. He leans against one of the kitchen units. Good idea, that's what I am going to do. When I turn and try to stand next to him, I nearly lose my balance again. The alcohol is taking its toll. I had already downed quite a few glasses of wine in the restaurant, of course.

'Hey, careful now, don't fall over!' Romeo catches me round the waist. He is very close to me suddenly. Blimey, he smells good. And his hand, what a lovely firm grip. I could stay like this for hours, preferably with my head against his chest. My head is feeling rather heavy at the moment.

'Julia . . .' says Romeo.

I nestle in his arms. I think we should stop talking now, we should enjoy this intimate moment.

'Julia,' Romeo says again.

'What?'

He forces me to look at him. 'You've got issues.'

I burst out laughing.

It reminds me of a scene from *Ally McBeal*, in which she gets told exactly the same thing. Also by a black man. He is the boyfriend of Ally's flatmate and she steals into their bedroom at night because she wants to see them lying in each other's arms. It's a fairly sick thing to do, but Ally is like that. Her face is right

242

above the black man's head when he suddenly wakes up.

You've got issues. It's a curious phrase. It means: you have problems. There are subjects that are difficult for you. There are things that keep bugging you. You have worries. You have your own agenda. There are things going on in your life. Things with which you struggle on your own, day after day.

Romeo is not amused. 'I'm serious, you have issues,' he says again.

I dig my finger into his chest. 'I have issues, you have issues, everyone has issues. What are your issues, Romeo? Would you care to share them with me?'

Silence.

'See, you have them too.' I pick up my glass from the worktop.

'Mine aren't as serious as yours.' He glances at the glass in my hand.

It annoys me. Already Mr Gigolo thinks he has the right to tick me off about my alcohol consumption. I knock back the rest of my glass in one go. 'You worry too much. All I have done is take some time out. People should do it more often. It's very good for you. Gives you a chance to have some new experiences. Without my issues, I would never have met you. Tell me honestly, Romeo: why did you come and sit at my table in the restaurant? Did you do it because you wanted to, or merely because you spotted a potential client?'

'It doesn't matter.'

'This is precisely what I hate so much.' I bang my empty glass down on the worktop. 'I am honest with you, and immediately you withdraw. *You* are the one with issues. You don't know how to treat real people.'

'Oh, no?' Romeo pulls me towards him and presses

243

his lips on mine. He overwhelms me, not tenderly, not in Leni fashion: he pushes his tongue into my mouth, I let him, his hand slides over my neck, squeezing me hard.

He stops just as suddenly as he started and pushes me away. 'I've been wanting to do that for a long time. I hesitated. You are not an average client, Julia, you are dangerous. You are the sort of woman a man can lose himself to, you know that bloody well yourself. If you keep looking at me like that, there is no way back, do you realize? Within five minutes we can be in bed together, and it will be out of this world. But then what do we do? We will want more and more and more. We can't have that.'

I touch my lips. He has kissed me. Entirely free of charge.

'Do you see what I'm saying?' he asks.

His words have largely gone past me, I have only caught the last sentence. 'Why can't we have that? I want it, you want it. What's the problem?'

'I'm a gigolo, Julia. I can't start an intimate relationship with one of my clients.'

'I don't have to be your client. I could just be your girlfriend. Or your one-night stand.'

He lowers his eyes.

'Do you have a wife?'

No answer.

'Hello? Hello?' I tap him on the head repeatedly. 'Anybody home?'

His face breaks into a smile. He understands. We have the same sense of humour. We make a good couple.

'How about another drink?' I reach for the bottle. 'With me it's fairly simple, Romeo. I want sex or drink.

To be precise: lots of sex or lots of drink. Preferably the former and if that is not available, the latter.'

'You have had more than enough.' He takes the Bacardi from me. 'Shall I take you up to your bed?'

'One last sip.' I reclaim the bottle and put it straight to my mouth. It goes over my chin but I manage to get some in.

'You really do have issues,' Romeo repeats.

I wipe my mouth. 'Let's go upstairs. Give Mummy a hand, and I'll take you.' Things don't quite go according to plan. Romeo has to support me as I can barely stay upright. 'X, y, z, Romeo and Julia go off to bed,' I giggle.

'You are going to sleep,' Romeo says pointedly.

'Hello! You are a gigolo. We are going to have sex. I can't wait any longer. I will pay you tomorrow, I promise. Do you know I've never done it with an enormous—'

'Don't you worry, we will do it,' he interrupts me. 'We've got plenty of time.'

We get to the staircase.

'I'll stay right behind you. Do you think you can manage, or shall I carry you?' he asks, concerned.

'Of course I'll manage.' I am not giving in. That's number one. There is step number two. And number three.

'Number four, it's such a bore. Number five, I'm still alive.' I find myself very droll. 'Number six, let's get some kicks.'

'What was that?' Romeo asks.

'Number seven, my brother is in heaven.'

I pause a moment to catch my breath.

'Number eight, the doctor came too late.'

Two seconds' rest.

'Number nine, his choice, not mine.'

Mark time.

'Number ten, dead and what then?'

The tears are flowing down my cheeks.

'Number eleven, it was over by seven.' I turn round to Romeo. 'It's true! It really is. Do you believe me?' At last I am speaking his language.

'Who are you talking about?'

'Jimmy, of course.'

We get to the top of the stairs.

'Where do we go next?'

I point to my bedroom; he takes me through the door. Too late, I remember that I haven't allowed Stella into my room for several weeks. The consequences are quite noticeable. My bed is unmade, the bottom sheet is covered in stains and smudges, some light brown, others menstrual-red, there are bottles and dirty clothes all over the floor, a collection of greasy glasses adorns the bedside table and beside my pillow I notice a small white ball, a panty liner that I pulled out of my knickers, when I was half asleep, a couple of nights ago. The only thing missing is graffiti on the wall saying 'Tracey Emin was here'.

Romeo sums up the situation at a glance and sits me down in a chair. Without a word he begins to remove the bedding. I bury my face in my hands. Everything is spinning – I feel sick.

'Where are the clean sheets?'

'In the cupboard,' I answer without looking up. 'You don't have to do this, Romeo, my cleaning lady is coming the day after tomorrow. Go home. To your hotel, I mean. I'm sorry. Forgive me. Forget everything I said. You don't have to stay. I'll give you a good reference.'

No response. I can hear him rummaging about in the room. Love Service is cleaning out my pigsty.

'Do you have any bin liners?'

I am about to get up.

'Stay in your chair, where are they?'

'In the kitchen, under the sink,' I say feebly.

Romeo goes downstairs, taking the dirty glasses.

I feel ashamed. Why didn't I think to tidy up my bedroom when I knew he was coming? I could have directed him to a different room, there are plenty of others in the villa.

He comes upstairs again. He goes round the room and collects all the rubbish in a bin liner, humming a tune to himself. He pulls out an empty bag of crisps from under the bed and changes the sheets, as if it is the most normal thing in the world. 'Where is the laundry basket?'

'In the bathroom. Two doors down.'

I don't understand how Romeo can be so cheerful.

'Get undressed!' he shouts from the landing. 'If you can, that is . . .'

Slowly I stand up. I manage it. The spinning is not so bad. I take my clothes off and worm myself into a soft-yellow strappy top.

Romeo comes in. 'Fine pair of legs you've got there. Do you work out a lot?'

I blush. He throws back the top sheet invitingly.

'Are you coming in too?' I ask.

He shakes his head. 'I'd better not.'

Disappointed, I go to the bathroom, propping myself against the wall a couple of times en route. He doesn't want to go to bed with me. I have a villa, I have a fine pair of legs, I have money, and yet he refuses to please me. I shouldn't have had so much to drink, of course, that's it: men find drunk women a turn-off. I have a pee and brush my teeth. I zigzag back across the hall to my bedroom.

Romeo is sitting in a chair right beside my pillow. I

can't say I am surprised: probably he is a woman whisperer as well.

I flop down onto the bed, face up. I wish the spinning would finally stop. I close my eyes. The clean sheets smell delicious. Not quite so delicious as Romeo, when we were in the kitchen earlier, but lovely all the same. I am so tired, I could be in the land of Nod within the next five minutes. Perhaps that would be best.

'Julia,' whispers Romeo.

'Hmm?'

'Do you want to fall asleep straight away, or talk some more first?'

I open one eye.

'Let it all out, Julia. You can tell me anything. Your secrets are safe with me'

I open my other eye as well, I turn my face to him. My secrets and my money too.

'You're in distress. My mother told me you should always help a person in distress.'

'That is very . . .' I search for the right word. '. . . noble of you. Thank you.'

'I mean it.' To emphasize his words he leans over and kisses me gently on the lips. His hand glides under the sheet, underneath my top, and moves up. When his hand reaches my left breast, he takes my erect nipple in between his fingers. He keeps looking at my face to register my reaction. My lips part, my hips begin to rotate restlessly. He lets go of my breast and slides his hand down into my knickers, touching me briefly between the legs.

'You're wet,' he concludes with satisfaction. He pulls his hand out again, brings his fingers up to his mouth and licks them. He stands up.

'Sleep well, Julia.'

Chapter Twenty-five

A few hours later I wake up with a start. Romeo. The minute he left the bedroom I went out like a light, too tired to think about what had and hadn't happened, and about what he had said: that I could tell him anything.

I switch on the light and look at my watch. Four fifteen. Jimmy died at four thirty. The house is deathly quiet. Just the same as then. Romeo has turned my life upside down. Presumably he is lying asleep somewhere, blissfully unaware of the havoc he has created. It's easy for him, I am just another client – it's just another day at the office. As it happens, this particular client comes with a story. He doesn't mind listening to me, he is helpful: it's all part of the service. I wonder what Jimmy would say about it. Of course, now that I want to ask him something, he doesn't show up. I decide to summon him.

'Hey, are you there?' I say out loud.

As soon as I have said it, I feel goosebumps on my arms: I don't really want him to respond, I feel frightened. I wish that he would leave me alone, that he would stop appearing in the back of my car all the time, that we could make peace, forgive each other. He can't expect me to keep quiet for the rest of my life. I am his posthumous spokeswoman, I am not a child any more. I have some ability to make my own decisions.

If I get up now and go to Romeo, there is nothing Jimmy can do to stop me from telling the whole story. What could he possibly do? There is no oxygen cylinder to roll against the door. His ghost is never going to be strong enough to force me back into my bed.

I decide to risk it, get out of bed, and creep to the door. Nothing. See? Too many worries, too many anxieties. I open the door and slip out onto the landing. Now I must find Romeo. Shall I go and look for him straight away, or quickly grab a drink first? I can feel a hangover coming on. Maybe not, I decide. Romeo is more important than a drink. He is bound to find me less attractive if I turn up reeking of alcohol all over again. After I have been for a pee I turn on the landing light. The door of one of the spare rooms is ajar. That's where he must have gone.

Gently I push the door a little further, I don't want to give him a fright. He is lying on his side on the large single bed, with a striped sheet pulled over him. I go a bit nearer. I stretch out my hand and pull the sheet down a little. Romeo looks less broad when he is lying down, and paler too, he is different, smaller, something is wrong, this can't be Romeo, this is, oh God . . . no. I want to storm out of the room but I am fixed to the spot. The figure in the bed jumps up with a start. The emaciated Jimmy looks at me furiously. He is different from before. He doesn't tease me, he is angry.

– What are you up to, Jules?

I must scream. I must call Romeo. If Romeo is here, he will disappear. I try to, but no sound comes out.

– It's night-time, it's almost half past four and you are creeping around the house in search of a member of the opposite sex. History is repeating itself. I hope that Romeo of yours realizes what you are capable of. You think you can get away with anything: desert your family, have your body remodelled, hire a gigolo and give the game away to a complete stranger. You are about to blow the lid on our secret pact to a porn star. And why? For a few good shags? Even Kaitlin wouldn't go that far. I'm really disappointed in you.

– It had to end sometime, Jimmy. I'm exhausted.

– Don't expect me to feel sorry for you. You are a winner, I was the sucker who drew the short straw.

– You know how awful I felt about that. I did everything I could, everything you asked, I don't think you ever understood how difficult that was for me.

– You could have left it all to Him.

– If you're going to be like that, I'm out of here.

– You haven't got the guts, have you?

He still thinks he can beat me.

– Just you watch, I can do anything.

– That's what you said nineteen years ago.

– Exactly. And I did. Remember?

He hangs his head. The next thing I know, the young Jimmy is back, the healthy Jimmy with rosy cheeks.

I feel a lump in my throat. It is heart-rending to see him. As if he were really there, as if he could get out of bed this very moment and join the living. Or better still: lead a real life of his own, that would be the best possible outcome, then I could have peace, but it won't happen, it will never happen. He will always be nineteen, going on twenty. He will never get any older, get married, acquire a potbelly or have children; my brother was never granted any of those things.

– I hereby officially declare our pact over, I say.

– Do you realize what you are doing?

– I no longer feel I owe you something. You made your choices – it wasn't always easy to understand what motivated you. Now I'm making mine.

– You won't see me again, he threatens. You may be relieved now, but you are going to miss me, Jules.

– I'll take that risk.

Chapter Twenty-six

There is a big man in the bed. He is fast asleep. For the second time I pull down the striped sheet slightly. I am in no doubt that Romeo will be naked. His body is gorgeous, his face completely relaxed. I kneel down beside the bed and inhale his smell. There is something about it that reminds me vaguely of Jim, my little Jim. I often sat next to him in exactly the same way, looking at him, sniffing and cuddling him and stroking his little mop of sweaty hair.

My son is growing bigger and getting older. I am not my mother, my son is alive, and I may enjoy him. I am not doing so. I am here and he is over there. His mother disappeared months ago. His father tucks him in every night, Jim doesn't know why.

Romeo wakes up. I am waiting for him to say, 'You've got issues,' again, but instead he just whispers my name.

'You were right, I need help.'

'What's the time?'

'Are you listening to me? You said that I could tell you anything. I'd like to.'

He picks up his mobile from the bedside table.

'How would you like to go about it? Shall we make it

one big session, or would you prefer me to break it down into little bits?'

'Julia, for God's sake, it's half past four.'

'Sorry, but this is important to me.'

Romeo has a good long stretch. His body is divine, he knows it, it's impossible to ignore it. 'Why are you down there on your knees? Come and lie next to me.' He moves up a little. A few hours ago he didn't want me beside him, now he behaves as if it is fully expected. I get into bed with him. He takes me into his arms. 'So tell me, what was so urgent that it couldn't wait till a more civilized hour?'

I feel his muscular body against mine. I don't think he is even wearing briefs. I am in bed with a clone of Will Smith: I must concentrate, I must enjoy this moment, there won't be many others like it, let's face it. Romeo hooks his finger under the strap of my vest and pulls it down over my shoulder. Leaving the top half of my left breast uncovered, he moves down the other strap as well.

The lace trim of my vest catches on my nipples, Romeo buries his face in my neckline. He kisses me between my breasts and pulls down the vest so that he can inspect the upper part of my body more closely. Thanks to the breast-lift he doesn't have to move down too far to find what he is looking for.

'Romeo . . .'

The man has just decided that he wants to take my left nipple into his mouth first. I get no answer.

'Is this work or pleasure? You can be honest. I can see you might regard it as work – essentially it is of course – I'm just curious to know what it's like for you?'

'Can't you for once shut up?'

I am flabbergasted. I have never shared a bed with

254

such a philistine. I can't claim experience of a great many sleeping partners; if I count them on two hands, I have fingers left over, practically a whole hand of them, but the guys I slept with were, without exception, gentle. Kind, tender, industrious: that's my experience of Dutch men. Not much rough and tumble; it is as though they are always holding something back when they are inside or around a naked woman, it's the way they are brought up. That's how we do things: you eat with a knife and fork, and you don't lick your plate, even if you've got a big appetite.

Romeo is an American. Sex is not about relaxing and enjoying yourself, it is about performance. He won't rest until he achieves his goal and when he achieves his goal he won't rest. The next victory is already waiting, there are always more prizes you can win, just like the Oscars or Olympic gold medals.

The master's hands slide over my body. It is as though I am made out of clay and he is shaping me, my hips, my thighs, they all have to be moulded by the artist.

Romeo turns me onto my back and pulls my legs apart. He goes down on me again. When he reaches my knickers, he doesn't pull them off but stretches the crotch over to one side. His fingers and tongue embark on a joint attack. After about thirty seconds I give in. My knees turn to jelly and flop sideways. I straddle my legs unashamedly, as wide as I can. It adds to the sexiness of the whole situation.

He slides his hands underneath my buttocks and pulls down my knickers. I move my legs together again so that he can slip them off. The vest is still stuck somewhere around my waist. Romeo carries on where he left off. Hardly varying his technique, he is very consistent in the way he moves his tongue and fingers.

It's precision bombing – highly skilled. If he keeps on like this I am going to explode.

'Romeo, please.' I lift his head and force him to stop. 'It's far too good, I'm about to come.'

'I should hope so,' he says wryly.

'I don't want to.'

He looks surprised. A client who doesn't want an orgasm, Love Service doesn't often get postmodern requests like that.

'I want one later, when we really do it,' I explain.

If possible, he looks even more surprised. 'Why not now as well as later?'

'Do you reckon?' I wonder how he knows my body's capacity. One climax is not bad, I find – especially if you are dealing with a new man: after all you've got to be able to surrender yourself quite a bit. 'I'm not really into multiple orgasms that much. When it's over, I like to roll over and fall asleep. So I would rather wait before I . . . you know?'

'You really do have issues,' he says with a laugh. 'You talk too much and you think too much. Relax.'

He is right. I must loosen up. The man knows what he is doing, he is a professional.

'All right then,' I say, pointing down awkwardly. 'You may carry on.'

He shakes his head and disappears again between my legs. His tongue gets there first. He is making a huge effort, I must say. His fingers catch up with his tongue. They caress, stimulate, push and feel, while spreading the juices around and sliding into every crevice there, going in and out, across and around, until the entire area is ablaze. Meanwhile, Romeo carries on licking me in the same predictable way, almost too deliberately. Before long, I am close to

256

climaxing again. It is a matter of seconds: I can let it happen, I can go into free fall, but I remain in control.

'Come over here, you,' I say in a hoarse voice.

Romeo raises himself up and finally displays his full regalia. His organ seems bigger than after his striptease. It is colossal, it is hard, it's a tree trunk.

'This is when I would normally want to fuck,' I say earnestly. 'But now that I can see you . . . I hope it fits.'

'You're about to find out.' He pulls out a condom and deftly rolls it over his penis. 'On top or underneath?' he asks in a businesslike manner.

'Sorry?'

'Do you want to be on top of me, or underneath?'

'Underneath, please.' I swallow. There is no return. I am on the point of being fucked by a large cock. Romeo's cock.

'Legs apart,' he commands. 'Look at me.' He takes my hands and presses them down onto the mattress. 'Are you ready for it?'

He doesn't wait for the answer. He forces his way in. He fills me up. He thrusts. He changes from a giver into a taker. 'Oh my God,' he moans. 'Oh my God, Julia!' He pulls his penis all the way out, he wants to mount me again, I tilt my hips to receive him.

'Fuck my brains out,' I encourage him.

He thrusts further, hard and deep, he touches my cervix. I groan, this time because of the pain, he notices and apologizes.

I think of my husband. It is the last thing you should do when a scrumptious black man is making love to you. For the first time in our married life I am straying, genuinely straying – that kiss with the young Portuguese fellow doesn't count. When I go back now, and Paul asks me if I have stayed faithful, I can no longer say 'yes'. I will think of something or other to add – that I became unfaithful the moment I got into the taxi. Without having an urgent reason, I walked out on my family, that in itself was an act of unfaithfulness. That a certain Romeo appeared on the scene, and that I ended up in bed with him, was nothing more than a logical consequence of what had gone before.

'Keep going,' I say. 'Please, keep going. Make me forget everything, except what we're doing, make me feel alive, make the stars fall from the sky, make me come as I have never done before, make it last a long, long time, and make it wonderful – so wonderful that Paul and God and everyone else will understand, and forgive me.'

We heave with exhaustion in each other's arms. After a first time, we did it again. Then followed a third time despite my protests, but Romeo wouldn't take no for an answer, he knew for a fact that I could manage another climax. He was right. I have just declared the zone between my legs a disaster area. It has been the scene of a battle: we won't be able to assess the damage until the smoke has cleared. Right now I am feeling completely senseless. It is as if my body is a glowing, warm, half-extinguished lump that has been ripped to pieces. The last soldiers are sounding the retreat, carrying off their wounded, moaning pals on hastily improvised stretchers. Beside me lies the field marshal. He looks fulfilled and takes a drag on his cigarette.

'I didn't know you smoked.'

'Only after sex,' Romeo clarifies.

'What do you do when you're at work?'

'There is a smoking ban on the set. Besides: that's work, not sex.'

Aha.

'You mean . . . this wasn't work?' I pull myself away from him and sit up straight so that I can see his face properly.

'Why is that so important to you?'

'I want to know what I mean to you.'

Romeo gets out of bed. He picks up a saucer from the window sill, drops his cigarette ash onto it, puts it on the bedside table and comes back under the sheet. 'What does it matter what you mean to me? Only a woman would worry about that sort of thing. What good am I to you? That's the question you should be asking yourself.'

'Well, what good are you to me?'

He smiles and puts out his cigarette on the saucer. 'If you ask me, you had a particular frustration, which I have just sorted out for you.' He reaches down with his left hand and gently squeezes his naked organ. The sight alone is enough to stir up another uprising in my forbidden zone. The soldiers reach for their rifles, the wounded moan and put their hands over their eyes. Please, not again, we're whacked.

'Maybe you only made it worse,' I say softly. 'Maybe from now on, I won't be able to settle for anything less.'

'You wanted to know what it would be like. Now you do. Otherwise you would have spent the rest of your life wondering what you were missing.'

Now I will spend the rest of my life *knowing* what I am missing, that is the ironic side effect of this excess. Even if Paul fulfilled his New Year's resolution and started to go to the gym three times a week, even if he had his penis extended by twenty centimetres, if he introduced more variety into our lovemaking, added something to the usual kiss-kiss-finger-finger-penetrate-done routine, he would still be no match for Romeo.

259

Romeo has sex appeal, Romeo is one of those men who make you feel faint, Romeo has charisma. It's hard to tell whether it would still be like that after fifteen years, but that is not my worry: Romeo is not a man you stay with for fifteen years, Romeo is someone who passes through your life, someone you can borrow for a while, you don't know who from, or when you will need to return him, you'll probably find that one day he's just gone and you will never hear from him again, but that makes him all the more attractive.

Yes Paul, I know, it is not fair and you haven't deserved it, but that is how it is.

'It's getting light,' my lover observes.

Things seem better when it is light outside.

That is a lie, everything is a lie; in fact some things seem worse when it is light outside. Some memories are unbearable. You'd like to cut them out of your brain, but you can't. No surgeon would want to take the risk, there isn't a knife that is fine or sharp enough. They are like vicious growths: they entrench themselves inside your brain, they can be big, they can be dormant, they can seem small and harmless, but they are extremely painful and they destroy you without finishing you off. Ergo: you are still alive. The living are obliged to make something of it. Curtains! The start of a new day.

'Open the curtains,' I say briskly. 'A new day begins.'

When Isabel was small, she used to say crutains instead of curtains, and macroni instead of macaroni. She was one of those little girls you can watch for hours on end. I have a photo that says it all: Isabel is sitting in her big nappy on the wooden floor in the middle of the room, toys scattered around her. Next to her is her babywalker. She's waving a colourful rattle, she has dimpled cheeks and laughs at the photographer. I am sitting behind her, wearing a wide, greyish-white T-shirt, a pair of faded jogging bottoms and gigantic tiger slippers with holes in the soles. My hair is uncombed and short – too short, according to Paul – I am wearing no make-up, there is a cup of coffee on the window sill rather than on the coffee table because Isabel might push that over. My arms are folded and I have my eyes fixed on the focal point of my life: my face beams with pride and maternal joy. I don't care if the world falls apart, if bombs go off; it's all the same to me, as long as our house remains standing. Isabel and I, we'll be just fine, we are one. Secretly I think that she can feel everything I feel, that she knows everything I know, that she can read my thoughts, that she understands me without words. Paul, the photographer, my husband, her father, is not part of our pact. I gave birth to her, he will never understand it. It's not his fault.

Ten years later Paul and I have swapped roles. I have become the onlooker, I am the one who takes the photos, I no longer feel at one with any of them, not with Isabel, not with Jim, not with my husband. Now it's Paul who is beaming in all the digital pictures, it's he who is lighting the candles, helping them in and out of their little coats, being both a father and a mother to them. He has outdone me on all fronts. I became superfluous ages ago. That is why I could leave.

'What did you say?'

'Nothing.' Quickly I wipe away a tear from my cheek. 'Do you fancy something to eat? Or would you like to sleep, or do you want to have another er . . .'

'As if you're up for that.'

I produce a vague smile.

'You look tired,' says Romeo. 'You should get some sleep. When you wake up again, we'll talk further.' He pushes the sheet away and steps out of bed.

'I don't want to talk any more, I just want to have sex and eat and drink. Is that OK?' I ask.

He takes a towel from the cupboard. The naked god will be getting under the spray of my shower in a minute.

'Last night I wanted to tell you everything. Now I'm not so sure.'

Romeo throws the towel over his shoulder. 'Why?'

'Perhaps it isn't such a good idea. There are things that nobody knows. About my brother, about me.'

'The brother who is haunting you?'

I nod. 'He was here last night. He was lying in your bed. He doesn't want me to tell you our secrets.'

'You talk to him?' Romeo asks gently.

'He talks to me. He gives me advice. It's what he did when he was still alive, Jimmy was a highly articulate person. Before he died he gave me detailed instructions. There are certain things I will have to keep to myself for ever.'

'How long have you been doing this?'

'Nineteen years.' Exactly the length of his life. Jimmy has been running things from his grave for nineteen years now.

Romeo looks at me, full of awe. 'But that's inhuman. You can't expect that from a girl of . . . how old were you?'

'Seventeen.'

'Even so. I've no idea what it's about, Julia, but I'm sure it would do you good to get it off your chest.'

'Jimmy gets angry if I say it out loud. It would bring bad luck.'

He pulls something out of his suitcase and puts it in my hand. It's a blindfold. Not one of those red and black thingies that you buy on the plane – this one is made out of leather and looks as though it has come straight out of an S&M mail-order catalogue.

'Wear this, it will make you sleep better. It all seems simple enough to me: if you can't say it out loud, you write it down. I've got a laptop with me, you can borrow it if you want.'

If he knew just how much I have already written about Jimmy. Diaries full. I was still dreaming about becoming an author one day. I wanted to go to university and study Dutch literature, and Jimmy's story was to be my first work. Dad thought I didn't have enough talent and that you couldn't make a penny out of writing books unless your name was Ludlum or Cartland. It would make more sense for me to come and work in his office. That way I would have the security of a fixed income, which would allow me to build up a pension, and, in any case, he needed me: he was desperately short of staff.

The problem with Dad was that no one could ever stick it out with him. He insisted on only appointing female members of staff and then wouldn't be able to keep his hands off them. Initially he got away with it, but then it became awkward, the thing was given a name, people set up helplines, you could end up with a court case on your hands, the same hands that you hadn't been able to keep to yourself. Some cases would come out, family members would say it was an absolute disgrace, in the end my mother became so embarrassed that she didn't want to be seen in public any more.

It ended with good old Jules regularly giving up her school holidays to sit in the office and deal with overdue accounts. If she puts her mind to it, she can probably manage it in six weeks and if it's his own daughter, Dad won't be tempted to try anything on, that is how they justified it. Dad was indeed nowhere to be seen. He would be out on his boat, or having a fling somewhere, or having a fling on his boat. Jules would be spending the summer at his desk putting into order the pile of papers that he had flung in a corner. The only person who sometimes dropped by was Patrick – the darling. He kept hoping that one day I would realize he was the one for me.

'Come on, beauty, everyone is lying on the beach. Lock up shop and come with me, your father won't notice if you take the day off, he isn't even here himself.'

I wished him a good time, showed him to the door and carried on with my invoicing. I was so bloody loyal to my family, always have been. It may sound odd, but I would find it hard not to be. If I look far enough into my heart, I feel a stronger sense of duty to Dad, Mum, and Kaitlin – and of course Jimmy, always Jimmy – than to Paul, Isabel and Jim. Every string of DNA in my body has been programmed to believe that without me, those four are hopelessly lost.

The other three, on the other hand, don't need me so much. In fact, they are probably better off without me, let's face it. Essentially I am a pretty disturbed woman. My CV fits onto a postage stamp, I have been working in the office of an alcoholic since I was eighteen, I have never had the chance to go to college or university, none of my stories have ever been published, I have hardly been through any kind of experience at all, except for one wild holiday on Corsica and my brother's death.

I have chosen my husband on the grounds of his durability and reliability. My marriage is suffering from a serious lack of passion, and that goes for the rest of my life too. What can I give to my children, what can I tell them about the world, in what way can I be a shining example to them? If anything, I am an example of how *not* to do things. That is the kind of example I grew up with myself, and look at the sad result. The only advice I can give to my children is that they shouldn't do what I did. I would like them to feel they don't owe me anything, the best thing is if we can leave each other in peace, I want them to develop their talents without being burdened by a depressed mother. I must tell them that. Soon. One day.

'Writing something down is every bit as bad as saying it, Romeo, perhaps even worse.'

'What does it matter? Tell your story, type it, whatever you prefer. Let it go. Set yourself free.'

Look at him, standing there starkers. No shame and too big for his boots.

'Put that thing over your eyes.'

'Yes, sir.'

The sudden darkness comes as a pleasant surprise. I take a couple of deep breaths and try to relax. Romeo bends over me, I can smell him: he still smells of sex.

'How do you say "clouds" in your language?' he asks.

'*Wolken*,' I say.

'And "girl"?'

'*Meisje*.'

After he has stuck the words together and I have corrected him, I feel his warm mouth on mine. He kisses me, my lips part, his index finger moves over my bottom lip. 'That is what you are,' he whispers, 'you are my *wolkenmeisje*.'

On the barren plain that is my heart a flower opens up its petals. Inside my head a child's voice begins to sing: '*Lo, how a Rose e'er blooming from tender stem hath sprung! It came, a floweret bright, amid the cold of winter. When half spent was the night.*'

It has taken me thirty-six Christmases. I have decorated, and taken down the tree dozens of times without a connection or understanding, and now, here, in the Algarve, in the Casa da Criança, in Tomás Taveira's finger exercise, behind my S&M blindfold, I have this sudden revelation. This must be it. This is how my mother sees God. I don't see God, but I can smell him. He smells of sex. His name is Romeo and I love him.

'What's your real name, Romeo?'

'Are you sure you want to know, Julia?'

'Yes.'

'Absolutely sure?'

What if his name is Jimmy?

He can feel me go rigid and strokes my chin. 'It's not what you fear. It is . . . er . . . I hope it doesn't disappoint you. I'm called Javis.'

Djeevis.

Javis?

Javis!

'Night, Javis,' I mutter. I grope for his head, pull it towards me and kiss him back.

'Goodnight, *wolkenmeisje*.'

'Can I still call you Romeo, Javis?'

'You can do anything you like.'

'Bye, Romeo.'

'Bye, Julia.'

Chapter Twenty-seven

The summer my brother died was a real scorcher. 'Just our luck,' Kaitlin said. 'This is July, we're in Holland, the weather is just too good to be true, and still we can't go to the beach because we're stuck in the house with a cancer patient.'

Kaitlin could come out with pretty awful remarks sometimes, but we all forgave her. That is to say, Jimmy forgave her, which is what mattered.

He was running out of time, our brother. One day he came home and the cancer had spread everywhere, it was out of control.

'Do you know I can feel it roaring through my body, Mum?' I heard him say to my mother as I was standing in the hall. I wished I hadn't. I didn't like the idea of such a malignant thing roaring through my brother's body. It shouldn't be there, I wanted it to go. The cancer had messed up his red blood cells. They had become self-destructive, they couldn't do what they were supposed to: transport oxygen to vital organs. As a result he felt more and more ill and became very short of breath.

Every three days Jimmy would go to the hospital in my mother's old Volkswagen, to have a blood transfusion. Afterwards he would perk up for a little while. He began to mention euthanasia. My mother refused to listen. Jimmy brought in his prethumous spokeswoman and Patrick to convince her.

'It's not working any more, Mum, he's had it. He is worn out, completely worn out. He is living a nightmare, that's what he calls it, he wants it to be over,' I said.

We were sitting at the kitchen table. Kaitlin was in the living room, Jimmy was on the sofa. They were playing Frustration. Kaitlin threw for Jimmy as well, and also moved his counters for him.

'That's right,' Patrick came to my rescue. 'He sees how difficult it is for you, but it's even worse for him. He can hardly do anything any more, it just gets worse all the time. If he were allowed to choose the moment he goes, he'd feel there was at least one decision that was still his.'

My mother got up and started to wipe the kitchen dresser even though it wasn't at all dirty. 'It isn't right,' she said without looking at us. 'It shouldn't be his decision. I am against it.'

'He wants it, Mum. Patrick and I are going to arrange it for him, whether you agree to it or not.'

She carried on scrubbing with her back to us, refusing to speak. Patrick said that he would come back the following day and went home.

That night my father came over with the Toyota. It was a sports model in Jimmy's favourite colour. Dad had told only me that he had bought Jimmy a car: I had no idea how he would respond. Just ring the bell, I had said to him, we'll soon find out which way the wind is blowing.

Kaitlin spoiled the surprise. She happened to be looking out of the window and saw Dad turning into our street.

'Blimey, come and see this!' she shouted. 'The old man has bought a new car. He's parking it right outside our house.'

'What is he doing here?' Jimmy asked Mum sharply. She raised her hands to let him know she had no idea.

'Do you know about this?' he snapped at me.

Before I could say anything, the bell rang.

'You're not letting him in, Mum,' Jimmy ordered.

She stood up, picked up her rosary and went to the door.

'I think he wants to surprise you,' I whispered to Jimmy.

'What with?'

'The car. It's for you. It's a Toyota sports model.'

Jimmy turned onto his side, with his back to me. Mum and Dad were talking by the front door. Bits of their conversation filtered through to the living room.

'Surely, I'm allowed . . . just a couple of minutes . . .'

'. . . really not . . .'

'But I've got . . .'

'Just leave . . . he doesn't . . .'

'Can somebody . . . a lift . . .'

Mum gave some unintelligible answer. We heard the door close. She returned to the living room. 'Your father has given you a car,' she said to Jimmy's back.

No response.

She put a bunch of keys down on the coffee table.

'It's a cool, car, Jimmy,' Kaitlin said. 'Why don't you give Patrick a call? Then we can all go to the beach tomorrow.'

I watched Dad walk to the end of the street. He didn't

look back over his shoulder, he didn't wave to us as he used to in the old days, when he was still welcome.

'You don't need to feel sorry for him, Jules, it's his own fault,' said Jimmy, who in addition to his cancer had developed a sixth sense.

The next day, to my surprise, Jimmy decided that he wanted to go to the beach with us after all. Patrick had to be the driver. He had just passed his test.

'Are you sure you trust me to drive that car?' he asked at least three times.

'You can park it up a tree, if you like. I couldn't care less,' Jimmy replied, shrugging his shoulders.

Patrick and I helped Jimmy get up from the sofa and supported him on the way out. My mother wanted him to wear a coat and a cap. He had lost his hair because of the chemo. Jimmy refused. My mother said that she would pray for a safe return.

Jimmy began to giggle. 'That would be such a good joke: if you had to call Dad this afternoon and tell him, "Jimmy is dead. He was in a car crash. By the way, the Toyota is a complete write-off." I wonder what would upset him the most.'

When he had stopped laughing and recovered his breath, we were ready to go. We took him to the car.

Kaitlin was all excited. 'It's fantastic. What do you think, Jimmy?'

He said nothing, trying to hide his reaction, but I thought I could tell he liked it. I told Dad so later, it seemed only fair that he should know. Patrick and I heaved Jimmy into the front of the car. Kaitlin got into the back with me. My mother came running out of the house with an oxygen cylinder. We put it on the floor.

Just before the town of Halfweg Jimmy became sick.

270

We had to stop on the hard shoulder. Patrick held onto Jimmy while he leant out of the door to throw up. He spat, he cursed. He was having to wear nappies because he'd become incontinent a few days before. He was beginning to hate his life more and more. 'Turn round,' he said after Patrick had wiped his mouth.

'Come on, Jimmy, just hang on a little longer, we're nearly there,' said Kaitlin. I poked her in the ribs.

'We could see how it goes, couldn't we? I've brought my new bikini. That yellow one that's got white flowers on it, Jimmy.' Earlier that week Kaitlin had put on a show, modelling her bikinis.

Jimmy's breathing was getting more and more difficult.

'It's just the smell from the sugar factory, it's making me feel sick too,' Kaitlin insisted.

Patrick glared at her furiously.

I got the oxygen cylinder and fed the mask between the seats to Jimmy. He took it and inhaled.

At a snail's pace, Patrick drove on.

'I'm going to take the next turning,' he said. Kaitlin put on her sunglasses and stared out of the window.

'I want you to settle it with the doctor for next Saturday,' Jimmy said, once he could breathe again.

'And what about Mum, then?' I asked.

'Is she the one with cancer or am I?'

None of us said anything.

At the traffic lights in Halfweg Patrick turned left, into the village.

'Do you want to get something to drink somewhere?' he asked Jimmy.

'Home,' he said. He'd had a bad afternoon, he had stopped making jokes and so we didn't dare to either.

Patrick turned and drove back onto the motorway,

towards Amsterdam. A couple of minutes later the smell in the car was getting terrible. It wasn't the sugar factory, it was Jimmy, who had soiled himself. Kaitlin got out a handkerchief and held it against her nose. I had to retch, and tried with all my might to resist the feeling by taking little breaths in and out through my mouth.

'Do you know what I really like about Kaitlin?' asked Jimmy, talking to no one in particular. 'She's only ever interested in Kaitlin. In her own little pleasures. If Kaitlin wants to go to the beach, she wants to go to the beach. If her fatally ill brother nearly dies on the way, she doesn't care.'

'Sorry, Jim,' said Kaitlin through the handkerchief.

'Don't say sorry, I'm enjoying it. You aren't going out of your way to please me, you're just being yourself.' He coughed. 'It suits you. If you want to get out and hitch a lift to the beach, go for it.'

'I don't want to any more.'

Jimmy started giggling again. 'That's what I mean. If she'd really wanted to, she'd have got out. That's our Kaitie.'

Kaitlin hated it if he called her Kaitie.

I didn't really like what Jimmy was saying. Mum, Patrick and I were really doing more than our best. Even Dad was trying hard, in his own way. What was wrong with that suddenly? Sometimes I couldn't understand Jimmy, even if I was his prethumous spokeswoman.

'So what is actually going to happen with the Toyota in a while?' asked Kaitlin.

'In a while?' squeaked Jimmy. 'Could you be a bit more specific, dear sis? When do you want the keys, after my cremation, or before?'

I burst into tears.

'Jesus, I didn't mean it like that,' Kaitlin mumbled.

A couple of days later Jimmy and Patrick went for another drive in the Toyota. A few months before, Jimmy had borrowed some money from another student and he wanted to go and give it back in person. It was nothing really, you couldn't have bought a packet of cigarettes with it. Patrick offered to drop it off for him, but Jimmy insisted he wanted to come himself.

'Why don't you go past Dad?' I suggested. 'He'd love that.'

'Bad idea, Jules,' said Jimmy.

When they were gone, I called my father to tell him that Jimmy was out in the Toyota again.

'Does he think she's beautiful?' asked Dad.

'If he could, he would stay in her all the time, he loves her so much. He asked me if I could thank you,' I lied.

'I knew he would, I knew it,' said my father, cheering up.

The student lived in a flat. He wasn't at home. Patrick told me later that he was glad of that, otherwise he would have had to heave Jimmy into the lift. After Patrick had shoved the money in the letter box, they had gone to the beach after all. Jimmy didn't get out, he was too tired. For a while he looked at the waves from the avenue. Patrick couldn't bring himself to say anything. 'For the rest of my life the sea will remind me of your brother, Julia.'

'Did you get asked for anything else after that?' I asked. It seemed like the kind of moment Jimmy would have chosen to do such a thing.

Patrick nodded shyly.

'What did he ask you?'

'Nothing in particular.'

After the weekend my mother drove Jimmy in the Toyota to hospital for a blood transfusion. It was to be his last blood transfusion and his last ride in the Toyota.

'It is not going to go on much longer. The day after tomorrow the doctor is coming. For euthanasia.'

It was Thursday afternoon. Jimmy was lying in his room asleep. I called my father in secret.

'Does he still not want to talk to me?'

'I'm sorry.'

Dad sighed. 'I'm going to write him a letter. I'll put it through the letter box tonight. Will you give it to him?'

'I'll do my best. He's really stubborn.'

'He always has been. He gets that from your mother.'

The whole evening I kept going to the letter box and back. It really got on my mother's nerves.

'What is it? Are you expecting something important?'

I shook my head.

'Is it to do with the doctor? Has he brought it forward?' My mother couldn't bring herself to use the eu-word, she still wasn't willing to acknowledge it and she put all her energy into avoiding it. Her rosary was doing overtime.

'I can still hear you, Mum,' mumbled Jimmy. All three of us felt caught out. He was lying on the sofa, breathing heavily with his eyes closed. His moments of consciousness were few and far between. He seemed to be fading away from us: we didn't think he would make it to Saturday.

I cleared my throat. 'The doctor is coming the day

274

after tomorrow. At the stroke of nine in the morning. Jimmy wants you to put something nice on, Mum. Jimmy wants all of us to put on something nice.'

'That's right,' we heard from the sofa.

I went to the letter box again.

'Have you got a lover?' Kaitlin teased. 'Is he scared of coming into the house? Does he think cancer is contagious?'

Jimmy started making choking noises. If you didn't know him you would be frightened to death, you wouldn't realize that he was laughing. Cancer is not contagious, but sick jokes certainly are.

No letter came on Thursday night. I was disappointed. It pissed me off. Jimmy is right, I thought, the old boy isn't worth the effort. If his son dies in the night, he will have missed his chance. What a prick.

My father was lucky. Jimmy woke up as usual the following morning. I was with him. I'd been sitting at his bed from six thirty, as I did every morning. I always had to be the first there.

When he opened his eyes, he smiled. 'Tomorrow I'm going to die,' were his first words.

He said it quite cheerfully. It wasn't intended as a joke, he clearly meant it.

'We can postpone it, you know. We can wait until after the weekend. Or your birthday.' I tried, though I knew it was pointless. I thought of Mum, I thought of Dad's letter, which might still come, and I thought of myself. I didn't want to miss my brother yet, not today, not tomorrow, not ever.

He took my hand. 'Even when I'm gone, I'll always be here, Jules. You can call me.' He hardly had the strength to hold my hand properly. His bodily functions were rapidly going downhill, he could see less well, he was losing his sense of taste; only his hearing was still functioning as it should, in fact it seemed to be better than ever.

'Mum has bought lots of delicious things. She wants to cook you a five-star meal. Gran would like to come over one more time, and Patrick . . .'

'I've already said goodbye to Gran, and Patrick is dropping by this afternoon. The four of us will have a meal together this evening.'

The general let go of my hand and picked up his mask.

Patrick came over that afternoon. I had never seen him look so serious before. He went straight to Jimmy's room and stayed there for at least an hour. When he came out, his eyes were red with crying. He gave me a nod and left. The next time I saw him, Jimmy was dead.

With hindsight, I suspect that Patrick would have been a better husband for me than Paul. I think that, after Jimmy, he is the only person in the world who truly understands me. He adored me. Which is why I ignored him. I thought that love should be mysterious and unattainable. I believed in the fairy tales written by Leni Saris. Later, much later, when I'd stopped believing in those, it was too late. I had lost contact with Patrick – I had heard he was living with someone, a girl he had got pregnant. It had been an accident, but they wanted to make a go of it. I don't mean that in a cynical way, accidents can sometimes turn out wonderfully, people should have more faith in them. More than in love, whatever that is.

At ten past five on Friday afternoon an envelope fell into the letter box. I'd given up hope and had to control my desire to tear it up immediately.

'There's a letter for you from Dad,' I mentioned to Jimmy. 'Shall I throw it away?'

He turned onto his side with difficulty. 'Read,' he said.

I did as he asked. It was actually not a bad letter at all. During our last telephone conversation I'd given Dad a couple of ideas and he'd really gone to some trouble. He wrote that he was proud of his son, that he admired his courage, that he'd love to be with him and support him through the final moments of his life. But that he'd respect Jimmy if he preferred otherwise. Despite their differences, he couldn't have wished for a better son. Goodbye Jim, my son. See you, one day.

'He still doesn't get it,' Jimmy concluded.

'You've never explained it to him.'

'Is it my job to explain to him how he misbehaved? He should apologize, he should be made to lick the dust. Do you remember when Mum was in London?'

I did.

My mother had gone to London for a long weekend with a friend. My parents hadn't separated yet, they were having an amnesty. I think I must have been roughly eight at the time, Kaitlin nine and Jimmy eleven. My father took us along to an aunt's birthday party. She lived in a block of flats, on the top floor.

We'd taken our bikes. During the party Dad drank white wine. He drank one glass after another, no matter how many times Jimmy told him he'd had enough. Towards the end of the evening he could barely keep himself upright.

A woman with big red lips offered to take us home. Dad said she was a sort of aunt of ours, though we had never seen her before. In the lift Dad conked out, and Jimmy and the woman had to heave him up. Kaitlin

277

looked the other way, pretending she wasn't one of our group. Dad reeked of alcohol and spoke with a thick tongue.

'Don't breathe a word to Mum, girls,' he jabbered. 'And you too, young man.' When we were on the bikes it got even worse. He zigzagged along the street, the aunt sitting on the back of his bike. It was extremely dangerous.

'Watch out, Daddy, watch out! Dad! There's a car behind you, watch out!' I can still hear Jimmy's shouting.

The aunt stayed the night. Dad and she made so much noise that the three of us grew frightened and huddled together under Jimmy's bed. We fell asleep there. The next morning Jimmy called my mother at her hotel in London. Could she please come home? She said no, this was the first time ever she had treated herself to a foreign trip. She asked Jimmy why he wanted her to get the next boat home. He thought for a moment and then answered that she needn't bother, he'd be OK.

'After that weekend I'd really had it with him. Do you understand, Jules? I felt I was superior to him. I couldn't take him seriously any more. Every second I spent thinking about that man was a second wasted. And I still feel that way – all the more so, now that I am ill. He's the last person I want to spend my energy on. I've got so precious little left.'

Jimmy could state things so categorically that it wasn't until later – much later – that you might realize some of his arguments were flawed, that they weren't the absolute truth. No argument is watertight, only you haven't had time to find that out when you're seventeen.

'Two things,' said Jimmy. 'First, I want you to burn this letter straight away. I don't wish to see it ever again. Second, I want you to come to my room at four thirty tomorrow morning.' He gasped for air.

'Why?'

'I'll tell you tomorrow morning. And now I want another piece of cherry pie.'

I went to the kitchen and told my mother Jimmy wanted more pie. You couldn't do my mother a bigger favour than ask her for something to eat. I think that preparing and serving out meals really made her feel she was a good mother. When our need subsided, when we could make our own food, she no longer seemed to know how to deal with us. You might say it was a positive aspect of Jimmy's illness that the three of us would eat at home almost every night.

Chapter Twenty-eight

The two of us are sitting by the pool. Romeo is lying on a towel doing sit-ups. He is just wearing his boxer shorts. I have nothing on besides my knickers. I have Romeo's laptop on my knees and am paddling in the water with my legs. I hold the screen with my left hand while using my right index finger to scroll through the document that I have named 'Jimmy'. If Paul saw me like this he would go berserk. He would never lend me his laptop again.

Today is a good day. I haven't taken any Valium so far, nor had alcohol. I was woken up by Romeo entering me. I was lying on my stomach. He lifted my buttocks and then pushed it in, in one. It was a new experience to be shagged awake by someone. I rather liked it.

'I want to do it everywhere with you,' he murmured in my hair. 'In the kitchen. On the worktop. On the stairs. In the pool.'

He didn't mention money. Neither did I.

Romeo took me from behind while fingering me from the front. He gave me such intense pleasure and I was so relaxed that I came before I knew what was happening. Romeo allowed me no time to enjoy the afterglow, he dragged me out of bed and propped me up against the bedroom wall. He had planned it so that we could see ourselves in the wardrobe mirror. 'Watch me screw you,' he commanded.

I did.

I saw myself standing against the wall, with flushed cheeks and dishevelled hair. I observed how a muscular man with an enormous penis lifted me up. How I put my arms round his neck, gripping his hips with my legs, how I let myself slide down over his organ. I watched myself bobbing up and down, becoming completely immersed in the process, Romeo doing the same. I saw our movements grow wilder and wilder, our mouths falling open as we squeezed our eyes tighter and tighter. I heard my shouts, I heard his. I heard how he peaked and as I heard him – because I heard him – I climaxed too.

Romeo went off to have a shower. I wanted to get back under the duvet for a few more minutes but he insisted I go with him. We had only just turned the taps on when I felt the top of his glans pushing against my clitoris. How on earth did this man manage so many erections? He pushed, he turned, he gently thrust, and before long I was getting wet again.

'I want you,' he said.

I opened my legs. I was defenceless, he was welcome: he could do anything he wanted.

Romeo stepped out of the shower to get a condom.

I leaned against the wall of the cubicle. I had never had such good sex before. It was primal sex – my previous experiences had been child's play.

My lover came back again. The condom was already on. He fucked me against the wall of the shower. The water was going cold, the boiler had run out but we hardly noticed. We carried on until we were saturated.

Romeo dried me. I put my white linen dress on. He handed me his laptop and sent me out to the terrace. 'I'm going to the shops, you carry on writing.' I did as I was told: I would have done anything he asked, because I knew he would shag me again as a reward.

Romeo disappeared. I sat down under the sunshade, opened up the laptop and began to type. I was completely engrossed in my text when he returned with coffee, freshly squeezed orange juice and scrambled eggs with bacon. He put the laptop away, and laid the table. We sat eating the nicest breakfast I'd had so far at the Casa da Criança. As we polished off the last mouthfuls our eyes met.

'Not again?' I said.

He laughed.

'No, Romeo. Please, don't. This is really getting too crazy.'

His T-shirt disappeared over his head. How many times had we done it now? This would be the fourth time. I had never done it four times in a row with anyone.

Romeo stroked my breasts with the back of his hand. I left him to it. He pulled the dress over my head and put the cushion of the deckchair down on the ground. In a matter of seconds I lay on my back, legs apart. He came inside me. We were becoming a better team all the time, it was getting easier, Romeo knew exactly what he had to do to get me where I wanted to be. It was so exciting it was becoming addictive. How on earth was I going to do it with Paul again without yawning?

A couple of minutes later we were lying side by side, satisfied.

'We're ill,' I said.

'No we're not.'

'We are.'

'Let me show you something.' Romeo went inside to fetch a book he had brought with him. It was a book by a Japanese photographer who had taken photographs of couples making love, or about to. They were in bed, in alleyways, in a hotel room, and in the car. The photographer had caught them in the act, some with their trousers hanging down on their knees, others frantically trying to assume impossible positions. The couple in the car give the photographer a disturbed look over their shoulder: they were just settling into a good position.

'Don't you find them beautiful?' Romeo says almost tenderly. 'They all want just one thing. The drive is so strong that they are willing to put up with the risks: the risk of being found out, catching a disease, getting pregnant.'

Romeo depends on that drive for his living. He doesn't take any risks, he always wears a condom. I would let him do it with me without protection, but he doesn't even try. Romeo controls his urges. I wonder if that means that he can't fall in love with me.

'Read me a little,' says Romeo.

I translate a few passages about the Toyota, the drive to Halfweg, about Patrick and Kaitlin, and about Dad.

'Did you find it difficult to write it down?'

'Not that difficult. It's just impossible to describe it as it was, what it *actually* felt like at the time.'

'You paint quite a good picture,' he says. 'Kaitlin strikes me as a rather special lady.'

Of course. Men are always fascinated by Kaitlin, even when they have never met her, and only heard a few things about her.

'Do you have brothers or sisters?' I ask, to change the subject. It annoys me that he is interested in Kaitlin.

'I have one half-sister, my mum's first child, she's twelve years older than I am. I call her auntie. Apparently my dad fathered several other kids, but I don't really know, I'm not in touch with him.'

'Just like Jimmy,' I say quickly.

'He rejected me, not the other way round. He left my mother when she was pregnant.'

'Have you ever tried to find him?'

'He doesn't want to be found.' Romeo's voice conveys no emotion whatsoever.

I save the document and shut the laptop. 'It must be strange not to know your father.'

'It's the way it's always been for me,' he says.

I take my legs out of the water.

Romeo sticks his sunglasses in his hair and looks at me piercingly. 'When did you have those operations done?'

'How do you mean?' I ask, feeling found out.

'I recognize the scars. You've had liposuction and they've done something to your breasts.'

'So?'

'Did you really need that kind of intervention?'

'I did, for my own sake. And yours, actually, because you saw me before the operations and you can't even remember.'

He puts his sunglasses back on and looks away from

me, staring into the splendid landscape. 'That was in Faro,' he says in a meaningful tone.

Something happened in Faro. He clearly doesn't want to talk about it. I bet it's something to do with a woman.

'Do you know what love is, Romeo?'

He calmly turns the question over in his mind. After a while he nods slowly.

'What is it?'

He takes my hand and pulls me up. 'Look me in the eyes and you'll see,' he says.

Does he mean what I hope he means? My heart begins to race. I take off his sunglasses with trembling hands. His eyes are soft, so soft that I can hardly bear to look at them. I am in pain. My belly hurts, my chest – I didn't know it would be so painful.

– You did know, Jimmy whispers, you've always known. Pain is the underlying feeling.

Romeo is going to kiss me. If he doesn't, I will kiss him. But before we do, I want to be sure, I want to know once and for all – this is the moment of truth.

'I don't need to pay you, this isn't work for you. You're doing this for me because you . . .'

Have feelings for me, I want to say. He puts his finger over my lips.

'Quiet, *wolkenmeisje*.'

I want him to say it, I want to hear it from his mouth, but his kisses silence me. 'Romeo . . .' I say after a moment. 'Please tell me that I'm right.'

'To love is to trust, Julia. Don't listen to me, don't listen to anyone, only listen to your heart.'

'My heart has been shouting out your name very loudly since last night. It's . . . it feels so big, it frightens me.'

'You don't need to be afraid. I'll stay with you.'

'For ever?'

He smiles. 'For as long as you need me.'

'That *is* for ever.'

'You should get back to work.' He points to the laptop.

I want to open my mouth to ask another question, but something stops me. A rustling shrub. There is a breeze but there is no wind. A shadow passes over the terrace.

– It's OK, Jules, you have my permission. Write it down. Do it. The time has come.

Chapter Twenty-nine

As always, I followed his instructions to the letter. At four fifteen my radio alarm went off. At once I hit the off button: nobody was to hear me. A torch lay ready underneath my bed. I sat up and stretched myself. Every morning at half past six I sat by Jimmy's bedside. I didn't understand why he wanted me to be there so early today. We had asked the doctor to come at nine. Another four hours and forty-five minutes and then it would happen: Jimmy would be put to sleep with a drug and then he would be given something else, something fatal. I didn't want to think about it.

Like my mother, I hoped things would take an unexpected turn, that he would change his mind, or get better, or die peacefully in his sleep. Maybe it had already happened, it was so quiet in the house. Who knows, perhaps he'd had a premonition, and had asked me to come for that reason. It always gave me the creeps to check whether he was still alive, but at least on other mornings it would just be getting light. Now it was pitch dark.

I picked up my torch and switched it on. Then I sneaked barefoot to his room. The door was shut. Very gently, I pushed it open just a little. I heard his

287

breathing straight away, you couldn't miss it: thank God, everything seemed normal. I opened the door further, went in and shone the torch over his bed. He was lying motionless, on his back. How thin and pale he had become – he looked less and less like my brother.

'You're twelve minutes early.'

I dropped the torch in terror – he had said it without opening his eyes. The bulb flickered briefly and then went out.

'Ever so sorry. I'd set my alarm for quarter past, I didn't want to be late.'

I fumbled for the bedside light and switched it on.

Jimmy gestured in the direction of the oxygen cylinder. He had uttered one sentence and was already out of breath. You could understand him. I would probably have begged for a doctor in his place. This was unbearable.

'How do I look?' he asked after he had taken a drag.

'Normal. The same as yesterday.' In fact he was looking a little worse, but I didn't want to say so. You should never dishearten a patient.

'Do I look peaceful?'

'I suppose so. Why?'

'We're going to answer Mum's prayer, Jules.'

Mum's prayer. What was the last one about again? She prayed round the clock these days, I had lost track of all the things she mentioned in her prayers. Jimmy saw my confusion.

'She is praying that I will go before the doctor gets here,' he said patiently. Too late now, I was about to say. But then it dawned on me.

'No,' I said.

He just nodded.

288

I shook my head resolutely. 'I refuse to be drawn into this. I'm going back to bed, I'll come back at six thirty. Goodnight.' I wanted to turn round, but I saw his eyes grow wide. They burned in the dark, deep sockets. They forced me to stand still.

'You are staying here,' he said, wheezing. 'And you do exactly as I say.' The general was ready for action. For the very last time.

I bit my lip. My brother was going to die. Now, or in a few hours' time, his fate was sealed: the die had been cast. We were allowed to stay alive, we would do all the things he would have liked to do. Well, almost all.

During his first year at university Jimmy had told us that he wanted to get a job at the morgue, washing bodies. It seemed a valuable experience, it felt like a useful thing to do and, besides, it would provide a welcome addition to his student grant. Kaitlin and I were appalled at the thought. 'They're dead anyway. What could possibly happen?' Jimmy said in his coolest voice. My mother, who rarely if ever contradicted her son, responded with such horror that he had to give up his plan, and got a job as a barman instead.

Now, almost two years on, Jimmy wanted me to make sure that he would end up in a morgue after all. Did I have any choice? He would find it selfish: we were blood relations. He felt I should be there for him, who else could he ask? A stranger? A doctor, someone in a white coat? The people in white coats had failed to cure him, it seemed unfair that they of all people would be granting him his last wish. The situation was unfair enough as it was. I was his prethumous spokeswoman, he didn't need to explain it to me, I could see

289

it for myself. There was no point in refusing him anything. It was my duty to be there for him, and that was that.

I relented and gave a salute. 'OK then.'

Jimmy smiled gratefully. He pointed to the cushion lying at the foot of his bed. It was a large fluorescent green velvet cushion, with a flimsy purple heart embroidered in the middle, and golden tassels on the corners. Kaitlin had made it for a Mother's Day, or Father's Day – I can't remember which, it had been in the house for so long. It was a hideous threadbare thing but we were used to it.

'I want you to push it down over my face. Firmly. For fifteen minutes. Keep an eye on the clock.'

I nodded and swallowed hard. Now was the time to be brave. Like him.

Jimmy picked up the mask and inhaled. 'Then you put the cushion back. The worst will be over. You must take a good look at my face. If it doesn't look peaceful, then I want you to make it so. You can raise the corners of my mouth.'

Tears welled up in my eyes, I couldn't help it.

'Don't be sad, Jules. I am not, either. I'm happy. I love you. Because you're doing this for me. Because you're my sister. This is our secret. For ever. *Capisce?*'

I smiled through my tears. Don Jim. I was going to miss him so much.

'I'm not taking any more oxygen now,' he gasped. 'That makes it easier. For you. Do we have a deal?'

I nodded.

'Promise me.'

'I promise. I swear. I'll do what you want me to.'

'And . . . you won't . . .' He could barely finish his

sentence. I passed him the oxygen mask, but he pushed it away. '. . . tell . . .'

'I won't tell anyone,' I promised. 'Cross my heart.'

He made a gesture. I picked up the cushion. 'Aren't you afraid?' I asked. 'Is there anything else you want me to do?'

Beside his bed lay an open book of poetry. Jimmy had become an avid reader of poetry since falling ill. 'It comforts me,' he would say. He had always had spiritual leanings anyway. Mind you, not in the same way as my mother – he didn't worship God, or any other Supreme Being. He was more interested in the meaning of life, reincarnation, life after death, that sort of thing. He discussed it all with Patrick. They would talk about it for hours. I don't know if they ever managed to find the answers, you never really get to the bottom of such questions, I think. It keeps the discussion lively.

Jimmy saw me look, and faltered.

'Shall I read something?' A little reprieve, for him as well as for me.

To my surprise he nodded.

I picked up the book. It was by Sirkka Turkka. Must be a pseudonym; no normal person would be called that. I began to read where Jimmy had put a pencil mark.

You, too, get ready, little bush,
licking my window with black flames.
Get ready and be prepared.
For death is kind
when it comes.
It holds you against its breast.
Wordless, it lets you know your childhood lullaby,

bringing it to you behind your bent back,
from beyond years, decades.
It gives a gift to your childlike hand, a gift
that you keep looking at with bleary eyes.
It gives you the song you thought you had forgotten.
Its shoulders and breasts are covered with flowers.
It is hollow, in order to take in the whole being.
It grabs you by your edges.
It spreads you out:
it tries to understand you.
And then it has grasped.
It nails your eyes open,
opens your mouth, from where
the tumult of life is escaping.
And you look, no longer at me,
but through me
beyond me
to your own death.
And to the white flowers
that have blossomed
around the tiny house.

Blimey, it was as if Sirkka had written it specially for the occasion. Uncanny almost. Jimmy had closed his eyes. His chest was moving regularly. The poem seemed to have had a soothing effect.

'"It tries to understand you. And then it has grasped,"' I repeated beseechingly. '"Get ready and be prepared. For death is kind."' My voice was no longer tremulous. Sirkka's words had prepared me for what lay ahead. I took a deep breath. 'Bye Jimmy. Have a good journey.'

No response. Presumably he was already on his way. I placed the cushion over his head, with the heart facing me. I wasn't sure how to press down, so I just lay down on top of the thing, my breasts pressing against the purple heart. Jimmy's arms were by his sides. He clenched his fists. I glanced at the clock. The first minute had started.

I tried as hard as I could not to think about what I was doing. I forced myself to concentrate on something else, something that would distract me, something safe and nice. Cherry pie: there was one piece left, maybe I would be allowed to have it. Kaitlin's new bikini. Patrick's eyes. Dad: as usual oblivious to it all. The Toyota: parked outside the house. Jimmy would never drive in it again. No! Wait, stop, that was dangerous territory. Something safe, something nice. Television. Was there anything good on tonight? I hadn't watched anything in weeks. *Sesame Street*, I'd really like to see that again. *Sesame Street*, with Grover.

The blue monster always made me laugh. That episode when he is in the supermarket waiting at the till, and he keeps letting everyone go in front, so it never gets to be his turn. A little bald man says he is having a pickle party and insists he must go first. In the end Grover says he'll just go to the party as well: all the tills are closed, there is nowhere left to pay for his shopping. That was so funny, Jimmy would have—

Jimmy's arms suddenly started to flail about uncontrollably. Was he having second thoughts? I automatically relieved the pressure a bit. His arms kept moving. The rest of Jimmy joined in as well – he lay there thrashing about in bed. Barely two minutes had passed. What now? I took my weight off the cushion and lifted it up. We looked each other in the face, both seized with shock – me a bit more than him probably. His translucent skin looked blue-grey.

'Have you had enough?' I asked. 'Do you want me to stop?'

He shook his head. He was breathing in gasps, unable to slow down, just like the cancer in his body, it occurred to me.

'You suddenly became so restless . . . I thought . . .'

He couldn't speak, he reached for a scrap of paper and pencil. Sorry, he wrote. It just happened. Carry on. Ignore it.

I began to giggle, I couldn't help it. He grinned as well and then pointed at the scrap of paper again, looking anxious.

'I'll burn it later. Jesus, Jimmy, what a business. I was just thinking about *Sesame Street*.'

Jimmy looked at me, puzzled.

'Forget it.'

He put on the mask and helped himself to one more puff. 'Can you remember . . .' he paused, 'what my last words were?'

I shook my head, I had no idea.

'Me neither.' He laughed again, almost choking.

'Whoops,' I said.

We were both laughing now, Jimmy silently, and I with tears rolling down my cheeks. Actually, we were half-crying, half-laughing.

'Was there something else you wanted to say?' I asked finally.

He thought deeply. 'Hey diddle diddle, the cat and the fiddle.'

It didn't seem funny to me, but it did to him. He was in fits. I picked up the cushion again. Time was short. Soon Mum or Kaitlin would come into the room, we couldn't have that.

Jimmy cleared his throat. 'What is life? It's the flash

of a firefly in the night. It's a buffalo's breath during winter. It's a tiny shadow gliding over the grass, disappearing into the sunset.'

Unbelievable. And without a single pause. I nodded. I would try to remember it.

He closed his eyes. I placed the cushion over his face again – it had to be over quickly this time. I pushed down with all my strength, more firmly than before; I didn't want him to start moving about again. But he did: after a couple of minutes his arms began to flap. He also kicked about with his legs. He was clearly fighting a struggle. A death struggle. I managed to ignore it. It wasn't easy, but then no one had said it would be. The force of his blows was bound to fade: everything fades eventually. Such is life. I was proved right: first his legs became floppy, then his arms. After a while the occasional light shock wave passed through his body – that was all. I sensed I probably didn't need to keep pressing so hard, but I did so anyway.

At a certain point, well before the fifteen minutes had passed, the movements stopped altogether. All the time I kept my eyes on the clock, counting the seconds. To make absolutely certain, I waited a full twenty minutes – I was sure Jimmy wouldn't have minded. When the time was up I lifted the cushion, averting my eyes. There was a damp patch on the back of the green velvet.

I didn't want to look at his face. I had to force myself, I had promised. I held my breath. Do it quickly, Julia, just get on with it, think of Mum, think of Kaitlin, of Dad even. You are doing it for them.

I had expected to see Jimmy, but all I saw was Death. He grinned at me like a vicious dog. Death had not been kind, Sirkka Turkka had lied. I fiercely rubbed away its traces. I could do that, because I was alive. I was stronger, infinitely stronger – that is where Death had been wrong: I could have carried my brother up to heaven single-handed.

I shoved the cushion under Jimmy's bed, picked up his note, put his arms and legs in a decent position, pulled the sheet up to his chin and picked the broken torch up from the floor. Then, without saying another word to him, without looking at him, I slipped out of the room.

When I got to the landing the torch suddenly flicked on. The light shone brightly, more brightly than before. Jimmy came with me to the door of my room. As soon as I entered, the light went off again – I never even touched the switch.

Later I thought, and hoped, that the whole thing had been a dream, but on the back of Kaitlin's cushion, which my mother found underneath Jimmy's bed the next morning, there were white marks that wouldn't wash out. My mother didn't notice them. After Jimmy's death my mother noticed very little. I lay down on my bed, and stared at the ceiling, wide awake, waiting for dawn to break, and for the acting to begin.

Chapter Thirty

It is bizarre to be sharing a house with someone from one day to the next. I keep having to remind myself to close the bathroom door and to slap on some lipstick in the mornings after my shower – I stopped bothering with make-up unless I was going out, ages ago.

Bit by bit I had been letting myself go: before long I would have turned into a Jane Goodall with long grey hair. Within two weeks I could have adopted a couple of chimpanzees. In all likelihood a pack of stray dogs would have attached themselves to me. Slowly but surely, I would have separated from other people, spending the rest of my life in perfect harmony with nature and Taveira's creation. It could easily have gone that way, if it hadn't been for Romeo.

We are driving to Monchique in his Maserati. The weather is beautiful. The weather is almost always beautiful in the Algarve. It makes you forget things, it makes important things seem trivial. Tomorrow, you think: it can wait until tomorrow or the day after, or the day after that, even. The sun can blind you, just like love.

All I want is Romeo, day and night. I eat him, drink him. Now I am chalking up a high every second. I have written down the whole story and read it to him. I have revealed my true nature to him: he knows my biggest secret and he hasn't rejected me. Far from it: he took me into his arms, comforted me, wiped away my tears and said that he understood. That anybody would, and that everything was going to be all right in the end. That he knew what to do and that I should trust him. He said some other things as well but I only half heard them – I was so relieved he wasn't walking out on me immediately. I scrutinized his face as I told him what I had done to Jimmy. I could see no disgust – the thing I most dreaded – no loathing. Just sympathy, really.

'So that was the cloud you were shrouded in,' he said after a long silence. 'How did you manage to keep it up? All your life you have been pretending.'

I put the laptop down on the bedside table. We were lying in bed. The doors to the balcony were wide open, allowing the typical sweet smell of the Algarve night to drift into the bedroom. Countless stars shone brightly in the clear sky and the cicadas were making a racket. I pointed out the Plough to Romeo – you could see it perfectly from one of the windows. I wanted to be his lover, I wanted to forget everything and only do what lovers do: show each other the Plough, feed each other delicious titbits, whisper sweet words into each other's ears, and make love.

'Would you like to talk about it?' Romeo asked with a nod in the direction of the bedside table.

I shook my head. 'It's fine. I got it off my chest. It's in the past, it's over.' As soon as I'd said it I began to cry. Reading out the text had affected me more than I realized.

Romeo handed me a tissue. He was prepared for all eventualities, this man: wherever he went he carried his condoms, tissues, business cards, and – most importantly – his fabulous organ. 'Tomorrow I'll take you to the mountains,' he said.

I snuggled up against him and let my hand slip inside his pants.

'It's going to be 38 degrees Celsius tomorrow. Wouldn't it be better to spend the day in bed with the air conditioning on?' I massaged Romeo's biggest asset. It was warm, it was getting hard: in a moment it would be digging into me, like a rocket with a red-hot tip. Romeo wanted me to get some sleep but I managed to seduce him: first in bed and then in the moonlight out on the balcony, under the Plough.

In the morning, as we were getting ready to go to Monchique, Romeo retaliated. I was turning over the eggs in the kitchen, when he suddenly lifted up my skirt, pulled down my knickers and penetrated me point-blank. After breakfast I walked to the car, bandy-legged and with a grin on my face. We were about to drive off when Eddie came running up to us. I got out of the car, Romeo stayed in his seat.

'Everything all right, love?' he asked anxiously. 'We stopped hearing from you and we saw a car we didn't recognize in the drive.'

'Everything is fine, Eddie,' I assured him. 'This is Romeo, a friend of mine.'

Eddie peered curiously at the man behind the wheel, covered in gold and nodding benignly. 'Is he an actor too?' he whispered. 'If you need me again, just give me a call, OK?'

'Yes, he's an American colleague,' I replied with a smile. 'But he's off duty. He's here on holiday.'

'I see,' said Eddie.

The next moment Stella arrived on her scooter. The

only ones missing now were Lotus and the midgets. She parked and seemed surprised to see me, Eddie and the Maserati.

'*Bom dia*, Stella,' I said. 'Can you give the master bedroom an extra good clean today? It's a bit of a, how shall I put it . . . tip. And could you change the sheets as well, please?' I gave Eddie a saucy wink.

Stella took off her helmet and nodded. I looked from Eddie to Stella and then to Romeo, and began to glow. My life was good: I felt at home, I felt secure. I had met new people – kind people who cared about me. I never thought it would happen so quickly, but it had. I had built a new life for myself.

'Eddie, what does Casa da Criança actually mean?' I had been meaning to ask him for ages but kept forgetting.

'Don't you know?' My landlord hesitated for a moment. 'It was Tomás Taveira's own idea. He once explained in an interview that his creative energy awakens his inner child.'

'I think Tomás's inner child had better be left in peace from now on,' I said laughing. I had seen Taveira's marina in Albufeira and thought it was just as ugly as the Casa da Criança, only much bigger. And to think they call it a tourist attraction.

Eddie didn't smile. 'You may find this painful: Casa da Criança means House of the Child.'

'Where are we heading?' I ask Romeo.

'To Fóia, the highest mountain in the Algarve.'

'Your decision is mine, darling.' I put my hand possessively on his leg. I am driving across the Algarve in a fancy car with the most gorgeous man in the world. What more could I want?

300

Romeo turns on the radio.

'What's special about the top of the Fóia?'

'You'll see when we get there.'

The Fóia is 902 m high. The surrounding landscape is bare and dry. There is a stiff breeze, I should have brought a cardigan. At the top is a building where you can get a drink and buy souvenirs. You've got to be dying of thirst though, because you wouldn't want to go and sit there for any other reason. A host of satellite dishes and television masts reinforces the desolate feel of the place. There are several tourists at the top taking pictures of each other.

'Great view. Very special indeed. Shall we go back now?' I stay in the car.

Romeo gets out. 'I didn't bring you up here for the view.'

'What then? Something naughty? You rascal.'

He opens the door on my side. 'Can you be serious for a moment?'

'I'd rather not.' I get out of the car. What else can I do?

'I've been thinking,' Romeo says.

Oh dear, I sense the onset of a bad-news conversation. If Romeo dumps me, I'm jumping off this mountain.

'The saga with your brother . . .' he begins.

'Forget it.' I make a dismissive gesture. 'That's in the past, I'm over it, it doesn't trouble me any more.'

Romeo opens the boot to get something: the laptop. 'I wanted to print out your story but I haven't got a printer. You're still shrouding yourself in the same cloud, you're running away from it, you seek refuge in alcohol, sex . . .'

'. . . love,' I correct him. I want to say, I love you, but

I don't want to appear too desperate so I water it down. 'I'm extremely fond of you.'

'You have a family, Julia. You have a husband and children. You can't ignore that.'

'Why not? I've been doing it for months.'

We walk to the panorama point. It is just a concrete platform. There isn't even a bench to sit on.

'I know why you left them,' says Romeo. 'Your sense of duty towards your parents and siblings is so strong that you can't handle the added responsibility that comes with having a family of your own. Plus, you're bearing a secret . . .'

'What difference does it all make, Romeo?' I am getting angry. It's ages since I felt so happy, I thought this was to be a romantic outing, but no, he has to yak on about my family and ruin my day. 'We're here now. Just you and me. Let's forget about the rest.'

'I can't.'

'It didn't seem to bother you this morning, when you came into the kitchen.'

'This morning we were having sex,' he says coldly.

I almost forgot. He is a porn star, he can perform to order, he doesn't need to feel emotionally involved – it's just an act and I fell for it.

Romeo opens up the laptop and closes it again. 'Are you thinking of going back one day?'

It is the question that has been preying on my mind for a long time and that so far I have been ignoring successfully. Of course, in principle, I intend to go home, that was always the plan – I wasn't going to stay away for ever. The family will be reunited at some point in the future. I just haven't reached that point yet. When I return home it will be for good. I don't want to pack my bags again a week later. It wouldn't be fair on the children. And Paul wouldn't accept it, either. When I am home I will have to get back to the grindstone: the shopping, cooking, the cleaning and washing, dropping off and picking up the kids. In short: run the house, call in on Mum regularly, and get back to the office.

A family comes and joins us on the platform. They look Portuguese: a man and a woman with a daughter. The little girl looks about four. She is wearing a light blue skirt and a white T-shirt. Her dark hair is tied back in a ponytail.

Romeo changes tack. 'What are your children's names?'

I put on my sunglasses and pretend to be admiring the view.

'How many children do you have?'

Oh all right, I suppose I might as well tell him. 'I have a daughter and a son.'

'Are they in good health?'

'I imagine so.' How long has it been now, since I last saw them? More than two months – I have lost track. I somehow managed to disengage myself from them. I had no idea that might happen, but it did.

The father takes a couple of photographs of his wife and daughter. When he is done he comes over to us. Romeo still has the laptop under his arm. The man offers me the camera expectantly.

I take it – what else can I do? Yes I understand, it is very simple: that button, just press it, *compreendo*, Bob's your uncle! I stick my sunglasses in my hair.

The family take up position, with their backs to the view so that the spectator gets the benefit of the beautiful backdrop. The mother lifts her daughter up.

The man puts his arm round his wife. He is proud and she is happy. The girl nestles her head against her mother's neck.

I capture the moment. The eternal onlooker, that is what I am.

The mother puts the child back on the ground while I return the camera to her husband. He thanks me. *De nada*, it was nothing. Quickly I drop my sunglasses down over my eyes. I don't want him to see how difficult it was. The family leave.

'Shall we go too? I'm cold,' I say to Romeo.

'Did you bring any photographs of your children with you?'

I shake my head.

'In the villa?'

'No.' I swallowed them in the Hotel Eva. Another secret. My life is made up of secrets. I am a bad person. Thoroughly bad. Thankfully, the Portuguese family didn't realize what monster took their innocent picture. It is a miracle I am still at liberty.

Romeo frowns. 'Sometimes I just don't get you.'

'I don't get why you insist on wanting to understand me.'

'It's my mission,' he answers.

My noble Romeo: he regards it as his holy duty to get to the bottom of me. It is never going to work, though. Those kinds of whimsical attempts only tend to make matters more complicated.

'Tell me why you've brought the laptop?' I ask. He doesn't look as if he wants to leave yet.

'I had two ideas. One was that you could stand here and shout out the truth about your brother . . .'

'Shout out? As in: out loud?'

'Sure, you might find it very liberating. But if it's too

304

embarrassing . . .' He removes a piece of fluff from his shoulder.

'Of course not! I've been longing to do it for years! I just hadn't come across the right type of mountain, that's all, but this one is perfect. You go and grab the megaphone while I run a brush through my hair, and then let's do it.'

He doesn't seem even remotely perturbed. 'Because I anticipated that you might react that way, I thought of an alternative. I want you to take my laptop and smash it to pieces – as hard as you can – here, from the Fóia.'

This man is not nifty at all, this man is a total crackpot. 'You want me to smash your laptop against the face of this mountain?'

He nods fervently. 'It contains all your words, all your secrets – that way you can leave them behind.'

'My dear Romeo, that's very sweet of you. Honestly, I'm touched. But there's no way I'm going to smash a brand-new laptop in perfect working order. Do you understand? I am Dutch. I am a skinflint!'

Romeo takes my hand. 'Very good, excellent. You see? You can do it. Come . . .' He pulls me along. Next to the concrete platform is a large mountain of smooth boulders. You can go to the highest point of the mountain, several metres higher than the platform. Hand in hand we scramble up, the only two people venturing onto the boulders.

'Don't worry, I'll help you through this,' says Romeo when we are at the top. 'Shout after me: "My name is Julia!"'

'My name is Julia,' I shout bashfully into no-man's-land.

'Louder please.'

'My name is Julia!'

'Very good,' Romeo says enthusiastically. 'And now: "My brother is dead!"'

'My brother is dead!' Am I imagining things or was that an echo just then?

'Was that difficult?' asks Romeo.

'Not too bad.'

'The next one is tricky: "I murdered him!"'

I swing round abruptly. 'It wasn't murder, do you hear me? He requested it. It was euthanasia.'

'Did you push that cushion over his face or not?'

'At his request,' I repeat stubbornly.

'Did you or didn't you?'

'It wasn't murder. Death upon request is not murder!' I shout down into the Algarve. 'Give me that laptop.'

He obeys me.

I lift the laptop over my head. 'This contains the truth and nothing but the truth. Let the world have it!' I hurl the machine away. It lands two metres down on a sandy patch between some boulders – the laptop isn't even broken. What a fiasco, this is useless. I'll have to climb down and try again.

'Be careful,' Romeo says. He doesn't stop me. Of course I lose my balance and fall over, grazing my arms. On my bum I shuffle down towards the laptop. I grab it, stand up and fling it away a second time, with more force. It bounces off the mountainside, deeper and deeper, until it lands somewhere in the far distance. I can't get to it any more. Nobody can. I make my way back up, satisfied with the result.

Romeo walks over towards me and holds out his hand to pull me up the last little bit. I stand next to him, panting. I shake the sand from my clothes.

The Portuguese family group have gathered at the foot of the little hill, ready to follow in our footsteps.

306

Holding hands – the daughter in the middle – they begin the final ascent.

'You're almost there,' Romeo says hurriedly. 'Repeat after me: "I murdered him!"'

Suddenly I don't care any more. 'I murdered him!' I shout in the direction of the laptop.

'I murdered my brother!' Romeo goes a stage further.

'I murdered Jimmy! Jimmy is my brother. I suffocated him with a cushion.'

The Portuguese have stopped. They look up, clearly wondering whether to continue, and wait.

'I pretended to be God!' I shout. I lower my voice and go on less confidently, 'Maybe He would have answered my mother's prayer that night. Maybe He didn't get the chance to because of me. Maybe He could have cured Jimmy. Who knows? But because I . . .' My voice falters. I break down. I break down on top of the Fóia. Romeo catches me. He takes me into his arms and gently strokes my hair.

'Very good. That is what you have been thinking. That is what you've been afraid of all this time. You believe that you overruled God. That you are the devil incarnate.'

My body is shaking.

The Portuguese man arrives at the top. He approaches us with caution. 'Is everything OK?' he asks.

'Sure,' Romeo and I say with one voice.

'He doesn't know yet that I am the devil incarnate.' I laugh through my tears.

We clamber back down the boulders, passing the mother and the child, who are now nearly at the top. The mother smiles at me supportively as if to say: I know what you are going through. When we get to the bottom Romeo puts his arm around me. We walk to his car. He holds the door open to let me in. Then he shuts it, walks round to the other side and sits down at the wheel.

'You are not the devil incarnate. You were a young girl who listened to her brother. If God had wanted it to be different it would have happened.'

'Are you in direct contact with Him?' I am not trying to be sarcastic.

He starts the engine. 'I believe things happen for a reason. You think that your brother is pursuing you, but really it's your conscience.'

'Why?'

'Guilt, fear. You did something that was bigger than you could handle. You pay for it in the end.'

Romeo reverses the car and drives off. After just a few hundred metres I ask him to stop urgently. He pulls up on the hard shoulder.

'Do you mind if I borrow your mobile?'

He nods, takes the phone out of his inside pocket and gives it to me.

'I'm just going to call home,' I explain. I've got to. I've got to do it now. It can't wait any longer, I want to hear my children's voices. I key in the number. The phone rings. Someone answers.

'Isabel de Groot here.'

For a moment I don't know what to say. My daughter. I have my daughter on the line. 'Hello Isabel, it's Mummy here,' I say.

'Mummy, is that you? Jim, come quickly! It's Mummy, Mummy on the phone!'

'How are you?'

'Jim! Did you hear me? He's coming, Mum. Don't hang up.'

'I won't. What were you doing?'

'Oh, nothing much. Where are you? Are you coming home?'

The same question that Romeo just asked me. I must try and think of a serious answer, but it hasn't come to me yet.

'I'm still in Portugal. Where is Daddy?'

'He's gone out for a minute. I'm looking after Jim.' There is rumbling in the background. 'It's Mummy, she's still in Portugal,' I hear Isabel say. And to me: 'Here he comes, Mum.'

'Hello!' says Jim.

'Hello love, it's Mummy.'

'Hi Mum.' His voice sounds just like Isabel's, only higher and thinner.

'How are you?'

'Fine.'

'How is school?' I can't think of anything else.

'Fine.'

'Good. Don't forget to keep working hard.'

'Yes, Mum,' he says.

'Has your sister been kind to you?'

'Yes.'

'I'm sorry I wasn't at your birthday party, Jim. You'll get a present when I come home.'

He says nothing. Presumably he is nodding. Isabel joins in the conversation. 'Tell Mummy,' I hear her say to Jim. 'You've got Mummy on the line now so go on, tell her, about what happens at night . . .'

'What is it, what must you tell?' I ask.

'I have bad dreams,' he says in a soft voice.

'Why is that?'

'Because you don't come and kiss me goodnight. If I don't get a goodnight kiss from you, I have bad dreams, Mummy.' He begins to cry.

'Sweetheart.' I don't know what to say. All I know is that I've failed on all fronts. Jim hands the receiver back to his sister.

'Does Daddy not kiss him goodnight?' I ask Isabel.

'Of course he does, but he only wants them from you. He's often upset in the middle of the night. Daddy doesn't know, but I do. I go and comfort him. I wrote about it to you . . .' I haven't been back to the post office.

'That letter must have got lost in the post, Isabel. Portugal is a funny country in that way.'

'When are you coming home?'

I glance to my side, to Romeo. If I go home, I'll lose him. If I stay here, my son will continue to have bad dreams every night. 'As soon as possible. How is that den you made?' I am glad I have managed to remember something topical.

'We've just had to move it, they were coming too close to us.'

'Promise to be careful?'

'Yes, Mum.'

'And give my love to Daddy, will you?'

'OK.'

'I'll hang up now. See you soon, love.'

I give Romeo his mobile back. Fortunately he doesn't ask any questions. We drive home in silence. We pass through the Portuguese landscape: the orange earth, the capriciously shaped almond trees, the white houses, the dusty roads – it's all inextricably linked with freedom. Freedom from care, and, above all, Romeo. We have only just met, I don't want to lose him, I want to go on enjoying myself just a little longer, a week, ten days – perhaps a few days more – surely that's allowed. Thereafter I will lead a virtuous life, incredibly virtuous, bordering on devout.

My mother once showed me a devotional picture she had inherited from her grandmother, my great-grandmother. My word, she was a devout woman if ever there was one. Compared with her, my mother seems like an atheist. My great-grandmother gave birth to sixteen children, never skipped a church service on Sundays, remained deeply religious until her death and died in the conviction that the Lord, her deceased husband, and two of her sons who died young, would all be waiting for her at heaven's gates.

According to my mother, her grandmother was an absolute gem: a good person through and through, kind to her children as well as her grandchildren. That type of woman has been discontinued – nowadays they have to be imported.

Part of me wishes that I had it in me: the dedication, the submissiveness. It must be wonderful to be able to trust God blindly, not to have to ask yourself complex existential questions, to do everything in His name, to do the right thing, always, and with a clear conscience, and to derive a sense of fulfilment from it. Deep down I know only too well, of course, that I have strayed. I don't need the Lord, or anyone else for that matter, to see that. I can work it out for myself, I am not dim. Dead brother or no, snoring husband or no, I must undo what I have done.

We are entering the grounds of the Casa de Criança when Romeo's mobile goes off. He has a ringtone from *The Sound of Music*, what a freak. He fishes the phone out of his inside pocket.

'Hello?'

'. . .'

311

'Yes, she's here.'

'. . .'

'That's none of your business.'

'. . .'

'If you carry on in that tone I won't let you speak to her.'

'. . .'

'Just a moment.'

Romeo puts his hand over the phone. 'It's for you.'

He has tracked me down. I have only myself to blame: Isabel told him I called and Romeo's number must have been on display still. How easy was that? Am I going to speak to him? Do I have a choice? I hold out my hand. Romeo gives me the phone. I get out of the car and walk over to the fig trees. The figs are a deep purple, some with slightly cracked skins, which means they are ripe; I eat several a day, they taste delicious. I have even made jam from them: Romeo was deeply impressed.

I hold the mobile against my ear. 'Hello, Paul.'

'Who was that guy?'

His tone is resolute.

'What is it, Paul? Why are you ringing?'

'It was *you* that rang. You told the children you're coming home.'

'That's the plan, yes.' I squeeze a few of the figs until I come across one that is soft enough.

'And you don't think you should discuss it with me first?'

I pluck the fruit from the tree. Romeo has also got out of the car. He sits down on the terrace, unfolds his paper, which is still on the table, and begins to read.

'You weren't there. The children asked when I was

312

coming back.' With my thoughts elsewhere I take a bite out of the fig.

'I hope you're not expecting a big welcome-home party.'

The line is beautifully clear. I can hear Paul as if he were standing next to me, but he sounds more distant than the 2,500 km between us. We're just completely disconnected.

'I'm not expecting anything,' I say with my mouth full.

'Are you eating?' he asks with unconcealed horror. 'Are you bloody stuffing yourself when, for the first time in months, I'm talking to you?'

'I'm not stuffing myself. I'm standing outside and eating a fig, which I picked off a tree. You should try one yourself, you'd find them delicious.'

'And that new guy of yours, would I find him delicious too?'

'I can understand you're angry, but—'

'Why didn't you reply to my letter?'

'Your letter?' I really must go to the post office.

'Oh forget it. I don't understand why I even bother to call you. Carry on with whatever it is you're doing, don't let me interrupt you.'

'Paul . . .' I begin. I should say something nice to him. That I love him, that I miss him. This would be a good moment. But I can't bring myself to say anything. My heart belongs to the man reading the paper on my terrace. I can't serve two men at once. I am no good at pretending.

My feelings for Paul have been pushed out, washed away with the torrent of emotions brought about by Romeo. My body belongs to him, my love is for him only. Everything in me yearns for him; I want to merge

313

with him, become one, and then stay with him for ever. It is the oldest song in the world, the most repeated story. It is a bubble, a Fata Morgana, but it is sweet, so sweet – sweeter than the figs, sweeter than my mother's cherry pie.

I must still love Paul, how could I not? I am sure the feeling will return once I am back with him. From then on I will be a good person again. It will look good in my obituary. It will make me seem more human: after a few mistakes she got herself back on the straight and narrow. The straight and narrow. There is no other way to go.

'I'm sorry. I'll be home soon.'

I break off, pick another fig and feed it to Romeo.

Chapter Thirty-one

The spirit was willing, but the flesh was weak. Seventeen days passed before I could bring myself to book a flight. Seventeen sweet, heavenly, carefree days. I had told Romeo that I was going to go back to my family. That I'd soon be a good mother again and that he needn't have any qualms.

Then I told him a lie. I said that Paul and the children were about to go away on holiday and wouldn't be back for almost another month. So, if he liked, we could spend a few more weeks together. We were floating around on the lilo when I mentioned it. He was lying on his back and I was on top of him. My hips were slowly rotating against his wet trunks. The drops on his broad chest were glistening in the sun, like diamonds. His gold Rolex was waterproof.

It is a pity that I am not a famous actress in real life. We'd be a real 'it' couple, him and me. I fantasized about being spotted by a photographer and how our pictures would subsequently appear on the front page of one of the tabloids: 'Julia's hot summer romance with American porn star.'

A week later we'd be in the news again because we'd had matching Hindu tattoos done on the inside of our ankles, symbolizing our eternal spiritual connection or something along those lines. The paparazzi would come and photograph my belly, and speculations would ensue about a possible love child. Witnesses were the only thing missing. Without witnesses our existence wasn't real.

I told Romeo that I wanted to buy a digital camera to remember our time together. He shook his head firmly, he pinched his lips. No photos. End of discussion.

'Why not?' I asked.

I didn't get an answer.

I bet he has a wife and children somewhere, I thought to myself. He's probably worried about black-mail. You can have several identities but you only have one body and one face.

It was too hot to worry about his lack of trust. Time was short so I let it go. Taking the decision to go back, being certain that I would be a good mother again, had relaxed me. The only thing I didn't want to do any more was talk. There was going to be plenty of explaining to do at home soon, so I made Romeo promise not to ask me any more questions. Not about the past, not about the future. I just wanted to talk about the present, about little everyday things. How do you want your eggs: fried or boiled? Shall we play a game of Trivial Pursuit or would you rather read? We're out of water, would you mind picking up a couple of bottles from the supermarket? I wanted to spend our remaining days together without conflict. Our relationship would die a quiet death – that was certain – and I had resigned myself to that. The deadline, the definite boundary put my mind at rest.

Romeo still had to finish off with a couple of clients. I knew about it: he had made it clear from the beginning. The first time he went, I had to take a few deep breaths and count to ten, but I coped. I didn't kick up a fuss, I didn't try to stop him. I didn't sulk. I just grabbed a black marker.

'Give me your foot.'

He obeyed. I couldn't immediately think of an authentic Hindu symbol so I drew a yin-yang sign on the inside of his right ankle instead. I also drew one on my own ankle.

'As long as this stays on your ankle you're with me,' I explained.

Romeo didn't mind. 'I'll be back in three hours,' he promised.

I kissed him and waved goodbye. As soon as he was out of sight, I slipped into my clothes and went to the hairdresser. Blondes have more fun, but they also have more worries: I urgently needed to have my roots done.

Romeo returned punctually from his date, leaped under the shower and dragged me into bed, as if he wanted to erase what had happened. His yin-yang symbol had faded a bit, and he asked if I would retrace it for him. From that moment on, I touched up both our ankles every day.

'We would make a good team,' Romeo said on day five.

'I don't know anyone else like you,' he said on day twelve.

'I'll miss you when you go,' he said on day seventeen.

Chapter Thirty-two

On day eighteen I wake up and stretch out my arm, expecting to feel Romeo's warm body. It is not there. I open my eyes. My lover stands in the room in his pants. His suitcase lies open on the floor and the television is on, with the sound turned down. He is half watching Sky News.

'I have to go,' he says. He puts a pile of shirts in the suitcase.

'To see a client?' I ask against my better judgement.

'To America.'

I cast a quick glance at his right ankle. The symbol is gone. His skin looks a bit red where it used to be.

'My husband and children haven't returned from their holiday yet,' I lie. 'We can . . .'

'I'm off, Julia.'

I am being kicked out of paradise. I don't want to go yet, it's too soon. I leap out of bed and hug him. 'Come back to bed for a bit.'

He shakes his head.

'Please.'

He gently pushes me away, giving me a strange look, as if I were someone else – someone with an illness, someone he should pity. 'You knew this would happen, Julia.' He grabs a T-shirt and pulls it over his head.

'The symbol has gone from your ankle,' I say accusingly.

He carries on packing.

'Is this it? Are you leaving me, just like this? Why didn't you say something? Only last night we were doing it, while you knew—'

'I didn't want to burden you with it.'

I feel my face growing hot. That sounds like an excuse. Surely it can't be. Romeo isn't like that. 'Burden me! Let me feel what it feels like. I beg you: let me feel something. Don't leave me like this. Not in this cold way.'

Romeo frowns. I feel confident enough to touch him again. I hug him, my hands disappear underneath his T-shirt, I stroke his chest. His nipples respond. If they respond, there is every chance the rest will too. I moan softly.

'Lie down on your front,' commands Romeo. He shoves me towards the bed. His gruff voice worries me, but I do as he says. 'So you want to know what it's like?'

He pulls up my buttocks, tears off my knickers and penetrates me. Roughly, he tugs at my hair until I'm on my hands and knees. This is rape, I asked for it. My lips mouth the word 'no'. Romeo thinks I am encouraging him. He thrusts deep, too deep and too hard. I moan louder, tears rise to my eyes. He doesn't restrain himself. On the contrary. I turn my pain-stricken face towards him. Can you please be a bit less brutal, I want to ask, but then I notice that he still has his eyes on the television. He sees me looking at him and laughs triumphantly. 'Are you satisfied now?' he asks. 'Have you learned something? Tell me what you learned.'

'Stop it, you're hurting me . . .' I say in tears.

He withdraws. I sigh with relief. It was a misunderstanding, a silly misunderstanding. There are probably women out there who enjoy this sort of thing, he must have thought I was one of them, that's all. I'll explain to him he made a mistake. I am about to do so, when he pushes the tip of his penis against the smaller opening. I protest, I try to pull away, but he firmly grabs my hips. He is stronger, he stops me. He enters me with a single, explosive thrust. A sharp, stabbing pain follows. Everything goes black.

'My name isn't Romeo. Or Javis. You mustn't believe everything, Julia. Fairy-tale princes don't exist.'

He thrusts three, four more times, I scream with pain until he ejaculates over my buttocks. When he is done, he pushes me away. I fall onto my side and double up, sobbing. Instinctively, I clutch my backside.

'This makes our farewell a lot easier. Don't you agree, *wolkenmeisje*?'

I hear him pull on his trousers and zip them up, then I listen to him packing the last few things before he shuts the suitcase. Without another word he walks out of the room and pulls the door shut behind him. He leaves the television on. I hold my right hand against my bruised parts and want to put my left hand over my mouth.

Then I notice there is blood on it.

Chapter Thirty-three

I lock up at the Casa da Criança for the very last time. I close the shutters and switch on the alarm. All my stuff is packed. After Romeo had left, I stayed in bed for ages. I only got up to fetch a glass of water and a Valium. I imagined I was feeling just like Marilyn Monroe during her last night. I had always had this image of her lying between the silk sheets, with a telephone and a bottle of sleeping pills, smelling vaguely of Chanel No. 5. Bobby Kennedy had either just left or had refused to come and see her. John F. had long since stopped returning her calls; the housekeeper was asleep in her own private wing of the house. Not surprising she went for the pills. Sometimes you need pills to live and sometimes you need them to die.

Hours went by. Every now and then I thought I could hear Romeo coming back. I asked myself what I would do. Fight it out, give him an earful and then take him back? Beg him to stay for one more day, one more week, one more month? I knew I would be capable of it. I could never have imagined that I would be so submissive. He had humiliated me and already I was prepared to humiliate myself again in order to be further humiliated. I would carry on begging for love, the way my children never stop begging for my love, even though I am not worth it.

I have bad dreams if I don't get a goodnight kiss from you.

I should have gone back the minute Jim said that. I should have listened. I hope they can forgive me – Isabel and Jim. I thank God I have them, I miss them terribly. What have I done to them, and why? I must make it up to them, I must make up for everything, I must buy presents – big presents – I must tell them it won't ever happen again. I'll have to eat humble pie, tell them I'd understand if they hate me, tell them they are allowed to hate me, that I will accept their hatred, their loathing, just so long as I can be with them, so long as they don't cut me out.

I belong with them. It is so obvious: we share the same name, we are family. I just didn't know what that meant any more, I had lost sight of it, my compass wasn't working properly – that is what I'll tell them – but now the needle is pointing in the right direction again, now I remember, it has all come back to me. Hold tight, dear Jim, just a little bit longer – one more night, two at the most, Mummy is almost home.

I fling my things in the boot of the Vauxhall. I haven't booked a flight yet, I'll have to find a travel agent but first I want to pass by Eddie's house. I hope I can leave today but if I can't I'll spend the night in Faro. Any hotel will do as long as it isn't Hotel Eva. Eddie is surprised to see me with the keys. The lease isn't up yet, there are still several days left.

'My husband called. If I don't come home soon, he'll come and get me,' I say. 'He can't manage another day without me.'

Eddie nods understandingly. 'Sounds good, Julia. And your . . . er . . . difference, has that been resolved?'

What difference did we have again? Oh yes, the adoption business, of course.

'He said he'd give me everything I want as long as I come home immediately.'

He looks radiant. 'Then your greatest wish will be fulfilled soon.'

I nod hastily, I want to keep it brief. He is going to ask me about Romeo next – he's certainly nosy enough. 'Say hello to Doris from me, will you? And sorry again about your cap.'

He snorts. 'We should have known better, Julia. They can't be trusted. You give them a place to sleep, you treat them, you work with them, and what do you get? Bloody bastards.'

'Where are your dogs, Eddie?' I ask to distract him.

'Doris has taken them to the vet.' Does Eddie's wife exist after all? It seems so.

'Are they ill?' The last time I saw them they were their usual hysterical selves, drooling all over the place.

'Fleas. An infestation, they were covered from top to toe. Just as we were going to take them to a show.'

'Oh. What a shame. Well, good luck. Must go. Thank you for everything.' I blow him a kiss and get into my car.

The travel agent's office is tiny and unbearably hot. I have to wait to be served, so I sit down in one of the plastic stacking chairs. An elderly couple, sprightly for their age, are in front of me. When I first observe them I find them quite endearing. He does all the talking, making vehement gestures, while she sits next to him, clutching her bag tightly in her lap, and nodding diligently after every word he says.

The girl behind the counter pulls out one leaflet after another from the cupboard. She gets out the atlas; the pile of papers on the counter is growing ever higher. They leaf through everything, discuss all the options, while the girl makes notes. The man takes a diary from his briefcase, they go over the dates, the girl looks something up on her computer: clearly this couple are booking the journey of a lifetime and are going to take their time – the entire afternoon if necessary. Meanwhile, I'm completely ignored.

After half an hour of listening to their babble – I no longer find them charming and am about to explode with irritation – I can't contain myself any longer. 'Excuse me, do you speak English?' I ask the girl.

The three of them look up, annoyed, as if they hadn't noticed another living being had come into the room.

'I need a single ticket to Amsterdam. That's all. A flight from Faro to Amsterdam. Can you book it for me?'

The man says something in Portuguese, sounding very angry. His wife glowers at me.

'I don't speak English,' the girl says in English.

As if by agreement, they all turn round again and carry on with what they were doing.

I sit frozen in my stacking chair. I can stand up and leave, I can accept my defeat and wait my turn, or I can kick up a fuss: those are basically the options. If only Romeo were here now, then everything would be different. He would get the girl to toe the line with one click of his fingers.

'Listen,' I try again. 'I urgently have to go home. My son needs me. He is ill. Can you help me?'

'You'll have to wait,' the girl says sharply.

The couple don't even deign to look at me again. I decide to go to the Tivoli Almansor. I can book a flight online using one of the PCs there. Why didn't I think of that before?

The Vauxhall takes me to the Tivoli Almansor, I mustn't forget to fill up the tank, the warning light has been on for a while. I put on my sunglasses and walk as casually as I can to the computer corner. A sweaty, sunburnt woman with a straw hat is using one of the PCs. The other one is free but you have to type in a password. I ask the man at reception if he can remind me what it is.

'Are you a guest at the hotel?'

I nod impatiently. Yes of course, what else would I be?

It is a miracle. The man comes out from behind his desk and types in the password. I log onto the Transavia website. I can still get a seat on the seven o'clock flight tonight. Good, I'll do that. The site asks for my credit-card details. I take my purse out of my bag. Jeez, it feels so light and thin.

How strange. It can't be. I got some cash out only the day before yesterday. Quickly I open it and see straight away that there is nothing inside. All my money has gone – the compartments are empty. My armpits begin to ooze. My cheeks go red. He has robbed me. First he raped me and then he robbed me. No wait, probably it was the other way round: he robbed me while I was asleep, and then he raped me. And now he is walking around somewhere with my money, my credit cards, my Air Miles card, my supermarket card, my Makro card, my car breakdown card and my Douglas Perfumery card.

I turn the purse inside out. There isn't a scrap of paper inside, no note, nothing. I want to cry, but there is no time. I must do something, immediately, before the bastard raids all my accounts.

I walk over to the man at the desk, tell him what has happened and ask if I can use the phone. I must cancel my cards, it is urgent. The man asks for my room number.

'I'm sorry,' I say. 'I don't have a room here. I lied. All I did was eat here once.' My T-shirt sticks to my back.

I must look pretty shaken. Without a word he hands me the telephone. Only then do I realize that the numbers to cancel my cards are all stored in my mobile. I daren't call Paul, I don't know Kaitlin's number by heart and I'd rather not bother Mum or Dad. Fuck, what am I going to do? I get out my Filofax. Somewhere at the back I scribbled down some of my friends' numbers.

Patrick.

His name leaps off the page immediately. There is a number beside it, a normal landline number, I must have written it down once. I know: it was when he sent me a card announcing the birth of his first child.

I dial the number. A woman answers. She sounds friendly. It is nice to hear a Dutch voice.

'Hello, this is Julia de Groot speaking. I'm looking for Patrick.'

'He is at work.'

'I am ringing from abroad, it's a matter of urgency. Do you have his mobile number?'

'May I ask what it is regarding?' She sounds a touch suspicious.

'I'm Jimmy's sister.'

The woman is quiet for a moment. I am sure that she

326

knows who Jimmy is. I'm sure she'll give me his number. She does. I call Patrick and get him on the line.

'Hi Patrick, it's Julia.'

'Julia?'

'Sorry to bother you. I need your help, you're the only person I dare ask. I'm in Portugal, I've been robbed, my money, my cards, I've got to cancel them but I have lost the numbers and—'

'Steady on, one thing at a time, please. You're in Portugal. Alone?'

'Yes.'

'And you've been robbed? By a man?'

'By someone I trusted.'

'I see.'

He simply listens, he doesn't condemn me. He doesn't start about Paul. He just asks me practical questions: which banks need to be notified, what were the account numbers, do I have travel insurance, what is my full address in Amsterdam? 'Good,' he says when he has written it all down. 'Don't worry, I'll deal with it. Was there anything else?'

'I want to come home,' I say timidly. 'I can't book a flight. And I've got a hire car which I've had for ages and haven't paid for yet.'

'Where exactly are you now?'

'In a hotel, at reception. They let me use the phone.'

The man behind the desk is beginning to look impatient. I shrug my shoulders apologetically.

'Give me the name and number of the hotel and go to the police to report the theft. Then go back to the hotel. I'll be in touch with you.'

'Patrick, you're an angel! I don't know how to thank you.'

327

'We'll think of something, gorgeous.' That's what he used to call me in the old days. He used to adore me. Whenever Patrick looked at me I'd feel beautiful.

The entire police force are on their lunch break. After an hour and a half, an officer finally turns up to help me. He looks as if he has just come out of nappies, a newbie, with olive skin, dark wavy hair and light brown eyes. As I start to explain my situation, he looks at me expectantly, with his pen poised. It wouldn't surprise me if I were his first encounter with a victim. A tourist who has been robbed, you can't really go wrong with that. A chubby man comes in through the back door. He sits down at a desk and leafs through a dossier. I assume he is the boss. The newbie listens to my story politely.

After a few minutes a frown appears on his smooth forehead. He attempts to summarize the information in broken English. 'You were robbed by an American? He was staying at your villa? He is black? You don't have a photograph of him? You don't know what his surname is? And you aren't sure about his first name either? He calls himself Romeo? Possibly his name is Javis?'

I dig around in my bag for Romeo's business card. Gone. The officer puts down his pen. 'I'm sorry to be so uninformative,' I say. 'I do remember that he was staying at the Tivoli Almansor before he moved in with me. At least, that's what he said. He drove a black Maserati. And a few months ago he was staying at Hotel Eva in Faro. That I'm sure of. Shall I give you the date?'

The boy nods, picks up his pen and notes down what I say for form's sake. The Portuguese *hermandad* won't give this case top priority. Since I made up my mind to

328

go home, everything seems to be going wrong. I should be returning like a new woman, energetic, in good spirits, radiant, irresistible. I should be a breath of fresh air, bring the sun back into the hearts of my family.

'By the way, he also raped me,' I tell the officer.

The newbie has eyes like saucers. His colleague closes the dossier and for the first time looks up at me. The boy straightens his back. 'When?' he asks.

'This morning. Before he left. I suspect he robbed me last night, while I was asleep.'

'At what time exactly?'

'The rape? Round about nine, I think.'

He scribbles it all down. His chubby colleague comes and stands next to him. 'Why didn't you call us straight away?'

'I wasn't sure if it was rape. It started as sex, but then . . .'

He stops writing. The colleague puts his hands on the desk and leans forward.

'. . . then he did something I didn't really want. From behind. Anal sex.'

They hang on my every word. They can picture it.

'*Todo lá dentro?*' the chubby one asks.

The newbie suppresses a smile. I glance at the pair of them, not understanding.

'Did he go all the way in?' the young officer translates, with a twinkle in his eyes. I don't understand why he thinks it's funny.

'The man is a famous porn star. The sex was good, very good. But this morning it wasn't how I like it. He forced me.'

As I say this, I realize there is a way we can track down Romeo. 'Do you have any pornographic DVDs

329

lying around in your office? I might be able to point him out to you. I'm sure I'd recognize him.'

The boy and the man simultaneously nod their heads.

'The only porn tapes we have here are Tomás Taveira's,' the chubby man says. He is smiling too now.

'Taveira? But he's an architect.'

'That's right. With an unusual hobby. Anal sex. *To-do lá dentro*,' he repeats slowly. He winks at the newbie, making a rude gesture.

I don't think I want to find out any more and suddenly feel rather uncomfortable.

'I suppose we could examine you,' the older man says. 'Have you had a shower yet?'

For a moment I don't know what he means. He notices, and explains himself.

'Perhaps we'd find traces of his sperm . . .'

This is getting out of hand. All I need is a crime reference number for the insurance company. Why did I mention the rape? Now the fat officer wants to stick a cotton bud in my rear end.

'Forget it,' I say. 'I won't be able to prove anything. I just want to report the theft.'

The fat officer retreats, disappointed. The newbie asks if I am absolutely certain. I reply that I am and he finishes off the crime report. I sign it and receive a copy.

On the way back to the hotel the car suddenly slows down, for no apparent reason. I step on the gas. It makes no difference: I have run out of petrol. I've gone on for too long, it's the first time it's ever happened to me. The engine stalls, the Vauxhall keeps going just long enough for me to steer it onto the hard shoulder. I pull up the handbrake and put my head down on the wheel.

After a while I hear someone pull up behind me. For a second I think it is Romeo. I lift up my head and see a black car, just not a Maserati. It's an Audi. The driver gets out and walks towards me. He is tall, completely bald and dressed in a smart suit. I bet he is a lawyer or an estate agent. I lower my window. Whoever he is, let him come to the rescue.

Amsterdam, 9 March 2005

Julia,

Since you left I have been thinking a great deal. I see now that family life doesn't always bring you what you are looking for. I know that I sometimes ask too much of you. I am prepared to change, to work at our relationship, including our sexual relationship. Let's try and make a new start together. Please come home.

Your husband,
Paul

Part Four

Paul

Chapter Thirty-four

Patrick has gone bald. His hollow temples age him, but his face is as friendly as ever. He takes my bag.

'Had a good flight?'

He was waiting for me at Schiphol airport, as arranged. At first I didn't recognize him. I remembered Patrick as a skinny nineteen-year-old but in the Arrivals Hall I saw a middle-aged man with a pot belly, who looked like Patrick's father. He raised his hand hesitantly when I smiled at him. 'Do you want to go home straight away, or shall we have a drink first?' he asks.

'What time is it?'

He glances at his watch. 'Quarter past two.'

The children come out of school in an hour. There is just time. We go to the pub at Schiphol Plaza. Patrick orders a beer and I a mineral water.

'You look great,' says Patrick. 'I didn't recognize you at first. Your hair is different.'

I look around me. It is weird to be back in Holland.

Patrick meets my eyes. 'Everything OK, Julia?'

'Sorry?'

'How are you?'

'Fine,' I answer.

'I didn't want to tell you over the phone, but your credit cards have been used. A considerable sum has been spent on jewellery and one or two other things.'

'How much?'

'It doesn't matter, you reported the theft in time. You only have to pay the excess.'

'How much did he spend, Patrick?'

'Just over six thousand euros.' Love Service has recouped its expenses from the Society for the Preservation and Protection of Families.

I open my bag, take out a bottle of wine and give it to Patrick. 'Monte Velho, one of the best reds from the Alentejo region.'

'Thanks.'

'You've helped me no end. I promise you'll get it all back.'

He makes a dismissive gesture. 'No rush.'

'If it hadn't been for you, I wouldn't have been able to come home.' I couldn't even have bought the children presents. They are not quite as generous as I wanted, but that doesn't matter.

'How long have you been away?'

'Three months or so.' I feel myself getting restless. It is good to see Patrick again, but it is exactly like it used to be in the old days. He is too nice, he doesn't excite me. I made the right choice; it wouldn't have worked between us. 'Shall we go?' I suggest.

He smiles. 'You're fed up with me already.'

'What on earth gave you that impression?' I sink back into my chair.

'You always felt that way about me, and you always will.'

'That sounds terribly fatalistic.'

'I don't mind. I know you think about me, and that you'll call me if you need me. That is enough.'

'Why are you doing this?'

'Because I promised your brother. And because I love you.' He says it as if it goes without saying.

'Is this how love ought to be? Unconditional and unselfish?'

'In theory, yes, though in actual practice we tend to expect more.'

I stand up and kiss him on the mouth. 'Will you still call me gorgeous when I reach eighty?'

He blushes. 'Of course I will, gorgeous.'

We are almost there. The journey took a long time: a lorry had overturned on the A10. You hardly ever see capsized lorries in Portugal, I don't know why that is.

'Just drop me off on the corner. I'll walk the last little bit.'

Patrick pulls up at the side of the road.

'Thank you again. I'll call you this week about the money.' I open the door. 'You're a good person,' I say to Patrick. 'He would be proud of you.'

He puts his hand on my knee. 'You were his heroine, Julia. He constantly talked about you. You were so brave, you did so much for him. It must have been very difficult for you.'

Perhaps Jimmy confided his plan to Patrick, perhaps he knows; it wouldn't surprise me. It has always slightly worried me, which is why I avoided Patrick after the funeral. But that's all in the past now.

I get out. Patrick lifts my bag out of the boot and hands it to me. We say goodbye. I walk into our street. Once I am past the bend, I see the building site. This is where the children's den must be, somewhere. The skeletons of the new houses are all there, they just need windows and roofs. Slowly I walk on. I've got about twenty metres to go before I reach the door. I don't have a key – hopefully somebody will be in.

The front garden is overgrown. Underneath the bell is a sticker that tells me someone has just been to collect money for the Heart Foundation. I ring. The door opens. My daughter stands before me. She leans against the doorpost and gives me a friendly look. She has no idea who I am. My word, she has shot up: I discover feminine forms that weren't there before. She has grown even more beautiful.

'Isabel,' I say. 'It's me, Mummy.' I take off my sunglasses and put down my bag.

'Mum!' she shouts. 'What happened to you? Your hair looks so weird! I didn't know you were coming. Why didn't you call?'

She flies into my arms. I hug her tightly. She smells different, older. 'Sweetheart, I've missed you so much,' I say with all my heart. 'Where's Jim?'

'In our den. Shall I go and get him?'

'I'll come with you.' We walk to the building site with arms locked tightly. She points to where the den is, behind the shrubs. When we are very close, I see Jim. He is alone. He is sitting on the ground, his legs folded. Next to him lies a skipping rope. He is wearing Isabel's old light blue coat.

'Ssh,' I mouth to Isabel. We sneak up even closer.

Staring into the distance, he doesn't hear us. I study his face. It has changed – the rounded innocence has been wiped away. This boy has been through a lot. I bite my lip.

Isabel tugs at my arm. A twig breaks underneath my foot – Jim starts at the noise.

'Mummy is back!' Isabel can't contain herself any longer. 'She's come home. I told you she would.'

His eyes dart from Isabel to me. He doesn't move. I stoop to get into the den.

'Hello Jim.'

'Hi, Mum.'

'How are you?'

'I'm OK.' He looks right past me.

'We'll catch up with you in a moment,' I say to Isabel. 'You go ahead and put the kettle on.'

When she has gone, I lower myself onto the ground and sit down next to my son. 'I'd like to kiss you, but I'm not sure I dare. I think you're angry with me.'

Jim remains mute.

'Am I right? Are you angry with me, Jim?'

No answer. I've messed up, he'll never speak to me again. Stubbornness is a family trait.

'I've been away for a long time. I didn't stay in touch enough. I didn't show up on your birthday, I hurt you, I know. I could try and explain it to you, but the damage is done now. Maybe one day you will understand that grown-ups don't always get it right either.'

He picks up the skipping rope and winds one end round his wrist.

'I'm very sorry, Jim, I hope you'll be able to forgive me.'

He moves a little closer to me and, with his free hand, ties the other end round my wrist. We sit together in silence for a while. 'Has the wall gone?' he asks.

'What?'

339

'The wall round your heart. Has it gone?'

'Yes,' I answer. 'It has.'

We have tea. Isabel talks nineteen to the dozen, Jim remains quiet. They each have a new pet; Jim a hamster and Isabel a budgerigar. They're called Frummel and Tweetie. While I admire the new animals, Frummel nips my index finger. A drop of blood appears. Isabel brings me a plaster.

I give them their presents. When it's coming up for half past five we hear a key in the door. Paul is home. I stand up and straighten my clothes.

Jim runs to the door. 'Daddy, Mummy is back!'

They come into the kitchen together. Suddenly I stand face to face with my husband. He is wearing a leather jacket I have not seen before. He has lost weight.

Paul walks past me and throws an opened packet of cigarettes on the table. 'Hello,' he says nonchalantly.

'Have you taken up smoking again?' I ask incredulously. He gave up after Isabel was born. Once you have children you've got to quit smoking, he said.

He kisses Isabel on her forehead. 'Cup of tea for you, Dad?' she asks.

'No thanks.' He picks up a half-empty bottle of wine from the worktop and starts to remove the rubber plug.

'Hang on, I've got something for you.' I produce the second bottle of Monte Velho. 'Comes from the Alentejo. Delicious.'

Paul examines the label. The corkscrew is in the usual place. I pass it to him. 'Get a couple of glasses for Mummy and me, will you?' he says to Isabel.

'I've still got tea,' I protest.

'Go on, you're back. Let your hair down.' He tears the

foil away from the bottle neck. I can't tell if his remark is intended sarcastically.

'We should be having champagne,' Isabel says. 'Real champagne for you, and children's champagne for us. Just like on New Year's Eve. Remember, we always do that, don't we, Mum?'

I give her a reassuring nod.

'How long will you be staying?' asks Jim. He seems to think I might be leaving again any moment. That I'm just dropping in to say hello.

Paul joins in the conversation. 'No one has actually said yet that she can stay, kids. I'm not sure I want this strange woman back in the house. We were doing just fine.' He pours two glasses of wine and offers me one. 'Cheers.' He takes two large gulps and lights a cigarette. Isabel puts down an ashtray in front of him. 'Have you cleaned out Frummel's cage?' Paul asks Jim.

He looks contrite.

'You promised you would do it today.'

'Sorry, Dad.' Jim pushes back his chair.

'And what about your homework, young lady?'

'I was about to get on with it,' Isabel laughs. She goes upstairs. The division of roles is clear, they understand each other perfectly. I feel like an intruder in my own family.

'They seem to be in a good state. You've done a great job,' I praise Paul.

He puts out his cigarette. 'Jim was very upset.' Now that the children have left the room, the teasing under-tone has gone. 'When you didn't get in touch on his birthday, he convinced himself that you were dead but that we were keeping it from him. He began to wet his bed, he got into fights at school. His teacher called me in because she didn't know how to handle him. On her advice I bleeped you so that he could hear your voice, but then you never called back. That only made it worse.'

I shake my head in disbelief. 'My pager never bleeped, not once, I swear. Are you sure you tried the right number?' I take the gadget out of my handbag. The screen is black – normally there should be a little red digit. Strange. I press the button. Nothing happens. 'Just try and bleep me again, will you?'

'What's the point?'

'Please. I want to know. I always had it with me, honest.'

With a sigh, Paul picks up his mobile and does as I ask him. The pager remains silent.

'I don't understand it.'

'What difference does it make? The battery must have run out.' Paul pours himself more wine. My glass is still untouched.

The battery. It never occurred to me to check, I'm such a cow. I open up the pager, fumble in a drawer and replace the battery. I hear a short bleep and a red zero appears on the screen.

'So all that time nobody could reach you,' Paul concludes. Obviously, he is right.

'I'm really sorry,' I say humbly.

'There is no need to apologize. If something had happened, you would simply have had to live with it.'

It's been fine, there have been no fatal accidents – but Paul seems to think that according to the laws of probability things can only go wrong. I change the subject. 'Have you been in touch with my mother?'

'Unfortunately, yes.'

'And?'

'She wondered what she had done to deserve losing

342

another child. Your father called a few times to ask when you'd be back at the office. He is now living with a Thai woman. They met on holiday.'

I burst out laughing.

Paul looks annoyed. 'Mae-Duna is very nice. We see each other regularly, especially since your father's stroke.'

'Stroke?'

'Did Kaitlin not tell you? She said that she was in contact with you, and that she'd let you know. Your father has had a stroke.'

'Nobody told me,' I say frostily. Just like Kaitlin to promise such a thing. 'How is he?'

'The left half of his body was paralysed initially, but he is almost back to normal.'

'And his girlfriend . . . er . . .'

'Mae-Duna. She's a terrific cook. Isabel and Jim adore her.'

'What age is she?'

'Mae is very young still,' Paul says quickly. It is the third time he has mentioned her name. 'I believe she is twenty-eight, or thereabouts. She speaks fluent English. You should hear her and Jim talk to each other. Very funny. And educational too. For Jim, I mean.' He fidgets uneasily on his chair.

Reading between the lines I sense that my destiny has taken an ironic turn.

'What does my father think?'

'About what?' Paul blushes.

I am surprised I manage to stay so calm. 'The fact that his son-in-law is doing it with his girlfriend. Don't try and deny it, Paul, it's blatantly obvious. And don't worry, I'm not going to get angry—'

'You're not going to get angry? Can we just go back to

the beginning for a second? I didn't know where you were, I hadn't a clue if you were ever going to come back, I couldn't get hold of you. Then Mae came knocking on our door . . .'

Fourth time. I take a sip of my wine, my first. I wasn't going to, I had decided to stay off alcohol for six months.

'. . . she'd moved to a new country, she didn't know anyone, your father had been admitted to hospital in an emergency. We were able to comfort each other, that's true . . .'

Paul's mobile vibrates. A text message. He opens it and smiles.

'From her?' I don't get an answer. He puts his phone away.

'Neither of us were looking for this, Julia. We didn't see it coming. Your father doesn't know yet. Mae wants to wait until he has made a full recovery.'

I think I feel an attack of migraine coming on.

Jim comes into the kitchen to inform us that Frummel has a clean cage again.

'Good boy,' says Paul. 'You can go and watch television in my bedroom, if you like.'

His children, *his* bedroom, *his* new girlfriend. I have been completely sidelined.

'Am I allowed to stay here with you?' Jim asks hopefully.

I stroke him on the head. 'Daddy and I just want to have a quiet talk, love. It's such a long time since we saw each other.'

'Is Mae coming tonight?' Isabel pops her head round the door.

Paul glowers at her.

'Please, don't take any notice of me.' I raise my hands

in the air and succumb. Perhaps I should book a hotel for the night. Or better still, a single ticket to Faro.

'She was going to show me how to make Thai soup,' Isabel explains.

Paul steps in. 'Mummy is here now, so we'll do that another time. I'll give Mae a quick call later. I think we've got enough rice left over from yesterday. Can you lay the table, please, Isabel? Jim, you clear the table after supper, OK? And then it's shower, pyjamas and straight to bed. No arguing, no fuss.'

Jim clambers onto my lap. I kiss him. He hangs onto me as if he never wants to let go again. 'Are you here for good now, Mummy?'

I carefully consider my answer. I don't want to alarm him, but neither can I promise him too much at this stage. My future depends on Paul. And a certain Mae-Duna. 'I am around for the moment, sweetheart. Tonight I'm putting you to bed, that's a promise.'

'And tomorrow?'

Chapter Thirty-five

Paul sits slouched on the sofa, with his legs on the coffee table. He has lit a cigarette. I can't get used to seeing him smoke. The children are in bed. Jim's eyes lit up when I came to kiss him goodnight. I gave him a hundred kisses, one for each night I'd been away, and a few extra.

'Do we have paracetamol?' I ask Paul.

He nods. I find the box in the usual place. I take a couple, walk back to the sitting room and sit down in the armchair.

'Port for you too?' Paul holds up the bottle. I decline. 'That must have set you back a bit,' he observes, 'your new body. I hope you got your money's worth.'

It is the first time he has mentioned it.

'I'm pleased with the result, if that's what you mean.'

'I'm sure you're not the only one.'

I massage my throbbing temples with my fingertips. 'Are you going to be like this all evening, Paul? Because if you are, I'm off to bed. I can go in the spare room, or to a hotel. It's up to you.'

'Did you honestly think you could come marching in here as if nothing had ever happened?'

'I didn't think anything, Paul, I—'

'Shut up and let me finish! I sent you a letter, begging you to come home.'

If only I had gone to the post office. I blame Romeo – if he hadn't raped me – but I can't tell Paul that. There is so much I can't tell him. You've got to watch out not to burden others too much with the truth.

'Do you have a copy?' Paul keeps a copy of every letter he writes.

'Why?'

'I didn't stay in Lagoa, I went on a round trip,' I lie. 'Please let me read it.'

He must have written the letter at a time when he still felt confident we'd pull through. It isn't too late. Perhaps he'll reconsider it when he reads over his own words.

'Why is this so important to you all of a sudden? You've known for almost three weeks that I wrote you a letter, I told you over the phone. Is this to do with Mae-Duna by any chance? Do you suddenly find me attractive because someone else wants me?'

I am unlikely ever to admit it, but he is right. I have come home because of my children, not because of him. I had no idea what would happen with Paul. I wanted to wait and see, but now Mae-Duna has put a spanner in the works. 'I think we should give our marriage another chance. We owe it to ourselves, and to our children.'

He takes his legs off the coffee table and sits up straight. 'I was prepared to make changes, I was prepared to work at our sexual relationship. I understood your situation. I told you so in my letter. My sympathy has evaporated, Julia. What possessed you to stay away for so long? It defeats me.'

347

'I needed to sort some stuff out. It had to do with Jimmy, with myself . . .'

'. . . and the size of my penis,' Paul reminds me. 'Did you accomplish your mission? Did you find a real man? Was it good?' He takes a drag from his cigarette and blows smoke rings. 'Mae-Duna makes me very happy. Do you know why? She takes me the way I am. She adores me. She doesn't complain about anything.'

That Thai slut has taken over my bloke. And he has walked right into it.

'Are you surprised? Thanks to my father she's managed to escape from Thailand. Any Western man she can get after him is a step up the ladder. You're that next step, Paul, you mean progress. She's getting ahead.'

He is unmoved. 'You're just jealous. Jealous and mean.'

'I am being realistic. That author of yours, Houellebecq, he'd agree with me completely. It all boils down to economics in the end, it's about the law of supply and demand. Your money and your status, in exchange for her servitude and twenty-eight-year-old body. Even my father was allowed to touch her – probably still is. Does she ever complain about that?'

'Have you finished?' He puts out his cigarette furiously. 'I'm not discussing this with you. You don't know what you're saying, you don't even know her.'

'I'm your wife, Paul – have been for the last fifteen years. There are two kids sleeping upstairs, our kids, we are a family. I went away, I know. And you're right, I haven't been faithful to you. But I came back. I'm willing to work at our relationship, like you—'

'How much do you believe in it, Julia? Be honest

348

with yourself. Do you desire me? I can't say I've noticed.'

It's as if I am talking to Jim. I have to weigh every word I say carefully. 'It's normal to feel less passionate as time goes by, isn't it?' I ask gently.

'I still want you,' Paul confesses. 'Maybe it's because I never completely possessed you. You are one of those women that no man will ever fully possess.'

Except for Romeo, I think. I gave myself up to him. But how healthy was that?

'Let's stay practical,' I say after some thought. 'We can do two things. We either have another go, or we split up. Neither will be easy. If we decide to go on together, you will have to break off with Mae. If we split up, we'll have to decide what to do with the children.'

Paul slowly shakes his head. 'I can't taste love, Julia. I can't go on with you, unless I feel you love me.'

'How can I prove it to you?' I ask desperately. 'I can't do it to order, I need time. So much has happened.'

'Perhaps too much. I asked you to be honest for a reason.'

He is slipping away from me, I'm losing him. No, that is not true, I have lost him already. I let go of him myself. A long time ago. Along with my SIM card, into the sea. I want to say something, beg him for one last chance, but the words won't come. My body begins to shake.

Paul gets up and pulls me into his arms. 'I'm not what you're looking for. You've had a taste of freedom and you want more. You shouldn't be ashamed. You could never be as happy with me now as Mae is. I always come first to her. And that's what I want. It's what I'm entitled to, what every person is entitled to.'

I can't stop crying.

'Hush now.' He strokes my back. 'It's going to be all right. You'll find someone. You'll come to accept Mae, because you're like that.'

'How can you be so sure?' I wipe my nose on his shirt.

'I know you better than anyone, Julia.'

THE END

With thanks to
Sandra, Marit, Tanja, Ingrid, Martijn, Peter, Leonard,
Marrit, Diana, Trix, Janine, Michiel.

With special thanks to
Olivia and Sam. Oscar, always Oscar.

With extra special thanks to
Marjanne. Thijs has not been forgotten.

THE WILDE WOMEN
Paula Wall

Meet Pearl Wilde, one of the unpredictable daughters
in the unforgettable family of Wildes. When Pearl
discovers her sister, Kat, dressed up in her favourite
pair of shoes – and in a compromising position
with Pearl's fiancé – she catches the very first
express train out of town. Five years later, Pearl
returns home to Five Points. This time, her claws
are razor sharp and her new demeanour is so
cool, the citizens of her home village begin
to doubt she even has sweat glands.

The Wilde Women is a funny, sexy, and bitingly smart
story of how love can turn to hate like wine can turn
to vinegar – and how one wise, wild woman can
turn that bitterness into a sweet, delicious tart.

9780552772488

BLACK SWAN